EX LIBRIS

The
Last Boat Home

Dea Brøvig

HUTCHINSON
LONDON

Published by Hutchinson 2014

2 4 6 8 10 9 7 5 3 1

Copyright © Dea Brøvig 2014

First published in Great Britain in 2014 by
Hutchinson
Random House, 20 Vauxhall Bridge Road,
London SW1V 2SA

www.randomhouse.co.uk

Addresses for companies within The Random House Group Limited can be
found at: www.randomhouse.co.uk/offices.htm

The Random House Group Limited Reg. No. 954009

A CIP catalogue record for this book
is available from the British Library

ISBN 9780091953768 (Hardback)
ISBN 9780091954291 (Trade paperback)

The Random House Group Limited supports the Forest Stewardship
Council® (FSC®), the leading international forest-certification organisation.
Our books carrying the FSC label are printed on FSC®-certified paper.
FSC is the only forest-certification scheme supported by the leading
environmental organisations, including Greenpeace.
Our paper procurement policy can be found at:
www.randomhouse.co.uk/environment

Typeset in Granjon by Palimpsest Book Production Limited,
Falkirk, Stirlingshire

Printed and bound in Great Britain by
CPI Group (UK) Ltd, Croydon CR0 4YY

For Nikolai, Lara and Jan André

The strongest man in the world is he who stands most alone.

HENRIK IBSEN, *An Enemy of the People*

But with me it is a very small thing that I should be judged of you, or of man's judgement: yea, I judge not mine own self.
For I know nothing by myself; yet am I not hereby justified: but he that judgeth me is the Lord.

I CORINTHIANS 4:3–4

For where God built a church, there the Devil would also build a chapel.

MARTIN LUTHER

Then

January, 1976

THERE WOULD BE pain, she knew.

Else looked for her mother at the window, but saw only the dark shape of the barn across the yard. The wind chased the snow, blowing flurries over the prints she had left behind. She would be back soon. Once she had walked the stretch to Tenvik's farm and used his telephone, he would drive her home and they would wait together for the hospital car.

Else rested her temple against the cold glass and imagined how it would happen. A tearing of the guts, a hatching, a birth. Even now, it did not seem real. She knew girls who, at that moment, were sitting in their classrooms counting the minutes until break, while she tallied the seconds between her last contraction and the next. When it began she gripped the edge of the dining table, taking deep breaths until it passed. She resumed her pacing between the window and the oven, moving in and out of its radius of heat. Wood smoke coiled under the ceiling. The room smelled of bonfires and she remembered the flames against the water on Midsummer's Eve. She wiped the sweat from her neck with hands that shook. She pressed them to her belly as if to soothe what was inside.

She would not think about the baby. She would focus instead on the certainty of pain, sharpening her fear to a single point to avoid the broader terror of what would follow.

Nothing had changed in the yard when Else next stopped at the window, but she lingered there and searched the pale landscape. The barn's roof was heavy with snow, but it was still standing. She closed her eyes and conjured up the gentle scrape of Valentin's saw, pretending for as long as she could manage that she was the girl of a year ago, who caught the ferry after school and arrived home to interrupt his labour with a dinner tray. She wondered where he was and pictured him sipping from a mug of coffee in his caravan, wrapped in a blanket, just as he had been on that last morning. The thought of the strong man fortified her and Else stirred and continued her journey across the floorboards. A new contraction folded her over the table. She clutched its edge and held on.

Now

2009

THE NIGHT MISTS have burned away by the time Else arrives at the harbour. In spite of the sun, the morning is fresh and she tugs her shawl tighter around her shoulders against the chill. She crosses the square where migrant workers have set up their stalls for the weekend market and stops by a trawler docked at the foot of the Longpier.

The fisherman greets her with a nod and she calls to him above the shrieking seagulls perched on his net.

'Any shrimp today?'

'Still no luck,' he says. 'They're predicting a bad summer for shrimp. I've got crayfish or crab.'

'Three crabs, then,' Else says. He selects the shellfish from a crate and, while he packs them in paper, she studies the fjord washing away from the pier, catching the sunlight as it goes, glinting silver, green and black like the scales on a mackerel's back and belly.

Else pays for the crabs and drops her bundle into the canvas bag she has brought with her before turning again to the square.

She lets her eyes skim the faces of the market's few customers, hoping for a glimpse of Marianne, though she doubts her daughter would surface here at this hour. Havneveien is deserted but for a pair of joggers, who advance at a brisk pace from the town hall. With a sigh, Else retraces her steps to Torggata and climbs the hill towards home.

She has come as far as the kiosk where Liv chooses her Saturday pick-and-mix when a voice startles her.

'Else Dybdahl,' it says. 'Is it you?'

A man stands in her path. He grins and a sour taste spreads over her tongue.

'Lars,' she says. 'Are you back? I hadn't heard.'

'Then things must have changed here more than I'd realised,' he says.

'Have you come for the summer?'

'You really haven't heard?' asks Lars. 'I took over my parents' place in March. Our plan was to wait for the kids to finish school before we moved down, but we got ahead of ourselves and came last week. A few extra days of sea air can only do them good. And I have some things to take care of at the shipyard.'

Else raises her eyebrows to show surprise, though he has not told her anything she didn't know. While he speaks, she is tempted to peek past him at her reflection in the kiosk window. She stares the impulse down, knocks it flat and sets her mouth in a line that she hopes will convey impatience.

'And how are you?' he asks. 'How is Marianne?'

'We're fine,' Else says.

'I hear she has a little girl now herself.'

'Now and for the past eleven years.'

'Eleven years!' Lars whistles. 'She'll be in school with my eldest. Her name is Liv, isn't that right? How does it feel to be a grandma?'

'Just fine,' Else says.

'And what of the old gang? Rune lives in Oslo, I know. Do you have any news of Petter?'

'I bump into him now and then,' Else says and inspects her watch.

'Well,' says Lars. 'We'll be seeing each other, no doubt.'

'No doubt,' she says.

'You look good, Else. Not how I remember my grandmother looking at all.'

Else's shoulders are tense when she resumes her climb, chewing her cheeks and keeping her eyes on the tarmac at her feet. She takes the corner at Krogveien and tightens her hand around the key in her pocket, pressing its grooves with her thumb. With each swing of her legs, the shawl that hangs loose over her arms flaps at her sides, tacking wings to her shadow. Her canvas bag knocks her thigh as she hurries to Vestheiveien, where the spruce trees between the houses smell of Christmas.

As soon as she arrives at number 43a, Else checks the coat stand in the hall. Marianne's jacket is still missing. She changes into a pair of slippers and pads to the kitchen to place the wrapped crabs in the fridge. She starts the coffee machine and waters her basil, pausing to glance at the oven clock, whose digits do not move fast enough for her liking. Her body is weary after a restless night. She closes her eyes and touches her chin to her chest, stretching her neck, rubbing solace into her muscles before she tiptoes into the corridor.

Upstairs on the landing, she lingers in the doorway of her daughter's room where, once again, no one has slept in the unmade bed. She shuts the door on the jumble of clothes that hides the carpet, on the tubes of lip gloss that clutter the desk along with perfume bottles and slivers of underpants and balled-up stockings. Else carries on down the corridor to Liv's room, expecting to find her asleep. The bed there is empty, too. In the hour since she last looked in on her, her granddaughter has kicked her duvet to the floor, where it sits in a heap of purple moons and shooting stars, a discarded universe.

She discovers Liv in her own bed, the double duvet pulled to her nose. Else lies down beside the figure tucked up in the middle of her mattress. Daylight pierces the join of the blanket-thick curtains, lifting the darkness enough to make out a flutter of lashes on Liv's cheek. Else can tell she is awake. She extends an arm across her granddaughter and nestles her forehead against her temple.

'Where were you?' Liv asks through the quilt that covers her mouth.

'I went out to get dinner.'

'Did you go fishing?' Liv asks.

Else smiles and, when she is done arranging herself, Liv turns into her embrace.

'Mamma didn't come home last night,' she says.

'There's nothing to worry about,' says Else.

'I know. She probably just met someone.'

'How did you sleep?' Else asks in order to change the subject.

'All right,' says Liv. 'I heard you downstairs.'

Else shifts her weight to free the arm pinned beneath her and begins to stroke Liv's hair. Her fingers are still sifting the strands that fall back onto the pillow when the front door opens and shuts like a handclap. Her shoulders relax for the first time since bumping into Lars and she holds her breath, straining to hear the click of her daughter's heels on the floorboards. She listens to Marianne climbing the stairs. Finally, there comes a tap on the bedroom door.

'Mamma?'

'You're home,' Else says.

A silhouette seems to float through the darkness. 'I saw you made coffee,' Marianne says. 'I brought up a cup.' She sets the mug on the nightstand just as Else flicks the reading lamp on. A soft light brightens Marianne's eyes. Her cheeks bloom with the chill of early morning and, at a guess, more than a few late-night glasses of wine. Her miniskirt shrinks up her thighs when she lowers herself onto the bed. Ignoring Else and Liv's protests, she crawls over their legs and slips fully clothed under the duvet.

'Did you have fun?' asks Liv.

'Yes,' says Marianne. She kisses Liv's cheek. 'I met someone. A Swede.'

'Did you go to Sweden to meet him?' asks Else. 'Don't you know what the time is?'

'Mads is his name. He's a dancer.'

'What kind of dancer?' asks Liv.

'A good one,' says Marianne and giggles. Else frowns and sits up to reach for the mug of coffee. She rests her head against the wall behind her and traps the liquid in her mouth, savouring its heat until she swallows.

Before long, Liv's breath meets her mother's in a tranquil tempo. She dozes with her spine to Marianne's chest. For some minutes, Else contemplates her girls. She puts down the near-empty mug and eases herself out of bed. She creeps to the bath-room, where she closes the door before flipping the light switch, not wanting to disturb their sleep.

Else undresses. She tidies her clothes into a pile on the toilet bowl, then twists the shower's knobs. The water pounds. The mirror over the sink shows sharp collarbones, a stern chin.

You look good, Else. Not how I remember my grandmother looking at all.

She purses her lips. Lars Reiersen has a nerve. Else pins her hair off her face and wonders what sort of father he is. He has two children, she has heard: a boy and a girl. He took his time, had his fun and now he has them, too.

Her own child is in the next room, wasting the day after another misspent night. If Marianne had had a father, would she behave differently? Else knows how this Saturday will evolve: the hours will pass and her exasperation will grow but she will let her daughter sleep, more relieved than angry. As long as she is here, the home that Else has built will be at peace.

Else inspects her reflection until it steams over. With an outstretched hand, she tests the water and, satisfied with the temperature, steps under the shower's jet.

VICTORIA REIERSEN ARRIVES with a jingle of the spa's bell. She shrugs off her boat jacket and drops her umbrella into a bucket by the door.

'What awful weather!' she says. 'It's typical, every winter you live for the summer, and every summer all it does is rain.' She shakes the water from her hair as her eyes flit from Else's face down the length of her body. 'You must be Else,' she says.

'Do you want a cup of tea before we start?' Else asks.

'Just water,' she says, 'if that's all right.'

Else excuses herself to fetch a glass. When she returns, her client has planted herself on a chair in what has been designated the 'waiting area' and chosen a copy of *Se & Hør* from the stack of magazines on the table beside her. It lies open on her lap while she punches the buttons of her mobile phone. She accepts the glass with an apologetic smile and places it on the table.

'I'll be ready for you shortly,' Else says and leaves Victoria to finish typing her text message.

Alone in the treatment room, Else sinks onto the edge of the massage bed and rubs her forehead with the heel of her hand. Victoria is closer to Marianne's age than her own. She is just as the locals have described her: dark and dainty, as delicate as a porcelain cup. How had a body like hers ever survived childbirth? Else imagines her shattering from the pain of it. She breathes in the blend of essential oils that her skin has soaked up during the day's appointments. This was a mistake. She should never have accepted Victoria's booking, but she had wanted to see Lars's wife for herself.

To shore herself up, she looks from the facial steamer to the magnifying lamp at the other end of the room. The wax warmer has been pushed to the wall under the Krøyer print that she hung the day before the spa's opening. Seven years later, she is still in business. She waits to feel the stirring of pride that often comes when she thinks about what she has managed. Today, the space seems shabby with its second-hand appliances. She pulls back her shoulders and prepares herself for work.

Victoria's nakedness is preserved under a towel as she settles on the massage bed. Her cheek rests on the stacked platform of her hands. Her head bobs when she speaks.

'At first,' she says, 'I wasn't sure about moving here. But Lars can talk me into anything.'

A self-conscious laugh mimics the sound of glass tinkling as Else opens a drawer. She scans the rows of bottles inside and picks oils that she hopes will send Victoria to sleep. Sandalwood. Lavender. Clary Sage. Floral notes scent the air as she taps a few drops of each into a bowl of almond oil.

'Do you have any pain or injuries?' she asks.

'Not specifically,' says Victoria. 'I'm just sore in general after the move. All of that packing and unpacking. It takes its toll.'

Else folds down the top half of the towel to reveal Victoria's golden back. There is not a tan line, not a single mole or blemish. She scoops the oil mixture from the bowl and rubs it warm between her palms before beginning at Victoria's tailbone. Her hands slide up her spine.

'There,' Victoria says. 'A little higher. Can you feel the knot?'

'Mm,' says Else and kneads the spot where she supposes she is meant to find it.

'I'm so relieved it's over,' Victoria says. 'Only death and divorce are more stressful. That's what they say. Than moving, I mean.'

'Mm,' Else says.

'All of that *stuff*! God knows where it came from. You don't realise how much you have until you see it packed into boxes in your living room. It'll be worth it, though. A little country living will be good for the kids. They just have to settle in. The main thing' – Victoria takes a breath while Else rolls circles into her flesh – 'is for them to make a few friends. Moving has been hard on them. I keep trying to remind them that Oslo is only a drive away.'

Without meaning to, Else jabs her thumbs behind Victoria's left shoulder blade. Her client gasps and she lets go her grip. Scolding herself, Else tries to soothe the area, keeping her touch light as her knuckles glide over skin.

Victoria's eyes close once more. Else decides that the oils are doing their work and, while tropical waves break from the stereo's speakers, she relaxes into the rhythm of her hands. Then Victoria clears her throat.

'We visited the school yesterday,' she says. 'It isn't at all what the kids are used to. But Lars was excited, showing them around. He had a story for every room.'

A tiny flare goes off in Else's chest, like the onset of heartburn. She turns to the counter to add a new drop of sandalwood to her bowl.

'He's always telling them stories about growing up here,' says Victoria. 'You knew each other then. Isn't that right?'

Else swirls her bowl. The blobs of oil slip and slither and never merge. 'A little,' she says.

'But you were friends, weren't you? Didn't your mothers know each other?'

'It's a small town,' Else says.

'I'd understood you were good friends.'

'It was smaller then,' she says.

Victoria opens her mouth as if to press her further, but her words melt into a sigh as Else resumes the massage. She leans into her arms, her oil-dipped fingers squeezing Victoria's tan up to her neck. Her thumbs grease the roots at the base of her hairline and Victoria groans.

'I'll feel better,' she says, 'once the house is in order. The kitchen can't have been painted since it was built. The walls are brown, for goodness' sake.'

Her back rises with a yawn and she says no more. Some minutes pass in silence before her breathing begins to thicken. Else keeps her strokes steady over Victoria's softening muscles and picks details from the recesses of her memory. A high ceiling. An American fridge. Countertops that span from one side of the room to the distant other. A pantry large enough to fit a family is stocked with tins and cooking chocolate, Solo and Cola bottles and foods she has never tasted. The view of the fjord from the window reaches for the horizon. Poor Victoria, she thinks, whose worst problem is the colour of her walls.

At four o'clock, Else wakes her client and leaves her alone to dress. While she waits, she washes her water glass in the bathroom sink and checks her schedule for the following morning. All day, she has been looking forward to spending a quiet night in with Liv. She has rented a DVD that she knows her granddaughter will like and, when the film is over, they will sit together and gossip until way past Liv's bedtime.

Her jacket is on and zipped to her chin when Victoria emerges from the treatment room. She takes her payment and deposits it in the till's drawer. Else collects the bags of groceries that she stowed in a cupboard earlier before seeing Victoria out. She locks the spa's door behind them.

'Thanks for that,' says Victoria. 'I feel like a new person.'

Else nods. 'My pleasure,' she says and turns into the rain.

———

When she arrives home, the house is in a flurry. A thudding music greets her from upstairs, boxing her ears as she hooks her jacket on the coat stand.

'*Hallo?*' she calls.

In the living room, Liv is watching television. Her face pops up from behind the armrest of the sofa. 'Hi, Mormor,' she says.

'What's going on?' Else asks.

'It's Mamma,' says Liv. 'She's meeting Mads.'

Else rolls her eyes before bending to kiss Liv's forehead. Her granddaughter pats the wet snarl of her hair.

'Did you forget your umbrella?'

'I did,' Else says. 'How was the last day of school?'

Liv shrugs. 'It's raining,' she says.

Marianne's shout interrupts them from the second floor. 'Where's my necklace?' Her footsteps thunder down the stairs. 'Mamma, have you seen my necklace? The one with the shell?'

'Where's he taking you?' Else asks.

'To the cinema,' says Liv.

'Is that how people dress for the cinema these days?'

Marianne makes a face and darts into the hallway. A cloud of hairspray hangs after her in the air. Else drops onto the sofa next to her granddaughter. She feels as if her body has been dipped in tar.

'I rented *High School Musical*,' she says. 'And I bought bananas and chocolate sauce for ice-cream sundaes.'

'Where are the umbrellas?' calls Marianne. Then, 'Never mind!'

She carries one in her fist when she breezes back into the room, her necklace's pendant strung up above her cleavage.

'I'm off,' she says.

'What time will you be home?' asks Else.

Marianne blows Liv a kiss. 'Have fun tonight. Don't wait up for me, Mamma.'

'Don't forget your jacket!' Before Else's sentence is out of her mouth, the front door slams. 'Well,' she says, 'I suppose that's that. Shall I make us a cup of tea?'

'I only have time for a quick one,' says Liv. 'I'm going out.'

'You are? Where are you going?'

'To Andreas's house.'

'Who's Andreas?'

'Andreas Reiersen,' says Liv. 'His family just moved down here.'

'But. We're having a night in,' Else says. 'I rented a film.'

Liv pushes herself off the sofa and raises her arms, showing her palms to Else as if to say the matter is out of her hands.

'But,' Else says.

She follows her granddaughter into the kitchen, where Liv holds the kettle under the tap and does not look at her. While the water boils, she finds the mugs on their shelf. She removes a slice from a bag of bread and takes the butter out of the fridge.

'Don't fill up on bread,' Else says. 'I thought we'd order pizza.'

'Mormor,' says Liv, 'I'm going over to Andreas's house.'

'I saw his mother earlier,' says Else. 'She didn't mention a thing about it. You have to ask permission for this sort of thing.'

'I did,' Liv says. 'Mamma said it was okay.'

'Well, Mamma was wrong. When did you meet this Andreas, anyway?'

'Last weekend,' says Liv. 'He was at the harbour with his dad. He's really nice, Mormor. He let me try his kayak.'

The tide of tar is rising over Else's head. She closes her eyes.

'All right,' she says. 'What if Andreas were to come here instead?'

'Not possible,' says Liv.

'Why not?'

'Because we're painting *his* kitchen, so we have to go to *his* house.'

'You're painting his kitchen? But his mother didn't say . . .'

'It's a surprise,' says Liv. 'She's so tired after the move.' She consults the oven clock. 'All of that packing and unpacking. I have to get ready. Andreas's dad is picking me up in four minutes.'

'But,' Else says.

Liv skips out of the room, the bread slice in hand. Else squints at the mugs on the kitchen counter. How can it be that that boy is already in their lives? And Lars – Lars will be here in four minutes. In spite of herself, she hurries out to the hallway mirror. Two smudges of mascara are all that remain from this morning's make-up routine. She is dismayed to see how old she looks without it. She tousles her hair and fastens it with a clip that she finds in the basket meant for keys. She licks a finger and rubs at the pockets under her eyes. The doorbell rings.

'Damn,' she says.

With a final peek in the mirror, she opens the front door to Lars. His build plugs the doorframe. Behind him, the rain falls in silver tacks against the sky. The boy at his side is a younger version of himself. He stays close to his father and peers past Else into the house.

'Else!' says Lars. 'You live here, too? I was expecting Marianne.'

'Marianne's out,' Else says.

'And Liv?'

'She's coming.'

Lars smiles. 'Long day?'

'What time should I pick her up?' Else asks.

'I'm sleeping over,' says Liv as she trots back down the stairs with her bag. She has changed into the denim skirt that Marianne says flatters her legs.

'Enjoy yourself,' says Lars. 'You look like you could use a night off. Ready, kids?' He claps his hands and Liv grabs her jacket from the coat stand.

'Ready,' she says and charges ahead of Andreas. 'Bye, Mormor!'

'Be good!' Else calls.

'Don't worry,' says Lars. 'I'll return her as good as new in the morning.'

Lars runs after the children to the BMW that is parked in the drive and slides into the front seat. The ignition roars and the car reverses into the road. Through the rain-streaked rear window, Else sees Liv sitting shoulder to shoulder with Andreas. She waves and Liv waves back. Then she is gone.

Else closes the door. She drifts into the living room and is grateful all at once for Marianne's music, for the television's din. She stops in the middle of the floor and stares at the screen until she realises she has been standing there for some time. With a sigh, she wanders into the kitchen to make herself a cup of tea.

Then

1974

IT WAS ON a blue-eyed Saturday afternoon in midsummer that Lars first kissed Else outside the toilets of the bus depot. She had woken up that morning wondering if he would. She hoped he would; it had been a while since he had tried his luck and she felt sorry for having turned her head away.

After breakfast, she caught the ferry to the Longpier and climbed Torggata to the top of the town. The racing had already started when she arrived at the depot. Two mopeds zipped along the car park in the shadow of the empty Kristiansand coach, stirring up clouds of dirt in their wake. Else recognised the yellow paint of Lars's bike, sleek and shiny next to its rival. She strolled to the mobile kitchen at the edge of the lot, where a group of boys hollered at the racers and stuffed their gums with chewing tobacco.

'Hi, Else,' called Petter.

'Back for more?' Rune said.

Else folded her arms over her chest and nodded at the bikes. 'Who's he racing?'

'Right now, it's Joachim,' Petter said.

'Who's winning?'

'Lars,' he said. He sounded disappointed. 'I'll be racing him next.'

The boys whooped and clapped when Lars crossed the finishing line. He raised a fist in the air before the yellow moped began to speed towards them. Else looked at her shoes. She studied her hands. A crust of dirt under one fingernail demanded her urgent attention.

Lars skidded to a stop in front of her. 'Do you want to go for a ride?' he asked.

'Not a chance.'

'Sure you do,' he said. 'I'll go slow this time. I promise I will. So are you coming?'

Else hesitated, but swung her leg over the seat. She shrieked when Lars twisted the handlebars and the moped shot forward. The wind was fresh on her bare arms and she wrapped them around his waist, tight enough to feel his stomach beat with his breath against her wrists. She buried her face into his neck, aware of her breasts crushed flat against his back. He smelled of cigarettes and of summer.

Stones clattered in the wheels of the moped as it whizzed around the car park. It circled behind the depot building and lapped the mobile kitchen twice.

'Hold on!' called Lars and tipped into a turn. He squeezed the brakes and swore as the moped toppled over. Else heard the screech of tripping tyres before her shins scraped the ground. She rolled into a puddle and groaned at the sting in her legs.

'Else?' said Lars.

Her eyes pricked at the corners. She sat up and prodded the bloodied skin below one kneecap.

'Are you crying?' Lars asked.

'No,' she said.

'Are you broken?'

'You promised you'd go slow.'

'Should I call an ambulance?' Lars helped her to her feet and she dusted off her shorts. The rest of the boys came running.

'Are you hurt?' asked Petter.

Else hobbled to the toilets. Once she had closed the door behind her, she turned on the tap and washed the muck and grit from her leg. She cleaned her knee with a wad of the paper that had been left on the cistern in a tidy pile, flushing it away before splashing water on her cheeks. When she opened the door, Lars was sitting on the bottom step. He jumped up and she limped down the stairs.

'Are you all right?' he asked.

'Are you?' she said.

'Just a couple of broken arms and two ruined legs.'

Lars lifted his hands to her shoulders and pulled her close. While greasy mists from the mobile kitchen settled over them like clingfilm, Else blinked at his grin. His lips gathered in a pucker before gluing shut her mouth. Hard, soft. Wet, rough. Her stomach seethed; bubbles danced along her throat. Between her ears. She was all fizz. It felt like laughing.

That afternoon, Pastor Seip was coming for dinner and Else had instructions from her mother not to be late. While Lars carried on racing against the other boys, she checked her watch, noting uneasily that she had just missed another ferry. She tried to catch his eye, but he was absorbed by the business of winning. It couldn't hurt to wait a few minutes more. Else sat on the bench between Petter and Rune and looked on as Lars took his fourth victory of the day. She picked a chip from a paper plate in her lap and a dollop of ketchup dribbled onto her T-shirt.

When she could no longer avoid it, she got to her feet.

'I'll walk you down, if you want,' Petter said.

Else smiled, but shook her head. 'See you tomorrow,' she said and started for the road. She had almost reached the end of the lot when Lars's moped drew up beside her.

'Are you leaving?'

'The ferry goes in five minutes,' she said.

'Want another ride first?'

'I can't. Pastor Seip is coming for dinner.'

Lars crossed his eyes and a snort of laughter shot up her nose like soda pop.

'See you at church tomorrow, then,' he said and spun away to rejoin the races.

Else gritted her teeth against the soreness of her knee and trudged down the hill, easing into a jog at the top of Torggata. She overtook one white timber building after another towards the harbour, where the water winked under the sun. The ferry was already docked at the Longpier. A handful of passengers had finished boarding the boat by the time Else hopped onto its deck and claimed a solitary spot at its stern.

The captain pushed off from land and steered them up the fjord, away from the Skagerrak and the cluster of islands that protected the port from the sea where, three hundred years earlier, merchant vessels used to offload their cargo. Bursts of salt air scrubbed Else's face as the curve of the mountain eclipsed the town. She checked her watch and her stomach pinched. She hoped her father would be in a fit state when she got home. At breakfast that morning, his breath had been foul with the onions he chewed to mask the stink of the homebrew. She knew all about the distillery he kept hidden in the boathouse. He had visited it several nights that week.

The ferry passed from one fjord into the next, sailing by islands scabbed with lichen and reefs that lurked at the surface like aspiring icebergs. In the distance, the Reiersen shipyard swelled. Its cranes pierced the sky as the boat swayed closer, until warehouses and construction sheds separated from the drab blur behind its empty graving dock. The shipyard sprawled on the waterfront, facing the opposite shore where the ferry put in. Else scrambled onto the public pier and across the road, where she had hidden her father's bicycle behind an oak tree. Her wheels sprayed dirty fans behind her as she set off down the zigzag of the track. Under her breath, she prayed that Pastor Seip would be late.

When she reached the farmhouse, her ears were buzzing. She left the bike behind the milking barn and ran inside. Her mother was in the kitchen, her apron flapping as she pivoted between the oven and her pots. Beside her, her father belted out instructions.

'That goddamned fish has to come out *now*!'

Else moved to the sink to wash her hands.

'You're late,' said her mother.

'Where have you been?' Her father's eyes were tinged with blood.

'The ferry didn't come,' Else said.

'Pastor Seip will be here any minute,' he said. 'Go and clean yourself up.'

After changing into her Sunday dress, Else raced down the stairs and began to wipe the dinner table.

'The potatoes! The potatoes!'

Her father hooted from the kitchen as she carried through a tablecloth still warm from the clothes line and shook it over the polished wood. The good plates were stacked in a high cabinet. Else climbed onto a chair to retrieve them.

'The butter! It's burning!'

A layer of dust had settled on the top dish. She rubbed it off with the hem of her dress and set a place at the head of the table for Pastor Seip. She saw him through the window stepping over the vegetable patch in the yard.

'He's here,' she called.

Her warning sent her parents scurrying into the hallway. They consulted their reflection in the mirror, smoothing stray hairs into place and dabbing foreheads with their shirtsleeves. Her mother opened the door just as the minister's fist was poised to knock.

Dinner was, by all accounts, a success. Pastor Seip doused his potatoes in melted butter, which floated on his plate like an oil spill. He polished off the ling he had been served and helped himself to seconds.

'Very nice,' he muttered afterwards, suppressing a burp behind his knuckles.

'We'll take coffee and cake in the Best Room,' Dagny said. She rose from the table and led the way across the hall to the pride of the house.

It was the first time they had used the Best Room since Dagny had hosted last month's ladies' luncheon, although Else had helped her mother dust its corners several times since. Now, sitting opposite Pastor Seip on a low-slung bench, she felt the chill that the room imparted to all special occasions. The pine walls were painted a midnight blue that drained the warmth right out of the air. Lace curtains filtered the sunlight, scattering it over the furniture like shards of glass.

Pastor Seip's stomach folded over his thighs as he leaned forward for his coffee cup. Else watched its progress to his lips, thinking how delicate it looked in his long fingers.

'I hear the catch has been meagre,' said the minister to Johann and took a slurp from his cup.

The china had been a wedding gift from Dagny's brother, Olav, a sea captain whose merchant ship had been wrecked in a typhoon in the North Pacific. Else had been a baby when it happened. Sometimes, when she had the farmhouse to herself, she would sneak into the Best Room and flip the lock of the cupboard to rescue a cup from the top shelf, cradling it in her hands. She would trace a fingertip around the outline of a gold leaf on a black sea and try to imagine where it had come from.

'I've been having some bad luck,' her father said.

'There is no such thing,' said Pastor Seip. He fixed him with a meaningful glare. '"Be sober, be vigilant, for your adversary the Devil, as a roaring lion, walketh about seeking whom he may devour."'

'More coffee?' Dagny said.

'Keeping vigilant,' said Pastor Seip. 'That's the point.'

Johann shifted in his chair and a creak filled the room. The minister looked at Else for the first time all evening.

'Amazing what we see,' he said, 'if only we open our eyes.' His gaze fell like an anchor and she stopped herself from trying to squirm out of its way. She thought of Lars's eyes, of how he had shut them tight when he kissed her. She watched as Pastor Seip deposited a cube of cake in his mouth.

'Another slice?' Dagny said.

'No, no.' The minister mashed the crumbs on his plate with his finger before slipping it between his lips. Then he stood and brushed his palms on his trousers. 'I have other obligations this evening, I'm afraid. Thank you for the fish. It was just as my mother used to make it, which is the best way I know.'

At the front door, he took his hat and turned again to Else. 'I trust you have been putting the lessons from last Sunday's sermon to good use?' he said.

Else nodded at her feet.

'Oh, yes,' said her mother. 'She certainly has.'

Pastor Seip pulled his hat down on his head. 'The years after one's confirmation are a delicate time in every young adult's life.' He bent forward at the hips, bringing his eyes level with Else's. His breath smelled of coffee. 'Remember,' he said, 'you must pray, and you must work. It is always possible, I believe, to work harder.'

The minister straightened up and strode into the sun. He crossed the yard to the milking barn and disappeared up the hill that would bring him to the road. From the doorway of the farmhouse, Johann stared after him, his jaw clenched and his lips thin. Without a word, he retreated into the Best Room and slammed the door shut behind him.

Else and her mother washed the dishes in silence. For a long while after Pastor Seip had left, her father sat alone, until the creak of floorboards and the groan of the back door announced his escape. Else knew he would be headed for the boathouse, just as she knew they would not see him again that evening.

'I'll have to dig up some more onions,' said her mother and added a chopped bulb to the fish bones in her pot.

ON A SUNDAY in early September, Else stepped from the ferry at the Longpier and made her way up the harbour towards the church. They were not long into autumn and the leaves of the trees in front of the town hall had just started to turn. The days were contracting in preparation for winter, gathering up their dusks and dawns and giving way to chilly nights – but today, in the late morning, it still felt like summer. Sunlight dripped onto the dock in golden puddles that warmed her ankles as she plodded through.

'Hurry up,' called her father, who had already reached Dronning Mauds gate. Else's good shoes chafed her heels as she ran to catch him up. She followed her parents and other stragglers up the hill, climbing towards the outburst of bells which called to them and the town of gravitas and observance.

In the churchyard, the steeple's weather vane spun in the breeze, throwing a cartwheeling shadow over the grass. Else shuffled after it to the church's open door and into the cool air of the nave. They were among the last to arrive and the pews were bustling with people. Women hushed butter-haired children, while their men adjusted suit jackets that some had first buttoned on their wedding day. Halfway up the aisle sat Lars, swivelled around on the Reiersen family's pew, wearing a glazed expression while he scanned the faces of the latecomers. He grinned when he saw Else, who did her best to ignore him as she settled onto a bench beside her mother.

The bells stopped tolling. In their wake, a shrill hum passed onto the air which the organist took up in a string of slow tones. The congregation stood and launched into the hymn that was chalked up on a board below the pulpit. While they sang, Pastor Seip thumbed through the pages of his Bible, glancing up now and then as if to measure their progress. Next to Else, her mother's voice lifted and soared to the psalm's final note.

'May the Lord grant you mercy, and bless you,' said the minister. 'Welcome, all, to this Sunday's service. We gather here in fellowship to praise Almighty God and to offer thanks for His wisdom and guidance.'

As Pastor Seip's greeting rang out in the church, Else ran her thumb over the weave of her psalm book's cover. She fidgeted on the bench that was too hard under her thighs and waited for her thoughts to carry her away. She felt cold in spite of the sun that fell from the window onto her back and shoulders. It skimmed the sails of the model schooner that hung from a ceiling beam at the foot of the altar, quickening the bronze of its hull, lending it the illusion of movement.

Pastor Seip began the first reading from the Book of Proverbs. '"I have taught thee in the way of wisdom,"' he said, '"I have led thee in right paths."' The minutes became elastic as he spoke, like wads of chewing gum pinched at either end and stretched. '"Enter not into the path of the wicked, and go not in the way of evil men. Avoid it, pass not by it, turn from it, and pass away."' In the portrait nailed to the wall behind him, Jesus spread His arms in Gethsemane, beseeching the heavens with mournful eyes while His disciples slept. '"But the path of the just is as the shining light, that shineth more and more unto the perfect day. The way of the wicked is as darkness: they know not at what they stumble."'

The parishioners stood for the next hymn and Else read the words on the page, though she could have recited them with her eyes closed. She sensed movement across the aisle and, when she peeked at Lars, saw him rocking on his shoes. His mother placed a hand on his elbow and continued to sing. Karin Reiersen's soprano aspired to the high notes. Her hair was tucked behind her ear, showing off a pearl as plump as a berry.

When the psalm was over, Else took her seat. The New Testament reading passed her by in snippets of scripture.

"'Destruction and misery are in their ways,'" said Pastor Seip and she wondered at how, after a summer spent anticipating her start at a new school, her journey to the Gymnasium on Elvebakken each morning had already come to feel ordinary. It no longer seemed strange to see Lars every day, nor did she notice the absence of those of her classmates from the old schoolhouse who had entered into apprenticeships. At the Gymnasium, students could come and go as they pleased in the breaks. So far, she and Lars had not ventured from the grounds.

"'And seeing the multitudes,'" began the Gospel reading, "'He went up into a mountain: and when He was set, His disciples came unto Him.'"

Else thought of Lars's hand warm in hers as he led her into the caretaker's shed, where they tended to stay until classes resumed. There, pressed against the grit box with Rune and Petter standing guard outside, they were safe from the prying eyes of teachers and townspeople alike.

"'Blessed are the merciful: for they shall obtain mercy. Blessed are the pure in heart: for they shall see God.'"

They had come a long way from the days when her mother used to bring her along to her luncheons, when the women would smoke American cigarettes in Karin Reiersen's parlour and Else and Lars would collect conkers behind the house. On afternoons when it rained, or when the snow was so wet that it seeped through the down of their winter suits, they would hole up together in the basement playroom that always smelled as if it had just been scrubbed with soft soap. She and Lars would dig in the toy chest for tracks for his train set or play Yahtzee or Ludo until they were bored and restless. Then they would sneak upstairs to admire the 'treasure' on display in glass cabinets: crystal figurines, silver platters and bowls.

The organist keyed a fresh chord and the congregation heaved themselves to their feet. Else flipped through her psalm book, only finding her place when the hymn's first verse had come to an end. During the second, Pastor Seip stepped down from the altar and climbed the stairs to the pulpit, his vestments sweeping the floor as he went. He studied the parishioners from this height until they were silent, his eyes watery worlds on the brink of brimming over.

He cleared his throat. 'Picture yourself dead,' he said, 'while the family who mourns you knows that you are damned to hell. Picture your husband or wife, your children, your parents, each weeping by your coffin for your forsaken soul. Some of you know that the path you have chosen is bound to lead you here at the end of your days. Others will look to your neighbours and deem yourselves absolved. But we are all of us sinners.

'"For all have sinned," said Pastor Seip, "and come short of the glory of God." Think on Paul's words in his Epistle to the Romans. Temptation takes many forms. Consider the unbeliever who rejects Christ, who turns away from the path of the righteous and instead embraces debauchery. It is easy, is it not, to name a man's transgressions against God when he flaunts them for all to see. But what of the man who indulges in a glass of brandy after a good meal? What of the women who draw their curtains before a game of cards on a Sunday evening? Are they not also sinners?

Do their sins count for less because they keep them hidden from their neighbours and friends?'

Else nibbled her gums and thought again of the caretaker's shed. She remembered Lars's lips against hers, his fingers on the small of her back. Behind the bus depot. Behind the oak at the public dock. She tried to empty her head and focus on Ivar Blåsmo's bald spot in front of her. Her mother shifted on the pew.

'The Lord bears witness to all,' said Pastor Seip, 'He sees into our hearts and knows our intentions. In today's Gospel reading Jesus begins the Sermon on the Mount, telling His disciples to be meek, to be pure, to hunger and thirst after righteousness. His instructions for entering into Paradise are clear, as is His warning to those who fail to heed them. "For I say unto you, that except your righteousness shall exceed the righteousness of the scribes and Pharisees, ye shall in no case enter into the kingdom of heaven." Who here can claim to be on the path of the righteous? And who amongst us has chosen a path to hell? There are many paths to hell, but only one way for the righteous. And there is no place for the sinner among the saved.'

A shiver darted up Else's spine. As guilty as she was, she let her gaze stray across the aisle to the Reiersen family's pew. Lars was watching her. He poked out his tongue. The skin at the nape of her neck prickled.

'The path of the just is as the shining light. The way of the wicked is as darkness,' said Pastor Seip. 'Search your conscience and ask yourself truly, which path am I on?'

This time when Else looked for Lars, his grin poked dimples into his cheeks. She dug her nails into her palm, but could not help herself from returning his smile. Lars winked and a giggle tickled her throat, until a pain in her leg put an end to her daring. Else tensed against the fingers squeezing her muscle. The curve of her father's wedding ring pressed the flesh through her skirt. In his urgency to scold her, he stretched across her mother, who leaned back to make room for him. His cheeks were flushed and his jaw worked to contain his displeasure.

'Submit yourselves to the will of the Lord,' said Pastor Seip. 'Serve Him. Fear Him. Enter not into temptation, for temptation is the Devil's summons.'

Else sat on her hands for the rest of the sermon. She dropped her eyes to the floorboards between her shoes and traced the grain of the wood long after her father had let her go.

When the service was over and the members of the congregation had advanced down the aisle to receive the minister's blessing, they gathered outside between the church doors and the gate, eager to exchange news of the week gone by. The sun was high above them, warming the crowns of their heads and toasting the lawn and the neatly sown graves. Else tailed her parents down the steps as her mother greeted their neighbours. She knew each face; week in, week out, they never changed.

Dagny met Karin Reiersen and Solveig Haugeli in the shade, while Johann wandered down the path to a huddle of fishermen on the grass. Else stayed with her mother, nodding politely when she judged it appropriate and biding her time until she would be able to slip away.

'Hasn't the weather been mild?' Solveig said. 'Do you know, yesterday afternoon Ole picked half a litre of blueberries behind the Aaby farm. Half a litre, this late in the season! They were a little bloated, but still good.'

'What did you make of the sermon?' asked Karin.

'It was very strong today,' Dagny said.

'But did you see Øystein Stormo?' said Solveig. 'Sitting straight as a flagpole next to poor Astrid. With all of that man's carrying on, I don't think he even flinched.'

While Solveig shook her head, Dagny frowned over her shoulder at Else, who excused herself and melted into the crowd.

She aimed for the outer ring of graves but walked the long way around so as to avoid the horse chestnut tree, where Lars whispered with Rune and Petter. As she wove through the parishioners she picked up scraps of conversation, much of it carried over from the previous week. There had been more reports in the papers about tankers put out of commission by rising oil prices and the reopening of the Suez Canal. Unwanted ships were dropping anchor in fjords and bays along the coast not far from here. Then there was the usual talk about the North Sea oilrigs.

'We'll be like the Arabs,' said Atle Aaby, who grinned when Esben Omland predicted that oil would make them rich. Esben was fixing to send his application in to Phillips. With the oil companies setting up offices in Stavanger, there would be worse places to raise a family.

The collective thrum of chatter followed Else to the relative peace at the rear of the church, where fallen leaves crackled under the soles of her shoes. She read the epitaphs chiselled into slabs of granite. To her left, a mound of earth marked a recent grave. Eva Bruskeland had been buried between her husband and the Tenvik children, whose two tiny plots were trimmed with autumn daisies. Both children had died before Else was born, though her mother had told her their stories several times. The first, a baby girl, had gone to sleep one night not long before Christmas and never again opened her eyes. The boy had pulled a pot of boiling water from the stove over his young body. A week later, he breathed his last in a hospital bed.

Else strolled to the cross at the centre of the Second World War plot and read off the names that had been cut into the marble. Gregor Sundt. Carl Hansen. Per Henrik Wiig. She stopped at the headstone that had been raised 'by grateful friends' for an English soldier, studying the dedication until Lars was in front of her.

'That was one hell of a sermon,' he said.

'What are you doing?' she asked.

'I wanted to check you were all right. Your father looked angry.'

'We can't talk here. You know that.'

'All right, then,' Lars said. 'What if I picked you up after dinner?'

'Don't be ridiculous,' Else said.

'How does five o'clock sound? I'll wait for you on the road. Just find an excuse to leave the house.'

'Lars . . .'

'Five o'clock,' he said.

'You know I can't meet you. It's Sunday.'

'Heaven forbid,' he said and stepped close to press warm lips to her cheek. Lars was slow and self-assured when he moved away towards the church, keeping his pace steady even when Pastor Seip appeared from behind its wall. Else turned back to the marble cross and reread its names. Gregor Sundt. Carl Hansen. Per Henrik Wiig. The minister must realise she and Lars had been together. She hoped he would leave, but was not surprised when she next looked to discover him standing there still. Pastor Seip watched her from his spot among the tombstones. Lars had already strutted from sight.

Else started across the grass with her eyes on her shoes. The minister called to her as she approached.

'Was there something of interest back there?'

'I was looking at the memorial cross,' she said.

'What were you doing with Lars Reiersen?'

'Nothing,' she said.

'Is that so?'

With an impatient wave of his hand, Pastor Seip dismissed her and Else hurried out of his way to the front of the church. The crowd was thinning as the parishioners set off for home. She found her parents by the gate.

'There you are,' her mother said.

'Where did you get to?' said her father. 'We'll miss the ferry.'

He led them onto the street, where a shadow fell from the trees at the roadside in long fingers that reached for the cars parked opposite. Lars was climbing into the back seat of his father's Cadillac, whose chrome and glass seemed alive in the sun. Reiersen leaned an elbow on the roof above the driver's door and fanned his face with the brim of his hat. Karin Reiersen smiled in the passenger seat at Dagny.

'See you on Thursday for the luncheon,' she said.

'See you on Thursday,' Dagny said.

Else trailed after her father down Dronning Mauds gate, glad to put distance between her parents and the minister. As they walked, the sound of an engine grew louder behind them. Reiersen's car raced by in a haze of churned dirt.

'Damned *dollarglis*,' said Johann of the Cadillac. He sucked in his cheeks and marched on to the Longpier, where the ferry was boarding.

Else changed out of her Sunday dress when she arrived home and crossed the garden to the milking barn. Once the cow had been fed, she returned to the farmhouse to help prepare dinner. Her mother gutted a coalfish while Else washed the potatoes that she had carried up from the cellar. She scraped her knife under their skins and carved out the bruises before filling a pot and setting it to boil.

When the carrots had been sliced and the peas shelled, she mounted the stairs to her bedroom and pulled on her bathing suit. Else skipped outside and bolted barefoot to the pier, wincing when she trod on the cherry stones dropped by magpies over the yard. This would be the last swim of the summer, she expected. There would be no more trips in Lars's boat to the skerry. She let her towel fall onto the rocks that separated the lawn and the pier and, as she stepped over the planks of timber to the water's edge, thought of the whirling in her stomach during those excursions, when she stood on the islands' high ridges and the boys shouted for her to jump.

Else dipped her toes into the fjord and drew them out with a sharp breath. She lingered in a patch of sun, anticipating the sting of the sea and glancing after her father, who was rowing his skiff inland to set crab traps in the shallows. In a single movement, she shut her eyes and pinched her nose and leapt. Her body plunged into cold that sealed around her. Her muscles seized up in the initial shock, until her foot brushed a slime of seaweed and she kicked and broke the surface. Near the *Frøya*'s anchor line, she paddled the feeling back into her limbs and swallowed air through teeth that chattered. Spreading her arms, she swam away from the splash of the waves against the stilts that lifted the boathouse from the water.

Across the fjord stood the Reiersen shipyard, its graving dock still empty. Else propelled herself towards it and thought of Lars. She knew it would be foolish to meet him later. Her mother would catch the bus back to town after dinner for the evening's prayer meeting at the *bedehus*, but her father would be home, smoking in the dining room as he did every Sunday on his night off. Johann was the last in a long line of shrimpers. He had been sailing the *Frøya* since the war, when the Gymnasium on Elvebakken was closed and requisitioned by Nazi officers for barracks. By the time the Germans had been driven out, his own father deemed he had learned more at sea than he ever would in a classroom. Day after day, year after year, the weather worked him over on his father's boat. The sun and the wind and the salt and the cold cracked his skin like a battered fender.

On most evenings after supper, Johann would put on his layers of wool and rubber and head outside to the trawler moored in front of the boathouse. Else would listen from the kitchen or dining room to the faint, thudding chop of its motor rupturing the silence. Its drum bounced off the mountains that climbed out of the fjord, echoing its farewell even after it had gone. She pictured her father rolling his first cigarette while he sailed under the eye of the lighthouse that signalled to the sea and, as the *Frøya*'s wheelhouse filled with smoke, unscrewing the lid of his thermos and treating his coffee to a squirt of homebrew. He would turn the radio off once he had heard the weather forecast and his boat would crash into the darkness ahead until, to the aft, beyond the trawl doors suspended like ears on either side of the net, there was nothing. No trace of land. No sign of home.

Through the night, the waves would pound the cabin walls to wisps and the prow would plummet and pitch. All the while her father would consult his charts, studying the markings that had been her grandfather's life's work. The lamp would swing a thin light over the deck as his net dropped into the deep and, when the time came to drag it up, he would spill his catch into the receptacle on board and sieve off the shrimp at the bottom of the container. He would set them aside to be stewed in a vat of seawater before slitting the throats of the cod, ling and coalfish and wringing the intestines of each flounder through an incision below the eyes. One by one, he would toss the fish into piles that leaked blood over his boots. At the end of the night, after five or six drops, he would deliver his haul to the Fish Repository in town.

Else had swum a hundred metres or more before she rested her legs and searched again for her father's skiff. She spotted him in the distance, saw the orange of his oilskins against the water. As she began to circle back to the pier, she thought of his fingers crushing her thigh at church that morning and resolved not to meet Lars. She changed her mind as soon as she had decided. She would have to go to him. He would be expecting her.

Else heaved herself out of the fjord, grazing her shins on the knots of mussels that were gummed to the bottom of the pier.

She wrapped the towel around her shoulders and scrambled to the farmhouse. When she appeared in the dining room dried and dressed, the tangles combed from her hair, the food was already on the table. She took her seat next to her father, who had docked the skiff minutes before. Side by side, they bowed their heads and folded their hands.

After the prayer, her mother served the boiled fish. Else stripped it of skin and cleaned it for bones. As she chewed, she contemplated the blade of sun that fell from the window, cleaving the room in two, downgrading each portion to cramped inadequacy.

'I thought,' she said.

'It'll rain tomorrow,' said her father.

'Do you think so?' asked her mother. 'There isn't a cloud in the sky.'

'The forecast said rain.'

'I thought,' Else said, 'I'd go and pick blueberries after dinner.'

'This evening?' asked her mother. 'But haven't you homework to do?'

'I've finished it.'

'There aren't any blueberries left now,' her father said.

'Ole Haugeli picked half a litre yesterday,' said Else. 'Solveig said so after church.'

'Wouldn't anyone like some more fish?' her mother asked.

'You won't find any blueberries now,' said her father.

'I won't see it go to waste. Else, pass me your plate.'

Else did as she was told. She tried to eat the fresh helping of coalfish, though her nerves trampled her appetite. Each mouthful tasted of dishwater and she sipped from her glass to wash the flavour away. Her father reached across her for the bowl of potatoes and a whiff of underarms lifted off his jumper. Else put down her fork and jiggled her knee under the table until the end of the meal.

When her parents had eaten the last of the fish, she scrubbed the cutlery and crockery in the kitchen and scoured the starch that had set in a film on the base and sides of her mother's pots. Then she stooped to the cupboard by the refrigerator and found a short stack of pails. Her mother stood at the counter spooning the leftover vegetables into a smaller bowl.

'Will you be going to the Aaby farm, then?' she asked.

Else nodded.

'Don't be late. You've school tomorrow.'

'I won't be late,' she said.

She eased a pail from the pile and, with her fist closed over its handle, retreated to the dining room, where her father had stationed his chair by the unlit oven. He glanced up from his rolling paper before she slipped into the hallway and through the back door. Else walked over the yard to the vegetable plot, past the lid of the old well and to the milking barn. She felt his stare like a fingertip poking her shoulder, commanding her to turn around. She almost did, but instead carried on to the hill at the end of the property. Under cover of the birch trees that bordered the path, she started to run.

Lars was waiting in a bend in the road. He kicked the pebbles in the dirt by his moped, whose yellow paint was bright beside the grey crags of the mountain. He beamed when he saw her jogging towards him.

'You're late!' he called.

'Come on,' said Else, 'let's go.'

'I'm glad you came.' He fumbled for her hand and knocked the pail with his knuckles. 'Why have you brought that?'

'I told my parents I was picking blueberries.'

'If you say so,' he said.

'Where are we going?'

'It's a surprise.'

Else climbed onto the moped behind Lars. With one arm looped around his waist, the other hand still clutching the pail, she buried her nose in the crook of his neck, breathing him in as the motor snarled awake. The wind whisked the smell of soap from his collar when he rolled the handle grips and the bike shot off down the track. Across the fjord, his father's shipyard dipped in and out of view.

The moped sped by the Aaby farm before it passed the public dock, where Else hid her face, though the last ferry had gone and the pier was empty. From there, the road pulled back from the coast. The fjord fell away as the bike veered inland. Else shut her eyes to the rushing countryside and leaned into the warmth that she felt through Lars's jacket. When she next looked, the rock at the roadside had given way to forest. A gap opened in the trees ahead. Lars slowed down as they approached.

'Hold on,' he said and tilted his weight. The moped glided onto a path. Tree roots split the earth, coiling under their wheels like fossilised snakes. Above them, branches sewed up the sky.

'We're going into the woods?' Else asked.

'For now,' said Lars. 'You'll see.'

He planted his feet on the ground and cut the engine. He dismounted from the moped after Else and set the kickstand with his shoe.

'This way,' he said.

Lars took her hand and led her into the forest, where the air seemed to clot around them. Chinks of sun filtered through the leaves to dapple the ground at their feet. With her free hand Else brandished her pail, swatting awkwardly at the insects that buzzed in her ears. She struggled to get her bearings among the firs that towered skywards, accepting at last that she had no idea where she was.

Somewhere nearby, a brook murmured. A thorny pelt of pine needles covered the mud, where mushroom caps peeped out from under fern fronds. Else noticed blueberry bushes in the scrub but, instead of stopping, tagged along after Lars into a strip of tall weeds. Moss sucked at her heels, slowing her progress as the shadows between the trees brightened to blue.

At the forest's rim, they stepped into a meadow. There were no fences that Else could see. Wild grasses and dandelion stalks grew waist-high in the paddock, whose limits appeared to be set by the contours of the land. Behind a hill at the far end of the field, she could make out the peak of a black-tiled roof.

'Who does it belong to?' she asked.

'Tenvik,' said Lars. 'He never comes here, though. Just look at it. It can't have been grazed all summer.'

He spread his arms at his sides and waded into the paddock, letting his flattened palms skate over the heads of the weeds. In spite of his assurances, Else met each rustle of grass in the wind with a nervous look. Knut Tenvik was her family's neighbour. She had cycled to his farm many times over the years to collect the jars of honey that, early in autumn, his wife sometimes promised her mother after church. Else knew the Tenvik property was vast, though she had never guessed it stretched this far. They must have come full circle. She realised with a twinge how close they were to home.

'Tenvik has more land than he knows what to do with,' said Lars. 'Pappa said he wants to rent some of it out. Did you know he went to Kristiansand some weeks ago?'

To their left, a path broke off from the field's perimeter and disappeared behind a copse. Else steered Lars away from it, pulling him deeper into the meadow.

'He went to a circus when he was there. He met the owner afterwards and offered him a deal.'

'A circus?' Else said.

'That's what he told my father.'

Lars's eyes glittered like snowflakes in the sun. He wound an arm around Else's waist and thoughts of home melted away.

'Can you imagine it?' he said. 'A circus. Right here. Elephants. Lions, even.'

At the heart of the field, the grass had sprouted so high that the tips of its stems drooped towards earth as if straining to return to the comfort of the soil. Else remembered the photos Lars had showed her as a child in the copies of *National Geographic*, whose yellow spines lined the bookshelves of Karin Reiersen's library. Elephants. Lions. She almost laughed at the idea.

'When are they coming?'

Lars shrugged. 'We'll have to see it together, you know.'

He tasted of oranges when he kissed her.

'I can't be late,' Else said.

He kissed her again. A wasp zipped by her elbow as she sank with him to the ground. Before long, her shirt was damp with dew and her head filled with the smell of the warm soil. Weeds swished around them like seagrass in a current. She vaguely wondered what had become of her pail.

When Lars dropped her off on the road by the farmhouse, Else stayed where she was in front of the mountain, unwilling to give up the easy feeling he brought, though it was already slipping away. She watched his moped speed off down the road before she trudged to the bottom of the hill, still straining to separate the whine of his engine from the soft stir of the land. Across the fjord, the sun had dipped behind the chimney stacks of the shipyard. Else rubbed the cold from her arms and hurried over the garden.

No lights were on in the farmhouse. She stepped inside and flipped a switch in the hallway. She pulled off her shoes and tiptoed to the dining room, where the fire in the oven was burning low. Else stopped beside it and held her palms to its embers, listening for her father through the floorboards above. The stillness weighed on the house. It smothered the relief she felt at finding no one home.

She did not need to look to guess where her father was, but still crept to the window for a view of the boathouse. Its walls were ragged against the dusking sky. At the top of its stairs, the door was ajar. Else moved away from the glass. She stood in the centre of the floor, unsure of what to do, before she turned the radio on.

THE WHISPERS STARTED some weeks later, a shared breath of disbelief at what Tenvik had done that passed from person to person like an infection. Rumours of a travelling show that had stopped along the coast at towns no bigger than their own were exchanged at the butcher's and bakery and carried home with cuts of pork and raisin buns. The mood in the Gymnasium shifted to one of celebration. Else stepped into the schoolyard on a Monday morning to find clowns' noses strung to the branches of its trees. The corridors and classrooms buzzed with invention as students described what they hoped to see, whipping up a giddy sense of camaraderie that felt precious and fleeting.

Else was standing between Lars and Rune by the caretaker's shed when Petter came charging through the school gate. By then, the weather had turned; the sun had gone into hibernation and, in its absence, a damp wind hacked down from the north. As he rushed towards them, she freed her hand from Lars's grip. She yanked up the zipper of her jacket and buried her chin behind her collar.

'Hey,' Petter said.

'Why the hurry?' said Lars. 'Spit it out.'

'You know how everyone's been talking about the circus?'

Petter placed his satchel on the ground and, after tossing back its flap, pulled a crumpled piece of paper from inside. His fingers trembled as he flattened it out. He presented it to Else, whose eyes grew wide when she realised what it was.

'It was pasted up outside of Arnholm's kiosk,' he said. 'I just tore it off.'

In the middle of the poster, a cartoon clown bared his teeth in an open-mouthed grin. His gloved hands pointed to a title in the top left corner: 'Circus Leona Is Coming!' A camel's neck popped up between splashes of purple and red. Four poodles stood on their hind legs in a row at the bottom of the sheet. To the right of the clown, there was a drawing of a man in a loincloth lifting a horse above his head. His arms bulged as round as the letters that proclaimed 'Circus Leona Is Coming!'

Lars let out a low whistle. He grabbed the poster from Else. 'What did I tell you?' he said. 'The fucking circus is coming.'

Three dates had been scrawled in black ink under the dogs' paws: 3rd October, 4th October, 5th October.

'Next Thursday,' said Lars. 'We'll sneak in next Thursday after school. It'll be busy on the first night, so it'll be easier to hide.'

'Won't you be going with your family?' asked Petter.

'So what?' said Lars. 'I can go twice.'

Else could not take her eyes from the poster that Lars had spread over his lap. The clown beamed at her beside the strong man's swollen torso.

'I'll come,' she said.

'Of course you're coming,' said Lars. 'None of us are missing this.'

During the next week Else's thoughts returned often to the poster, lifting off from familiar tasks and settling on a scene of poodles prancing on two legs. She would be doing her homework in the dining room and discover that minutes had been lost staring at the pages of a textbook, reading and rereading a single line but seeing clowns bouncing on the humps of trotting camels. Her excitement mounted with each day that brought the circus closer to town, quickening like a pulse under her skin whenever she overheard her mother muttering, 'Knut Tenvik must be out of his mind.'

The afternoon before the first performance, Else climbed Torggata on her way to the bakery. Petter tagged along, having just remembered that he, too, had promised his mother he would buy a loaf after school. He walked with his eyes on the pavement, skirting the puddles that had collected during the morning's rain. His silence made Else awkward. She wished he had not come or, better yet, that Lars had come in his place.

The bakery smelled of cinnamon when she opened the door. Inside, Ingrid Berge handed a paper bag to a customer.

'Who's next?' she asked.

'One loaf,' said Else.

'*Kneip*?'

'Yes, please.'

Petter ordered the same, as well as two raisin buns. He gave one to Else, who bit into its crust while Ingrid wrapped Petter's loaf. A shout from Torggata made her turn to the window, but all she could see was a slice of the empty street.

'In all my days,' said Ingrid. 'Someone is making a racket.'

The second holler was nearer than the last. Petter pocketed his change and dashed outside after Else, who collided with a boy racing up the hill.

'Watch where you're going!' said Petter over the trumpet of a car horn. Else looked up the road to the parade that the boy had been running to meet. Twenty cars or more rolled through the town behind a van. Across its bonnet, the words 'Circus Leona' were painted in purple and red.

'They're here,' Petter said.

The van's horn blared. Several others answered its call.

'Do you hear that?' he said. 'Else, do you see them? Come on!'

He set off at a sprint up the hill, leaving her to stare at the chain of cars that was edging towards her. The van's driver leaned out of his window to wave and grin at the crowd that was multiplying on the pavement. His face was flushed. The hair on his head crawled onto his cheeks in fat sideburns that fused in a bristly strip under his nose.

'Thursday! Friday! Saturday!' His letters tripped off his tongue with an exotic trill. 'Come see the animals and acrobats!'

The bakery door opened at Else's back.

'What's going on?' said Ingrid Berge.

'Thursday! Friday! Saturday!'

'Oh, my,' she said.

One after another, the cars passed. Vehicles in all shapes and sizes followed after the van. Volkswagens in various stages of disrepair towed trailers and caravans, while lorries and buses rattled in and out of potholes. From their seats in the cavalcade the circus troupe dealt out smiles to the townspeople, their dark eyes shining in dark faces. Else spotted a muzzle poking through an open window. A pair of nostrils quivered in the air, then disappeared.

The final car in the procession pulled a caravan whose walls had been mended with sheets of canvas and timber.

'Oh, Lord,' said Ingrid and bent her knees for a better peek at its driver. He was larger than any man Else had ever seen. His shoulders sprouted arms as thick as two knuckles of meat. He kept his eyes on the lorry ahead of him, not seeming to notice the crowd that inspected him with dropping jaws. Else felt the dip in her belly that always came when she cradled one of onkel Olav's coffee cups in her palm. Only after he had driven on did she realise that she had been holding her breath.

'Well,' said Ingrid, 'and now I've seen that, too.'

Ingrid withdrew into the bakery as soon as the spectators began to scatter. A staunch group made up mainly of children lingered at the rear of the parade, marching after it down Torggata and cheering with each bleat of the van's horn. Else searched the faces of those who remained and, when she did not find Petter, started to climb, realising with regret that her fingers had crushed the half-eaten raisin bun he had given her. At the top of the street, she looked back at the water. From here, she could see most of

THE LAST BOAT HOME

the town. White houses with black roofs speckled the hillside that tumbled to the fjord.

The procession had turned the corner at the Longpier and was now inching along Havneveien. At the end of the harbour, it picked up speed and pulled away from what was left of the crowd. Still the children ran, galloping after the column of cars as it receded from sight, keeping up with each other until, one by one, they fell by the wayside.

ON THE EVENING of the first circus show, Else walked the distance to Tenvik's farm with her head down, grateful for the rain that let her shrink under her hood, though water trickled down her jacket in streams that were soaked up by her trouser legs. Two cars sped by before slowing at Tenvik's gate and she crept after them onto his land, slogging through the mud in front of the farmhouse, whose windows were lit from within. To the right of his barns, a track decorated with red and purple sashes hooked away from the yard. Else's breath met the air in puffs of steam as she moved towards it.

Another car bumped onto the path behind her, catching her in its headlights, making her stumble. She turned her face to the bushes until it had driven on, then continued towards the music that was crashing through the dark. The band grew louder the closer she came to the paddock which, by now, she and Lars knew well. They had made the journey through the woods several times since he had first brought her there. As they lay in the shelter of its tall grass, they had tried to imagine what the circus would look like, where the Big Top would stand, where they would keep the animals, where the tickets would be sold.

Now, as Else stepped onto the field, the colours of the Big Top danced in a mist of white light. A winding queue of would-be ticket holders clutched money in their palms, anxious to escape the rain. She stole away from them, sticking to the shadows behind the generator and skirting the circus vans that were parked to one side of the tent. Between their bumpers she caught glimpses of bodies, a shimmer of costume, a whip of hair.

Lars was waiting by a row of boulders at the north end of the paddock. He stood with Rune and Petter, who sucked on a cigarette before offering it around. Else let Lars kiss her in front of the others and did not care that Rune swore, or that Petter looked away. She pressed Lars's hand.

'Ready?' he asked.

A voice bellowed inside the Big Top. 'Ladies and gentlemen,' it said, 'please take your seats.'

Else ducked into the gap between a car and its trailer, squeezing in behind Lars. He ventured forward and then drew back without a word. Two men hurried by, quarrelling in a language she could not understand. Once they had passed, Lars tried again. He dared a step, then another, and then he charged. From where she stood, Else watched him cover the distance to the Big Top in seconds flat. Next, a shadow darted from the trailer one car along. Rune and Petter were moving. She would have to be quick.

She took a deep breath. The air stank of horses. With one last peek around the corner, Else launched herself from behind the trailer's wall. Her shoes splattered mud. She was making too much noise: the whole circus would be able to hear her. She glanced left and right. A group had gathered at the rear of the tent. She could make out the silhouette of an animal, maybe two.

When she caught up with the boys, Lars was crouched on the ground with his fingers gripping the hem of the tent.

'Here we go,' he said. He lifted the canvas and crawled into the Big Top.

Else stooped after him, landing in sawdust which stuck to her palms and wet trouser legs. The band was walloping a tune to compete with the chatter of the audience, whose ankles dangled above her. On their hands and knees, Lars, Petter and Rune scrabbled under rows of shoe soles and scaffolding to the front, where restless feet revealed hints of the ring that lay beyond.

Lars dropped to his stomach behind a pair of boots and craned his neck to look for Else. She eased herself to the floor between him and Petter and sank into sawdust to meet the chill of the ground. The lights under the Big Top dimmed. A drum roll started.

'Good evening, dear ladies and gentlemen.'

The voice seemed to echo through the tent. A hush fell over the crowd. Petter's body stirred beside her. She could feel him trembling. Else found Lars's hand.

'Please allow me to welcome you. To the one. The only. Circus Leona!'

The Big Top exploded. First came the horses flashing white around the ring, their necks curved and their riders sparkling white from head to toe. Three sets of hooves thundered by, flicking dirt into Else's eyes. Next the clowns rolled in red and the acrobats flipped silver, green and blue, like mackerel straight out of the water. And everything was moving – spinning, flipping and rolling – and the colour was so bright, it was like landing on the sun.

The audience scrambled to their feet and screamed their delight and stamped the scaffolding which shuddered over Else's head. Cymbals crashed and the riders planted their feet on their saddles, though their horses galloped on. Another smash of the cymbals and the riders jumped and now they were falling in somersaults to the ground. They touched down with a splash in the sawdust and the Big Top shook with the crowd's jubilation.

'And now. For the first act of the evening.'

The microphone crackled and Else shivered. In a gap between a pair of legs, she saw the ringmaster stepping in from the wings to the centre of the manège. He wore a red top hat and tails embroidered with rhinestones. Even in his costume, Else recognised the driver of the van. The ringmaster smiled a glittering smile.

'I ask you to welcome. Ladies and gentlemen. From the bottom of your hearts. The Brothers Bezrukov!'

The spotlight blinked off and on. Now it pointed to the back of the ring, where two men jogged out with their arms open wide. A net as big as a fisherman's dropped from the ceiling to the floor and the first brother stepped up to wind his ankles in its mesh. The audience gasped as the net jerked, snatching the man into the air. His body twisted and twitched and became ever more tangled until his struggle tore the net in two. It dragged his legs into a split and tipped him upside down and he reached for his brother, who grabbed his wrists. Instead of saving him, he, too, was swept off his feet. He twirled up and over until both brothers were ensnared.

Else looked past their gymnastics to the spectators across the ring. In the grey light of the stalls, she recognised faces from school and even from church. Ingrid Berge appeared transfixed beside her daughter, Gro, who perched on the edge of her seat and pressed her palms in her lap. Behind them, Astrid Stormo's two sons had forgotten the blooms of candyfloss gripped in their hands. Tenvik sat in the front row and leaned forward in his chair, his fingers clutching the barrier rail. His eyes never strayed from the performers, though he shook his head from time to time as if unable to believe what they saw.

One by one, the ringmaster introduced the acts that followed the Brothers Bezrukov, each more wonderful than the last. A contortionist touched his ears with his toes before a clown proposed marriage to Tenvik's wife. Llamas and camels gave way to a quartet of poodles which sprang through hoops and balanced balls on their noses. A magician drove swords into a chest, while his assistant screamed her terror from inside. Trapeze artists swung and toppled, a juggler threw fire, a tightrope walker pirouetted under a red-and-purple-starred sky. The air smelled of sweat and dung and spun sugar. The tent was all twinkle and feathers and shine.

'And now,' said the ringmaster, 'for the night's final performance.'

The lights fell. Darkness smothered the murmur of the crowd.

'Prepare yourselves, ladies and gentlemen, to be dazzled.'

Petter inched closer to Else. Lars's fingers touched her elbow, sending a tingling up her arm.

'Here is the mighty. The unequalled. Please welcome, ladies and gentlemen. Valentin Popov!'

When the spotlight came on, a man was waiting in the middle of the ring, his fists resting on his hips. Above the hose that were moulded to his calves and thighs, his torso glistened in the light. It was the giant from the parade. Else remembered how he had seemed unconcerned by the townspeople gawking at him in his car. Any detachment he had shown then was gone. He glared at the audience, who welcomed him with raucous applause. He kept his stare level when a boy in a military coat led a golden retriever to his side. Valentin Popov noticed the duo and threw his hands into the air before scooping the dog up in his arms. After pumping the animal three times over his head, he put it back on the ground and shooed his partner away.

The boy returned, yanking a sheep by its collar. Its bleated complaint sent a ripple of laughter through the crowd. The man shook his fist at his accomplice and grabbed him instead of the sheep, using him as a dumb-bell before setting him free.

From the wings of the manège a honking horn announced the ringmaster, who appeared behind the wheel of a Volkswagen. The band pounded its drums as Valentin Popov knelt by the car's bumper and, with a groan, hoisted its two front wheels off the floor.

He held his load for some seconds before letting it fall. His chest heaved in the spotlight. His forehead gleamed with sweat.

Behind him, a rider guided a horse into the ring. She whispered into its ear and backed away. Valentin Popov's gaze swept the crowd and a rising chant from the stalls brought a smile to his lips.

He turned to the animal. Laying his palms on its underbelly, he jacked his thighs. A cry tore from his throat. He closed his eyes and a vein snaked down his forehead. As he lifted the horse towards the ceiling of the Big Top, a network of blood vessels sprang to the surface of his skin.

'Jesus Christ,' said Lars under his breath. The strong man's arms were swollen with mottled lumps of muscles when he opened his eyes and beamed at his supporters. They howled and clapped and stamped their feet while, above him, the horse tossed its mane in the air.

Now

2009

ELSE HAS COME as far as the town hall when she spots Marianne and Liv in front of the boathouses. She hides behind the crowd that separates them, feeling foolish but unable to help herself. In the gaps between the couples holding hands and the children white-tongued with licked ice cream, she watches Liv hop into the speedboat. Her granddaughter grins at Andreas and his sister. Lars clutches Marianne's elbow and she climbs aboard to where Victoria smiles in welcome.

Else takes a deep breath, swallowing the smells of frying waffle batter and hotdogs sweating in the sun. She presses through the throng towards her family, nodding her greetings at familiar faces as she walks by. Lars sees her first.

'There you are!' he calls. 'I was afraid we'd have to leave without you.'

'Mormor, have you seen this boat?' Liv throws herself onto the sunbed next to Andreas. 'Isn't it amazing?'

'I brought a box of white,' Else says and passes her Wine Monopoly bag to Lars, who places it in the shade. She ignores the hand that he extends, a puerile snub which he does not appear to notice as she steps onto the gunwale, testing her weight on the fibreglass before lowering herself into the boat. Once on deck, she finds a seat between Victoria and Marianne.

'How are you, Else?' Victoria asks. 'Oh, Thea, no. Not the steering wheel, darling. I said no, Thea. Come over here.'

Andreas's sister slides from the captain's perch and slots herself between her mother's knees. She sucks the whistle knotted to the collar of her life vest and scowls at Else, who pretends not to notice. Some hundred metres from the dock, a flotilla of boats waits for the signal to begin. Their flags beat in the breeze, flaunting their colours in a billowing stream across the sky.

Lars fits a key into the ignition and the speedboat's motor whirs. 'Andreas!' he calls. 'Get the ropes!'

His son scrabbles ashore to unpick the moorings and lobs them into the hull. When Andreas has reclaimed his spot next to Liv, Lars pushes off from the pier. They glide into the fjord and merge with the summer solstice parade.

It starts with a gunshot. A wooden *sjekte* garlanded with flowers noses out in front, slow-powering parallel to the dock while the rest of the vessels float after it in untidy rows. Trond Rastad shouts from the neighbouring boat.

'Haven't we been lucky with the day?' He beams when Lars agrees and tips a brown beer bottle at him. 'Welcome home!' he calls.

The boats putter on, following the line of the harbour. Victoria stands and, squatting by the door to the cabin, gathers up a column of plastic cups from the floor. She serves the first round of drinks: Coke for the kids, white wine for the adults. Else sips and narrows her eyes against the sun. In spite of her mood and the present company, her body responds to the nudge of the water. The motor's buzz tickles the soles of her feet. Her back teeth hum when she bites them together.

She takes another gulp of wine and tries to remember when she was last on a boat. It must have been before Tenvik sold his farm. While Liv and Andreas wave at the spectators on land and Victoria raves about her new kitchen, Else distracts herself with thoughts of their summer outings into the skerry when Marianne was a child. She recalls her daughter's excitement as she chattered in the bow seat, her chest puffed in an orange life preserver while Tenvik piloted his skiff and Else unwound her mackerel line into the deep, taking care not to snag her fingers on its hooks.

When the flotilla reaches the Longpier, it breaks apart. Lars spins the steering wheel to aim the speedboat at the islands that fend off the Skagerrak. At the limit of the no wake zone, he jams down the throttle and the prow cants into the air.

'Lars!' shrieks Victoria. 'Slow down!'

The speedboat races towards the sea, careening through a flock of seagulls that bobs on the water, launching them into the sky. The wind scrapes Else's hair off her forehead and she clutches her handbag close, not even letting go to wipe her leaking eyes. She is too old for this kind of ride. The children scream, thrilled when they slam into the first wave. Spray rains over the deck. Else wants to grab Marianne's arm, but makes do with gripping her handbag tighter.

She relaxes her hold when Lars turns into the calmer currents of a fjord and zips past the slower boat traffic to cut a path inland. Here, along the coast, summerhouses with mowed lawns and tended flowerbeds vie for space on the waterfront. Else marvels at the number of new properties, at the giant windows carved into their walls and the monstrous boats docked at their piers. In preparation for the evening's bonfires, piles of wood have been stacked on outcrops of rock. Already the odd blaze shines in the distance.

Lars eases back the throttle when the speedboat arrives in the skerry. The search begins for somewhere to drop anchor. Other boats have claimed the spots that are most sheltered from the wind and now their captains hurl ropes to fix their prows before leaping to land. On the islands, their families lay out picnics. Children scamper between the trees and inspect crab corpses dashed by seagulls on the rocks.

'That looks like it's going to be a good one,' says Liv, pointing to a tower of driftwood that has yet to be set alight.

Andreas calls over his shoulder. 'Pappa! That looks like a good one!'

'I see it,' says Lars. He guides the speedboat to the island and scouts its perimeter for a vacant space. On his second sweep, he settles on a slice of water between a sailing boat and a Winrace.

'There isn't room for you there,' says Else.

'Andreas,' says Lars, 'take the rope at the prow.'

Andreas crawls to the speedboat's prow and crouches with a rope in hand, preparing to jump while Lars manoeuvres them into the slot. He brings the boat in too quickly, then yanks the throttle into reverse and whirls the steering wheel. The seething of the engine attracts an audience on land.

'You're doing it wrong!' says Thea.

'There isn't room for you there,' says a man on the sailing boat. Petter Skoland is sitting alone in the cockpit, his eyes fixed on the speedboat that is threatening to ram him.

'Petter?' calls Lars. 'Is it you? How about a little help?'

Still watching the prow where Andreas clings to his rope, Petter gets to his feet and dips his upper body under the sailing boat's guardrail. He reaches out his bare arms and his palms connect with the fibreglass in time to save his hull. His biceps tighten as he leans his weight against the oncoming vessel's nose and Lars pushes a button on the pilot panel, releasing the anchor with a rumble from the speedboat's belly.

'You should have dropped the anchor earlier,' Petter says. 'Right her up. Right her up, I said!'

Petter heaves and Andreas throws himself onto land. The onlookers shake their heads and turn away as the speedboat wedges into place.

Lars directs his son in making the boat fast. When they have knotted the fenders and lifted their provisions ashore, he meets Petter on firm ground.

'It's been a while,' he says.

'Are you down for the summer?' asks Petter.

'We've moved here. We've taken over my parents' old house.'

'I hadn't heard,' Petter says. He nods at Else, then at Marianne. 'Enjoy yourselves.'

He climbs back onto his sailing boat and Lars leads the way to the centre of the island. With bags in hand, he navigates rock pools and fissures spattered with seagull droppings. Liv, Andreas and Thea wander off from the adults to a group of children in the shallows between this island and the next. A handful wade naked in the water, while others dangle crushed mussels and snail shells at the crabs. Liv peers into a bucket and beckons to Andreas, who stops at her side and peeks over the bucket's rim.

Close to the foot of the bonfire pile, Victoria finds an unclaimed patch of rock on which to set out the Tupperware containers that she pulls from an insulated bag. Marianne plucks the lids off smoked salmon, cured meats, scrambled eggs. Lars sees to the drinks, readying the nozzle of Else's wine box while she passes around cushions from an open rucksack. She hands out paper plates and arranges herself on a boulder slightly apart from the rest of her party.

Marianne digs into the scrambled egg with a plastic fork.

'Where's your boyfriend tonight, then?' asks Lars. 'I thought you'd be bringing him along.'

'He has a show,' Marianne says. 'He's in Grimstad tonight. He'll be in Kristiansand this weekend.'

'Does he usually travel so much?' asks Lars.

'He's a dancer,' she says.

'Ah. That explains it, I suppose.'

The boulder's stone is cold through Else's cushion. She fidgets with a tissue in her pocket, tearing it to pieces while her daughter answers Lars's questions about Mads. She has no appetite. She watches Lars rip the cover from a disposable barbecue and take a lighter from his pocket.

'So is he any good?' he asks.

'At dancing?' says Marianne. 'Mads is great at everything he does.' She bats lashes as thick as beetles' legs with mascara. Else rolls her eyes. She prods a slice of ham with her fork.

'Mamma doesn't like him,' says Marianne. 'She hasn't even met him.'

'Shouldn't you meet him first?' asks Lars.

'They've just met each other,' Else says.

'Well,' he says, 'then there's still hope for the boys of this town.' He winks at Marianne. '*Skål*,' he says. She lifts her glass and they drink. Marianne smiles.

The food is almost gone when the bonfire is lit. After the first burst of incidental flame a slow heat builds at its core, burning blue in places and shrivelling the kindling to ash. The children return from their play, the cuffs of their trousers damp. Else greets Liv with a towel and a lukewarm hotdog.

'Did you catch any crabs?' she asks.

'Andreas threw them back when we were done,' says Liv, a proud grin spreading over her cheeks. Else folds an arm around her granddaughter, rubbing at the chill that she guesses must have set under her skin, while Liv sniffs between mouthfuls. Behind them, the fire cracks and snaps and rises. Lars kneels and leans over the remains of the picnic, his finger cocked above the wine box's spout.

'No, thank you,' Else says.

'You'll have some, won't you?' He refills Marianne's cup. '*Skål*.'

'Maybe you've had enough,' says Victoria in a whisper. Then, to the group, 'Who was that man we met on the sailing boat?'

'Another friend from school,' says Lars. 'I heard that Petter got divorced.'

'That's right,' Else says.

'And his wife is remarried.'

'She is,' she says.

Lars prises the cap off a beer. He helps himself to another once he has passed the wine box around again. The families with younger children begin to pack up their picnics and he unzips the cool bag for another bottle. He staggers to his feet when Victoria announces it is time to go, stretches and stumbles away to find somewhere to piss. By now Liv is sitting with Marianne, who whispers into her ear while Else looks on, her heart filling up. Her girls pick shapes from out of the flames and huddle close and she feels an urgency to join them, to plant herself between them and those who would intrude. Instead she replaces the tops on the Tupperware and packs the containers into plastic bags. Her arms are weighed down when she moves off, leaving Victoria to gather their rubbish.

The night cools as Else retreats from the bonfire. She waits by the speedboat for the others to catch her up, glad to have some moments to collect her thoughts, to admire the evening without being disturbed. She thinks of her mother then, of how, on this day every year, while she was still able to, she would build a bonfire on the rocks by the pier of the old farmhouse, keeping it burning until long after dark. Beyond the ring of boats that are docked at this island, bonfires fleck the sky up and down the skerry, their reflections streaking the water like setting suns. Else hears a rustle of material from the sailing boat and peers over the guardrail at Petter in the cockpit. He is buttoning his boat jacket. He glances up and blinks at her through his glasses.

'Sorry,' she says.

'What for?' he says.

Else balls a piece of torn tissue paper in her pocket.

'How was the bonfire?' asks Petter.

'You can see it for yourself.'

'The picnic, then,' he says.

Else shrugs. Petter smiles and she peeks over her shoulder, fearing she has given too much away. Marianne and Liv arrive with Victoria, Andreas and Thea. The children search for shells to toss while the adults load the boat. When Lars reappears, he fishes the key from his pocket.

'You'd better give it to me,' Victoria says.

'Don't be silly.'

'The police are bound to be doing spot checks.'

'I'm perfectly capable of driving.'

'You're not driving,' Victoria says.

With an exaggerated sigh, Lars relinquishes the key. Liv climbs aboard after Andreas and they each choose a side to pull in the fenders. Victoria pushes a button and the anchor retracts before Marianne leaps from land, holding the end of the rope. She stows it away and the boat floats into the skerry. The island's shouts and laughter dwindle behind them. They have hardly begun their journey when Liv lies down next to Else, stretching across the cushions of the sunbed to place her head in her grandmother's lap. Else strokes her hair and considers the silhouette on the sailing boat. She wonders which way Petter's face is turned.

ONLY THREE CARS are parked in a shaded corner of the car park. Else crosses the empty lot together with Liv, who skips up the wheelchair ramp and leans against the door to the nursing home. In a reception area that smells of bleach, a girl dressed in a burgundy scrub suit is visible behind a window. She removes an earphone as Else draws close and the notes from a tinny guitar solo stray into the silent space.

'Knut Tenvik,' Else says. 'Don't worry. We know where we're going.'

The girl replaces her earphone and they continue down the hall, past the numbered rooms that house 'Assisted Living' residents. It is something quite different from the secure ward where Else's mother spent her final days. Even now, more than a year since her death, Else feels the guilt that comes with each visit to Tenvik. She should have done more, researched some new medication, but her mother was in a hurry at the last. She seemed to embrace her slip into dementia with a calm that pained Else almost as much as seeing her fade.

A staircase next to a wall plastered with drawings from the local kindergarten brings Else and Liv to the second floor. In the middle of the corridor a door opens into a common room, where a handful of the home's residents are gathered at a table playing whist. Tenvik sits in his wheelchair by the window, gazing at the fjord below. His hair has been washed. It springs from his skull in a dandelion clock's puff of white.

'Hi, Knut,' says Liv.

'Young lady,' he says. 'And there is Else. And Marianne?'

'Mamma's with her boyfriend,' says Liv.

'Well, that explains it,' he says. 'And what does Else make of that?'

'She doesn't like it.'

'I'm right here,' says Else. 'I can hear you, you know.'

Liv exchanges a smile with Tenvik before she darts to the kitchen to find an orderly who will make their coffee. While she is gone, Else carries two chairs to Tenvik's side.

'How are you feeling?' she asks. 'Any more trouble with that cough?'

'I'm fine,' he says. 'Tell me, how's business?'

'Fine,' Else says.

'Well,' he says, 'then everything is fine.' A laugh gives way to a splutter and Tenvik hacks onto his knees. Else waits for the attack to pass.

'Have the doctors said any more?' she asks.

'It's nothing,' he says. 'When are you going to take me out for lunch? It's the food here that's killing me, not the cough. One more meatball and I'll thank them for having me.'

Liv returns with a middle-aged woman, who places a thermos of coffee on the window ledge. She lifts cups from her tray, a jug of cream and a plate of biscuits. While Else pours the coffee Liv reaches for a saucer of sugar cubes, tearing the wrapper from one before handing it to Tenvik.

'Here,' she says and watches, delighted, when he pinches the cube between finger and thumb. He dips a corner into his coffee and the liquid bleeds into the sugar, staining its granules a caramel brown. Tenvik pops the cube into his mouth and sucks.

'That's more like it,' he says. 'Have you been to the house?'

'There hasn't been time,' Else says.

'You really must sell it. It's an asset, Else, you can't just leave it to rot. Stop by the farm while you're at it, will you? I want a report on how Karsten is treating my cows. Do you remember, young lady,' Tenvik asks Liv, 'what fun we used to have on the farm? You liked to drive the tractor, just like your mother used to. How about another sugar cube?'

Liv awards him with a second cube and he repeats the procedure. Then she stands and wanders to the television set. She flicks through the channels while Else fills Tenvik in on the town's gossip since her previous visit. The council has approved a proposal for a new supermarket behind the Statoil petrol station. Rimi, she thinks, or perhaps it was Kiwi. Janne Haugen mentioned it, but she can't remember now. Plans are going ahead for the expansion of the Solbakken pier into a marina. Janne said the work would begin in September. It should be ready before the summer season starts next year.

'What else?' Tenvik asks.

'That's more or less it.'

A frown puckers his lips. He touches Else's wrist with three crooked fingers. 'So it isn't true that Lars Reiersen is back.'

'Oh,' Else says. 'He's been back for a while.'

'Funny,' says Tenvik. 'You haven't mentioned it.'

'They've been here for ages,' says Liv, still watching the TV. 'We went out on their speedboat for *Sankt Hans*. We were in the parade. His son's called Andreas.'

'Is he?' says Tenvik. 'And what about his wife?'

'Victoria,' Liv says. 'She's nice. She's pretty.'

'She's young,' Else says. 'Not much older than Marianne.' She sips from her cup, angling the porcelain in a way that she hopes will hide her blush. 'He's doing something with the shipyard. I haven't asked what.'

'I'm sure you'll hear soon enough,' Tenvik says. 'You know how people like to talk.' His eyes are clear in spite of his age. They study Else's face for a beat too long before he throws up his hands and bellows to the room. 'Who's going to tell me about Marianne's new boyfriend?'

'Me!' says Liv. 'They've been together for ages.'

'Everything's relative,' Else says.

Liv points the remote control at the screen, which flashes and blinks out. She pushes herself from the armchair and recounts the details her mother has shared about the Swede. Else finds herself wishing the nursing home would serve something stronger than coffee. She checks her watch and pours herself another cup.

Once Liv has kissed Tenvik's sunken cheek, she leads the way home. Else pauses now and then while her granddaughter pulls a wild flower from the roadside. They take a short cut onto

Lundgata through the bottom of Terje Bull's yard, where they keep to the shade under the ash trees' branches.

'Do Knut's legs hurt him?' Liv asks.

'No,' Else says. 'He can't feel them any more.'

Liv stops to admire a dog rose that droops from its stem over a gatepost.

'Not that one,' Else says. 'That's from somebody's garden.'

'Why didn't you tell him about Lars?'

'What do you mean?' Else asks.

'That he had moved back.'

'I didn't think it would interest him.'

Else chews her top lip and points at a tangle of wild strawberry stalks that pokes out of the underbrush. She rummages in her pocket for a clean tissue and balances herself on her haunches next to Liv, who picks the tiny berries and places them on the paper cupped in Else's palm. The fruits are bruised, or else hard and yellow under the seeds that spot their skin. Else chooses a berry that is ripe enough and, with her tongue, mashes it into a sweet pulp against the roof of her mouth. She winks at Liv, anticipating her protests, the burst of indignation that will give way to laughter. Her granddaughter considers her with a solemn expression that stings her heart.

'I know about you and Lars, you know,' she says. 'That he was your boyfriend.'

'Liv,' Else says.

'Mamma told me,' she says. 'When you were younger. Andreas says he and Victoria fight about it sometimes.'

'Liv,' says Else, 'what a thing to say.'

'Why not? If it's true.'

'That's enough,' Else says.

'But is it true, Mormor? I want you to tell me.'

Else feels her throat is being scrubbed with steel wool. 'It was a long time ago,' she says. She avoids meeting Liv's eye, though she can sense that her granddaughter wants more from her. She pinches another strawberry from its stem and arranges it with the others, then supports herself with her free hand in the soil.

'Is it true?' Liv says and her voice is strange and Else hates herself for being the cause of its strangeness. 'Is it true that my grandfather was in the circus?'

'Yes,' Else says.

'Did you love him?' Liv asks.

Else looks at the fjord. It glistens in the gaps between the houses. The sun is bright. It hurts her eyes.

'Yes,' she says.

Her knees are stiff when she stands and carefully folds the corners of the tissue over the berries. 'I think that's enough for now. Don't you?'

Liv nods and follows her grandmother down the road. She slips a hand that fits exactly into Else's and presses the fingers and lets them go.

Then

1974

AFTER THREE DAYS of performances, the circus packed up and drove away. Its lorries and wagons and cars with their trailers disappeared without fanfare down the coast road, leaving behind a glimmer of possibility that seemed to Else to dull the colours of what had been there before. She treasured moments of solitude when she was able to return in thought at least to the sawdust at the edge of the ring to watch white horses galloping and tightrope walkers gliding across the sky. Often she would call to mind the circus troupe's performers and try to imagine the places they came from, far-away countries, towns and cities that bustled and buzzed under a different sun. She felt their departure like a promise revoked, but still remembered them hopefully. In three years, she would finish school. She would not have to stay in this town forever.

Several weeks passed before Else went back to the paddock. In that time, in the halls and classrooms of the Gymnasium, the students continued to trade stories from the Big Top as if each had seen a different show. As the only one of their friends to have visited the circus twice, Lars took charge of the collective testimony. Those whose parents had disapproved, who had spent the nights of the circus's stay in mourning for what they were missing, assembled in the yard by the caretaker's shed, where he recounted the wonders that he had witnessed in the manège. He described a contortionist folding his body into six segments and a strong man lifting a horse with the tip of his thumb until, little by little, his audience disbanded and talk moved onto other things.

Bjørn Fodstad brought an American football to school that an aunt had sent him from Wisconsin. For the next two weeks, Lars, Rune and Petter used the breaks to blunder after the oblong ball. Else cheered them on together with Gro Berge and Hanne Austbø, whose parents were Smith's Friends and who was the youngest of eight siblings, or else the girls would climb Torggata to the bakery and Gro would ask her mother for some of yesterday's raisin buns. Sometimes while Else was eating her roll, she would find herself listening for a blast of horns on the hill outside, though she knew the circus would not come back for another year, if at all.

A sombre sky settled over the town. Its clouds were low and tinged grey. After a stretch of days deprived of sunlight, the locals began to mutter about an ugly autumn. In the mornings before school, when Else stood at the public dock and watched the shipyard's boat ferry its workers across the fjord, her breath met the air in a thickening fog and she knew that winter would follow soon.

On a Saturday at the end of October, Else kicked through the rotting leaves on the forest floor behind the Tenvik farm. A torrent of rain had finally subsided and the brook thundered under the weight of new water. The paddock bore the scars of the circus's visit. The grass had been chopped before its arrival and what was left had been gouged by hooves and tent pegs or churned by feet and countless sets of tyres. Else's shoes sank into the soggy earth. She hesitated when she saw two trailers parked on the meadow.

Smoke spiralled from the remains of a fire in a ditch and melted into the sky.

Lars was not there. In front of one of the trailers a man leaned over the open bonnet of a Volkswagen, his ponytail wagging between his shoulder blades when he spat a gob into the soil. Else had begun her retreat when she heard a shout. Another man had stepped from one of the caravans and was yanking shut its door. He started towards her across the field.

'Hey!' he called. 'Are you looking for Tenvik? This is private property. Are you looking for the circus? The circus has gone.'

As the man approached, his scar came into focus. His left eyelid wilted across the iris that darted in his eye. He stopped too close to Else, who realised she was staring and looked away. He took his time to study her.

'You need something?' he said.

'I'm just waiting for someone.'

'Lucky someone,' he said.

'He'll be here any minute,' Else said.

'Maybe I'll keep you company while you wait. I'm Yakov. You want something? Coffee? Cigarette?'

'No,' Else said. She crossed her arms over her chest, her muscles taut even after Lars had ducked under a branch into the clearing. At first, he did not seem to notice her companion. He brushed the pine needles from his hair and then his hand dropped to his side.

'I know you,' he said. 'You're from the circus. You're the brothers with the net. You are, aren't you? I saw the show. I saw it twice. You and your brother were pretty good.'

A smile thinned the circus man's lips. He called to his brother, who was still bent over the car's hood. 'Do you hear that, Oleg? This boy says we were pretty good.'

Oleg aimed a fresh lump of phlegm into the mud.

'So what are you doing here?' asked Lars. 'This is private property.'

'That's what I just finished telling your girlfriend,' Yakov said.

Lars nodded. He stood almost as tall as the foreigner and met his challenge with an indifference that made Else shrink.

'We're doing some work for Tenvik,' Yakov said. 'If that's all right with you?'

'But what about the circus?'

'The season's over,' Yakov said.

The door to the second trailer opened and a man that Else recognised stooped through its exit. She felt her feet turn to clay. There was no mistaking the strong man. He straightened up to his full height, rising until he towered above the roof of the caravan. A dry sound scraped Lars's throat.

'We should go,' Else said.

'You just got here,' said Yakov. 'Do you have more questions for me, young man? Or is that all?'

While he spoke, the strong man lowered himself to sit on his trailer's top step. He started to roll a cigarette, sprinkling strands from a tobacco pouch that he pulled from the pocket of his trousers.

'What's your name?' Yakov asked.

'Lars.'

'Lars,' he said. 'Now, Lars, I think you can answer some questions for me. Does your father have a farm? We're looking for more work.'

'No,' Lars said.

'What about you?' he asked Else. 'Maybe your pappa has a farm.'

Else examined a patch of spoiled grass by her shoes. She wished that Yakov would stop staring at her.

'Well,' he said, 'it's always nice to meet the locals, but we're busy. So you'd better run along.'

'I know about things around here,' said Lars.

His boast took Else by surprise. She thought perhaps she had misheard him, but Yakov's grin told her she had heard him well enough. She peeked at the strong man, who smoked on the step and acted as though he were alone in the meadow. Still, his size made her nervous. She longed for the shelter of the forest.

'What kind of things?' Yakov asked.

'All kinds,' said Lars.

'Like liquor? You know about that?'

'I can get some, if that's what you want.'

'I'm leaving,' Else said.

'You'd better go with your girlfriend, or you'll wish you had later on,' said Yakov with a wink. 'Don't disappear, though. Do you hear? Come back soon. You, too, treasure,' he said to Else. 'Come back anytime.'

Else retreated into the wood, pushing a path between the tree trunks. She bowed her head to the branches that clipped her jacket, splashing mud up to her knees as she hurried through puddles towards the spot where she had left her father's bicycle. Behind her, Lars stumbled through the undergrowth.

'Else!' he called. 'Hold on! Where are you going?' He caught her arm. 'What's the rush?'

'What are you doing?' she asked. 'We don't know anything about those men.'

'They're circus performers,' said Lars. 'And they're camped in our paddock. What else do we need to know?'

'That Yakov,' she said. 'I don't like him.'

'He was just flirting with you. He thought you were pretty. He didn't mean anything by it.' Lars let go of her arm and touched his fingers to her cheek. 'Calm down. All right?'

'I'm cold,' Else said.

'I'll warm you up,' he said. He wrapped her in his arms. With her jaw pressed to his collarbone, Else looked for the circus men over his shoulder in the warren of shadow, bark and brush. Lars kissed her until she felt safe. The pounding of the brook smothered the whine of the wind.

———

'There you are,' her mother said. 'I was beginning to wonder if you'd got lost.' She smiled at her sewing as Else arrived in the dining room. 'Are you hungry? I took a loaf of bread out of the oven half an hour ago.'

In the kitchen, Else sawed the end off the warm loaf. She peeled the lid from a tin of mackerel in tomato sauce and, after heaping the fish onto her slice, carried her plate to the dining table and sat across from her mother. Between them on the table, lengths of fabric had been arranged in piles beside the sewing machine. Her mother squinted through her spectacles as she fed material under the presser foot.

'Who's that for?' Else asked.

'Ninni,' her mother said. 'I still haven't finished the dress pattern she brought me a month ago. What's the weather like out there?'

'Grim,' Else said.

'Your father's taken the trawler out early. They've forecast a storm tonight.'

Else watched her mother rub her forehead where concentration puckered the skin and tried not to mind the weariness of the gesture. Even so, the guilt that unsettled her each Sunday at church stirred her stomach like a spoon. She let herself imagine for a moment her mother's shame if she and Lars were ever to be caught. She crammed the remains of the bread slice into her mouth and returned her plate to the kitchen.

'I thought I'd go fishing,' she said from the doorway.

'Now?' asked her mother.

'That's what I thought,' she said.

'But it'll be dark soon.'

'I'll keep to the front of the house,' she said. 'I won't stay out long. Some fresh fish for supper would be nice, don't you think?'

The idea of doing something useful had already made her feel better. Else washed her dish and, in the corridor, zipped up her waterproofs and stepped into her shoes. She left the farm-house and made her way under the branches of the morello cherry tree to the boathouse. At the top of its stairs she laid a palm on the door, whose cracked paint flaked off when she gave it a shove. Inside, the vinegar stink of homebrew stung her eyes. It was stronger than it had been when she'd last had reason to come in here. Since then, a sponge mattress had been pushed against the wall beneath the pair of oars that rested across the ceiling beams. Its flower-print sheet was stained and dusty. The *Norges* jars her father used for decanting were lined up at its foot.

Else crouched by the workbench cluttered with fishing equip-ment and studied the distillery that was hidden under its shelf. While the fjord slapped the hull of the skiff docked under her feet, she followed the curl of a hose from a sealed pot into a bucket. She considered committing an act of sabotage – piercing the rubber with a fishhook, or twiddling the dial of the camping stove and emptying its gas into the air – but instead stood and chose a line from a tackle box, unsnagging its weight and hook before tugging open the trapdoor in the floor.

When she had finished lowering the oars through the hatch, she climbed down the ladder to the stacked rock ledge on one side of the boat. She loaded her gear before untying its ropes and clambering aboard. With an oar in hand, Else nudged its blade against the walls of the dank moorings, pushing the skiff from the cobwebs into open air. She left it there loosely knotted and crossed the pier to tear a cluster of mussels from the water, shaking the drops from the seaweed-sewn shells. After finding a stone with which to crush them, she balanced a foot on the skiff's gunwale and pushed off from land. The boat bobbed while she fitted the oars in the rowlocks. It turned on the current until, perched on the middle bench with her back to the shipyard, she started to row.

A slow ache crept into her arms as the farmhouse withdrew behind the trees. Else gritted her teeth and dragged the oars under white-capped waves. With each stroke, she resented the Johnson motor that her father had bought the previous year and forbidden her to use. It seemed to dare her from the stern of the boat, where it tilted its propeller out of the fjord, cocking its bulk to one side like the head of a sneering passenger.

By the time she had rowed far enough and decided to pull in the oars, the day's mist had graduated to a drizzle. Else drew up her hood and smashed a mussel with her stone, stabbing its meat with her hook before dropping the weight into the water. The line slipped through her fingers towards the schools of fish that she imagined streaking colour under the skiff, diving and weaving in synchrony as their scales gleamed in the black depths. She was glad for the rain that pocked the fjord's skin, knowing the fish would bite more readily because of it.

She thought suddenly of the Brothers Bezrukov tumbling and twirling in their net and yanked the fishing line. Perhaps Lars was right: they were men like any other. However Yakov had made her feel, all he had done was offer her a cigarette. Else recalled the strong man spreading his hands over the horse's belly and heaving her out of the sawdust towards the Big Top's roof. The animal had not kicked while he held her in the ring. She had not protested at all.

Else yielded to the bright daze that came with memories of the circus while the raindrops grew fat, skating over her water-proof trousers and beating the canvas hood that covered her ears. By the time her line jerked, the benches were slick. Water swished under the planking of the rowing boat. Her fingers were raw and clumsy with cold and she winced when the fishing wire nicked her flesh. She was surprised by how far the skiff had drifted. Behind her, the shipyard's empty graving dock carved a slab out of the shore. She let her catch fight the hook before easing it in and landing a coalfish in the boat. It thrashed, thumping the hull with its tail while its mouth gaped and its gills flared pink.

Else caught it in her palms and bent its neck until she felt a pop. She guessed its weight at around a kilo. It would do. After wiping the slime from her hands, she rescued the oars from the bottom of the boat and rowed for home. The cloudbank flashed like the inside of a shell. The coastline blurred behind sheets of rain as the boat pulled away, smearing the shipyard's construction sheds into brown dabs and washing the barns and farmhouses clean from sight. The old tomato tin that her father kept aboard for the job of bailing spun along the hull, thudding dully as the rain pelted its rust. Else strained against the wind that swept her off course no matter how her muscles burned.

When she craned her neck to gauge the distance to the farmhouse, the Aaby farm took shape in the murk. She backed an oar to correct her bearing and carried on rowing until, some minutes later, she looked around again. Else frowned at the choppy water that still separated her from home. She rowed with all of her strength, though her arms cramped with the wasted effort of fighting the current. The trees thinned and there was the boathouse, there was the straight stroke of the pier. Her mother stood at its end huddled against the downpour, clutching a sou'wester to her head. Else crossed the oars by her feet before raising a hand in the air to signal that all was well. Her knee connected with something hard. A rowlock jiggled in its socket and tipped overboard.

Even as she watched it sink from sight, Else thrust an arm after it into the water. Swearing under her breath, she ran her fingers along the gunwale for the missing cord that should have fastened it to the skiff. On the opposite gunwale, a shoelace secured the remaining rowlock. Else swivelled on her bench and shouted into the rain.

'Mamma!' she called. 'I lost a rowlock!'

Her sleeve leaked an icy stream down her arm when she picked up the oars. Every stroke sent the unfixed oar skidding along the slippery wood. Rain clattered in the boat.

'I lost a rowlock!' she called.

Her mother cupped a hand to her mouth, but Else could not hear her. She turned again to face the shipyard and seize the oars and, as she struggled to row, the skiff's prow wrenched to the portside. She glared at the Johnson engine, remembering her father's instructions. She baulked at the thought of openly disobeying him. Still, she lifted in the oars and threw herself at the petrol can that was pushed under the bench at the boat's stern, pumping its hose before grasping the motor's pull rope in her fingers.

The engine would not start. As Else checked the shift lever the wind snatched at the boat, driving it further from land. She tried again. The motor grumbled and spat smoke into the air before it died. Else eased out the choke and tried again. With each failure she looked for her mother, who paced the pier and waved her arms over her hat. Else tried again. And again. She jammed in the choke and tried again. She considered rowing again but the boat had drifted too far; she was too tired.

But this time, when she tugged the pull rope, the engine sputtered awake. Else twisted the grip of the throttle control arm, savouring the tremble of rubber under her palm. The tomato tin rolled down the hull's planking and bumped the toe of her shoe when she opened the throttle and the prow pitched out of the water. It juddered with each smack of a new wave, hurling spray into the rain as Else approached land.

Her mother ran up the pier to meet the skiff. With her hands on the gunwale, she guided it in.

'Are you all right?'

'Yes,' Else said.

'Thank God. What did I tell you about going out in this weather? We're lucky the boat wasn't damaged. You know we couldn't have afforded to get it fixed.'

Else killed the engine and, after tipping the propeller out of the tide, used the oars to manoeuvre the skiff under the boat-house. Her mother helped her tie its ropes before hurrying to the farmhouse, leaving her to hoist the oars out of the boat and through the trapdoor. Else climbed after them up the ladder. Once inside, she replaced her father's fishing line in the tackle box. With her fingers hooked under the coalfish's gills, she plodded into the rain and across the sodden yard.

THE *FRØYA* RAN aground around six o'clock that evening. Ole Haugeli and Tom Ivar Lund brought Johann home in borrowed clothes, which were tight over his shoulders and appeared to do little to relieve the chill that shot his muscles with a visible shiver. From her seat by the fire, Else listened to her father deliver the news that the trawler was gone. He limped away from his wife's questions, locking himself in the washroom even though she called after him from the bottom of the stairs.

Dagny's skin was ashen when she faced Ole and Tom Ivar, who shifted on their feet in the dining room. With their hands on their hips, they took turns to shake their heads in a slow, grave manner.

'We were the first to arrive,' Ole said. 'We saw his flare. He was lucky we did. There aren't many boats out tonight.'

By the time they'd reached the banked trawler, the rain had subsided, but still the water had been rough and roiling around the *Iselin*, launching her to the peaks of its waves and falling away before unleashing a new swell. The *Frøya* had been sinking. In seeking shelter from the worst of the sea, Johann had navigated behind an island group and been stranded on a scattering of rocks.

Ole had guessed from the speed with which the water claimed the trawler's prow that one may have punctured her hull.

As he and Tom Ivar closed in on the boat, they'd spotted Johann at its stern waving his flare gun in the air. Ole had steered the *Iselin* upwind, while Tom Ivar had prepared to float a lifebelt. It skated over the water to the *Frøya*'s starboard side and Johann had jumped overboard. Clutching the ring, he'd hollered for Tom Ivar to reel him in.

'He's had a shock, but he should be fine in a day or two,' Tom Ivar said.

'But can it be true,' Dagny asked, 'that the trawler is beyond saving?'

'It didn't look good when we left her,' Ole said. 'If she's stuck on a rock . . . With the sea as it is, it could do serious damage. She was listing badly.'

'If there's anything to be done, the insurance company will surely do it,' Tom Ivar said.

'But I don't understand. How could this happen?' Dagny asked.

Tom Ivar and Ole shared a look that made Else stiffen. She knew from the set of her mother's jaw that she, too, had noticed. In a strained voice, Dagny invited the men to coffee.

'Many thanks,' Ole said, 'but we'd best be getting off.'

Dagny saw them to the door and returned to the dining room to slump into a chair and stare into the oven with her fingers pressed to her lips. The glow from the fire made her cheekbones sharp. She let out a heavy breath that blew her hand into her lap.

'Your father will contact the insurance company first thing on Monday,' she said.

'How much will they pay?' Else asked.

'Goodness knows,' she said. 'Enough for us to manage while he looks for work. Though I haven't heard of anyone who needs a man on their trawler.' She reached for the Bible she had left on the sideboard. 'I've almost finished Ninni's dress. Perhaps she needs another one.'

'I'll help,' Else said.

Her mother forced a smile. 'You're a good girl,' she said and opened her Bible to the bookmarked page.

They did not go to church the next morning and neither did Dagny attend the *bedehus* meeting that night. While Johann recovered in bed, Else and her mother tuned into the radio broadcast of High Mass from Glemmen church in Fredrikstad. They cooked a meagre dinner of fish dumplings with cauliflower and carrots, which her mother ladled into a bowl and took upstairs. In her absence, Else lowered the radio and peered at the ceiling. Try as she might, she could not decipher her parents' whispered words through the floorboards.

The first of their visitors arrived just after four, when dinner was finished and the plates and pots had been cleared away. Solveig Haugeli parked her car at the bottom of the hill and began to march her bulk across the yard.

'Be quick,' Dagny said, 'and help me hide the sewing. We'll put it in the Best Room and take coffee in here.'

A gentle rain tapped the windows as Else gathered the fabric her mother had sorted on the dining table and bundled it across the hall. She placed it on a chair before shutting the door on the evidence of her mother's Sunday industry. In the hallway she rubbed her arms and waited for Solveig's knock, anxious to return to the dining room, where the oven burned the damp from the air. Her mother joined her in the moment Solveig hollered, '*Hallo?*'

Dagny pulled the front door open. 'How good of you to come,' she said.

'I brought a stew,' Solveig said. 'We've so much elk after Ole's last hunt. What a weather! Is this rain never going to stop?'

The pot was still warm from the hob when she passed it to Else and unbuttoned her coat, freeing the wool-clad breasts that dangled to her midriff like nosebags. Solveig raked the drizzle from her hair with her fingers and sniffed as her eyes darted up the stairs and between the coats hanging in the hall. They scouted the dining room when she followed Dagny to the kitchen, settling on the table and chairs and the fire smouldering in the oven, sweeping over the woodbox and the curtains and the sewing machine that Dagny had covered and shoved into a corner. Else wondered what she was looking for. She dismissed the idea that her father's misfortune had tainted their home, so that the farmhouse and all that was in it spoke to their guest of calamity.

'Can I make you a cup of coffee?' her mother asked and held the kettle under the tap.

'Please,' Solveig said. 'Now, tell me. How are you coping?'

'We're fine,' Dagny said.

'What a terrible shock you must have had. I understand from Ole that the trawler is unsalvageable.'

'That remains to be seen,' Dagny said.

'And Johann? Isn't he here?'

'He's resting. He's caught a cold.'

'Well,' Solveig said, 'if that's all.'

'It's nothing that bed rest won't cure.'

'He's lucky then, by the sound of it. Ole said that the boat was half-sunk when they found him. Before I forget, I have greetings from church. Karin especially asked me to send you her best. And Pastor Seip remembered you in his sermon.'

'How nice,' Dagny said.

While the coffee brewed, Else was dispatched to the Best Room to collect two of onkel Olav's cups from the cupboard. She wiped the dust from their bowls and, as she smoothed a finger and thumb around each rim, imagined the talk in the churchyard that day. She pictured Ole and Tom Ivar among the graves, shaking their heads as they had done the night before and describing her father's crash and rescue, while a crowd that included Lars, Petter and Rune thickened around them and muttered its horror at the news. Not for the first time since the two men delivered her father home, she remembered their discomfort when answering her mother's questions. Her face and neck grew hot when she thought about it, though she did not understand why she should feel ashamed.

Else was glad to be excused from going to school the following week. During that time, her father rarely stirred from his bed. On Monday afternoon, when Alv Knudsen arrived from the sheriff's office to take Johann's statement about the night of the accident, he stepped into the dining room swaddled in a blanket, his eyes red and his skin scored with wrinkles like ski tracks through snow. Now and again Else would come upon him in the corridor on his way to or from the bathroom, or when his shouts for water were not answered quickly enough. Coughing spells and rumbling snores betrayed his presence to guests, who stopped by bearing food and condolences. Dagny thanked Ninni Tenvik for a fish pudding and Sigrid Aaby for a walnut cake before serving her the last of their coffee. Else wished they would stay away. She took to hiding in her room until their visitors had gone.

On Thursday morning, the rain finally stopped. After tending to the cow in the milking barn, Else tramped over the grass, gripping the handle of her pail and watching the *Iselin* glide inland on the fjord. A sliver of sun caught on the boat's trawl doors when she turned on the glassy water towards the Dybdahl pier. Else started to run, but had to slow her pace when milk spilled over the rim of her bucket.

She set the pail on the floor of the farmhouse's hallway. 'Mamma?' she called. 'Ole and Tom Ivar are back.'

'What is it now?' her mother said.

Else hurried after her into the yard, her galoshes sliding in the soil to the pier, where Ole was putting in the trawler.

'Good morning,' he said. 'And how is Johann?'

'Much better,' said her mother. 'Isn't Tom Ivar with you?'

'It's only me today,' Ole said. 'I thought Johann would want to see the wreckage, now that the weather has cleared.'

'He isn't home,' Dagny said.

'That's a pity. Well. Perhaps you'd like to come instead? It isn't far. It needn't take too long.'

Dagny shook her head, but bit her lip before replying. She glanced over her shoulder at the farmhouse, whose black windows gave nothing away.

'Now that I'm here,' Ole said. 'So that the trip isn't wasted.'

'Else,' said her mother, 'go and get my coat.'

Else raced to the farmhouse to fetch their winter coats and hats and to exchange her galoshes for a pair of boat-worthy shoes. As she buttoned her clothes, she listened for clues that her father was moving in her parents' bedroom. She expected him to appear on the stairhead at any moment and to demand to be told what was going on. The house was silent when she slipped outside and returned to the pier, where Ole was helping her mother onto the trawler.

Else did not wait for an invitation before clambering on deck. She joined them in the cramped quarters of a wheelhouse that smelled of banana and pipe tobacco and bided her time until her mother ordered her ashore. Out of the corner of her eye, she saw her mother's brow furrow. Her jaw was stern with worry and it occurred to Else that perhaps she wanted her there. Still she hugged the extra layers that she had carried to her chest and kept quiet so as not to disturb her mother's thoughts. The motor thudded as Ole swung the trawler's wheel. He prodded the throttle and navigated the boat into the fjord.

The *Iselin*'s hull sliced through the water, transporting them past the shipyard and along the ferry's route until she broke towards the sea. Seagulls trailed after them in a dirty cloud that matched the tones of the recovering sky. They screeched their hunger at the empty net coiled at the trawler's stern, continuing their pursuit when she passed into the Skagerrak. Ole steered them north and, as they followed the coastline, Else looked from the dials of his instruments to the rifle that hung over the wheelhouse door. She realised she had been a child when she had last boarded the *Frøya*. Now, she never would again. She brushed her mother's arm.

'Wouldn't you like your coat?' she asked.

Her mother blinked. She sank her hands into the sleeves.

'We haven't much further to go,' Ole said.

When the *Iselin* dipped behind a knot of islands, he eased back the throttle and pointed. 'There she is,' he said.

Else moved to the counter by the portside window. She trawled the water with her eyes but did not see what she knew must be there: no floating timber, no glint of steel. Then she noticed a shadow darkening the waves like a sea creature. She focused on its shape, on its beginning and end, while the counter trembled with the engine, shooting a shudder through her stomach and thighs.

She glimpsed a wooden flank. The metal base of a mast. The awkward angle of a trawl door.

'The engine room must have flooded,' Ole said. 'That may be why she capsized. The keel will be badly damaged, too. She's for scrap, I'm afraid.'

Else stared at what was visible of the *Frøya*'s remains and felt her insides silting up. She imagined her smashed parts – broken glass, kinks of metal – scattered over the seabed or rolling with the tide towards Denmark. The boiling vat and sorting tank would have taken root in sediment to collect sea cucumbers in their basins and wait for the day when tufts of seaweed would slither through their rusting joints. Somewhere beneath them her father's net had caught on the rocks that had been the trawler's ruin, or else it wafted loose, stretching wide, snatching fish and hauling with it *Norges* jars tangled in its cords.

The thought of her father's decanting jars brought a sudden understanding of what no one had said and what her mother must already know. The whole town must know, either from Ole or Tom Ivar or, more likely, from both of them. Her father had been drunk. She wondered what Lars would say. She remembered Solveig telling her mother that Pastor Seip had mentioned them in his sermon.

'It's time we headed back,' Ole said, but he allowed them some minutes more before piloting the *Iselin* around. The trawler set off the way she had come, tracking the scrape of oil from her motor that silvered the water's surface.

To Else's relief, Lars did not mention either her father or the *Frøya*. On the morning of her return to the Gymnasium, she sat in Paulsen's classroom through maths and natural sciences and jotted notes while Hjerde read aloud from their New Norwegian textbook. The break brought her outside and across the schoolyard to the caretaker's shed, where Lars twined his fingers with hers and volunteered a wry smile.

'Welcome back,' he said and that was enough. More awkward were Petter's efforts at commiseration. Standing by the door to the shed with Rune, whose upper lip was fat with chewing tobacco, Petter wrung his hands.

'I'm sorry,' he said, 'about what happened. The crash. I'm sorry about that.'

'Come on,' said Lars and led Else inside.

It was the start of the month and Lars's father had given him a rise in pocket money. Each afternoon when school was done, the boys would climb down Elvebakken to Arnholm's kiosk and choose salt toads, sour bombs and tins of hockey powder. Else waited for them outside, her nose dripping while she scanned the street and ducked her head if any acquaintances strolled by. She saw the ferry drift into town and out again and ignored the whisper in her ear that told her it should be taking her home.

Her father had rallied over the weekend, while she and her mother were at church. They had hurried off down Dronning Maud's gate as soon as Dagny had shaken the minister's hand and assured him that Johann was almost himself again. When they returned to the farmhouse, her father was gone. Her mother searched for him in every room, in the bathroom and Best Room and finally the cellar, before storming to the old outhouse and the milking barn at the end of the yard. From the dining-room window Else watched her approach the boathouse, where her firmness of purpose seemed to falter. She scaled the stairs with an old woman's deliberation, pausing to knock on the door before pushing her way inside.

Else stamped her feet on the pavement by Arnholm's shop and reflected on what she thought was a kind of duplicity, when she caught the boat to town and endured lessons and kissed Lars as if everything was as it had been before. She did not know when her father installed himself in the boathouse, only that he was there in the afternoons when she arrived home. Often, her mother was at the *bedehus*. Apart from Sunday gatherings, there were meetings during the week if they had a visitor – a travelling preacher, a song evangelist, the representative of a mission who passed around photos and crafts made by foreign hands – as well as Friday's choir practice, and now, she said, she would help organise the Christmas bazaar and Christmas tree party. Else spent the early hours of the evening alone with the radio turned up until her mother shuffled in, when they would work together on the sewing pile and keep wordless watch on the lantern that burned in the boathouse window.

A pink glaze on the horizon narrowed under a dull, swelling darkness. Else checked the time: it was half past three. She wriggled her toes in her boots as she glanced at the fjord, where a lonely skiff with a sagging tarpaulin was docked at the Elvebakken pier. Her knuckles were winter rough. She brushed the coarse peaks across her lips before tucking her fists under her armpits. She wished she had remembered her gloves. She would have to be sure to bring them tomorrow.

When she squinted up the road and noticed Yakov Bezrukov, it was too late to steal into the kiosk unseen. The circus performer seemed not to care about the woman hunched in her coat who gaped when he closed in on Else.

'I thought we would have met again before now,' he said. 'Have you been ill?'

'No,' Else said.

'I'm glad to hear it. Then why haven't you been to the paddock with your boyfriend?'

The kiosk door opened, spilling a hot coffee smell onto the street. Petter and Rune followed Lars out of the shop. He clapped Yakov on the shoulder as if greeting a friend.

'And here he is,' Yakov said. 'The man who knows about things.'

'How's work?' Lars asked.

'Not good. We're thinking of moving on.'

'You can't do that,' Lars said. He tore open a packet of Prince and offered it to Yakov. 'Do we still have a deal for Saturday?'

'We do,' Yakov said.

He helped himself to two cigarettes, balancing one behind his ear before biting the other between his teeth. He levelled his gaze at Rune for the seconds it took him to produce a matchbook from his pocket.

Once Rune had lit Yakov's cigarette, Else returned to her study of the road. She was not convinced by Lars's plan to smuggle homebrew to the circus men, however infectious his excitement might be. The risk of being found out was too high, and what would her mother do then? The weeks since the accident had been hard enough. Else thought of her bent over the sewing machine, her eyes on the cloth and her slipper steady on the foot pedal as if the back door had not just crashed open and her father was not reeling down the corridor. When his snoring began, her mother would snip the thread with her scissors and tidy away her sewing box before joining him in their bed.

At the top of the hill, a man wearing a *lusekofte* emerged from the grocery. Else measured his descent and lifted her rucksack over her shoulder.

'I'll see you tomorrow,' she said.

'But I bought gum,' said Lars. 'Don't you want any?'

'I have to go.'

'See you tomorrow,' Petter said.

'Are you catching the ferry?' asked Yakov. 'Well, so am I. I'll walk you down.'

'I'll come too,' Lars said.

Yakov snorted two jets of smoke through his nose and he and Lars accompanied Else to Havneveien. They matched her strides while Lars reviewed the details for Saturday night: how much liquor to bring, when the boys would arrive at the paddock. Else surveyed the harbour before bolting under the ash trees that lined the pavement. At least there were not many people about. The thought of sitting with the circus man all the way across to the public dock made her mouth dry. She hoped the ferry would be empty. She hoped it would be full.

At the base of the Longpier, Lars's hand grazed her elbow. 'Stay a little,' he said. 'You still have time.'

Yakov grinned and sucked a long breath from his cigarette. He tossed it into the water and climbed aboard the ferry.

'I've been thinking,' said Lars, 'of where we could go, now that the paddock's been taken over. Can you meet me on Friday?'

'I don't think so,' Else said.

'I'll be at the bus depot at seven.'

'I don't know,' she said and again her eyes swept the harbour to check if anyone was watching. She was about to refuse, but saw herself sitting alone once more in the dining room when she could be with Lars. Why shouldn't she meet him? No one would miss her. It would be easier than it ever had been before.

'Where would we go?' she asked.

'Somewhere warm,' Lars said. 'I'll make sure it's comfortable.'

'All right,' she said.

The ferry's engine rumbled, dirtying the air with petrol fumes. Else jogged down the Longpier and jumped onto its deck. She slid open the door of the passengers' cabin, bracing herself for the journey that lay ahead. Inside, Yakov sat beside the strong man. Pastor Seip inspected his nails on the opposite bench. A look of relief smoothed the lines of his forehead when he saw Else hesitating in the entrance.

'Hurry up,' he said. 'You're letting in the cold.'

Else yanked the door shut and sank onto the bench next to him. The ferry's motor towed them into reverse.

'I was just on my way to visit your father,' said Pastor Seip. 'I trust he has fully recovered now?'

Else's stomach turned to vinegar. 'Yes,' she said.

'Good, good,' he said. 'I expect we'll be seeing him at church next Sunday, then. And how is your mother?'

'Well,' she said.

'Good, good,' he said.

The captain guided the boat around and into the current. Across from Else, the strong man's curls skimmed the ceiling. He grasped the folded lip of a paper bag from the hardware store and blinked through the window at the gentle crests of the waves. Yakov smirked at Else. He crossed and uncrossed his knees and fondled Lars's cigarette and burped once and scratched his neck. Pastor Seip cleared his throat and scowled at the strong man's shins. He combed his fingers through his hair before patting it flat over his head.

The town receded into a dwindling twilight while, on either side of the ferry, the fjord reached for an uninviting coast, where trees sprouted into branches that seemed feeble without the finery of their crowns. Else sat on her hands and suffered Yakov's attentions. A chill seeped through her coat from the wood panel at her back.

'And how is school?' asked Pastor Seip.

'Fine,' said Else.

'You're managing at the Gymnasium?'

'Yes,' she said.

'It's an adjustment for everyone,' he said.

When Else next peeked at the minister, his eyes were closed. She buried her chin behind her scarf and tried to think. In all likelihood, her mother would be out. Her father would have spent at least part of the day in the boathouse. Else would have to rouse him, clean him up, get him dressed and present-able before Pastor Seip arrived at the farmhouse. She would cycle ahead. Perhaps today would be different. Her parents would be in the kitchen brewing coffee, already prepared for their visitor.

Darkness had extinguished the last traces of colour from the sky when the ferry moored at the public dock. Else stood and pulled open the door to the deck.

'I have Father's bike,' she said to Pastor Seip over her shoulder.

The conductor released the chain that secured the ferry's exit and she bounded ashore to retrieve the bicycle.

'Now, Else,' said the minister and she rested a foot on one pedal and kicked onto the road and away from him. She swerved to avoid the circus men, who had wandered out of the lamplight that pooled on the pier.

'Careful there, treasure,' Yakov said. Straightening her legs, Else rose from the saddle. She pumped the pedals and bounced over rocks into the night.

No lights were on in the farmhouse. The boathouse window shone with a candle's flame. Else propped the bike against the wall of the milking barn and sprinted over the earth, trampling the vegetable plot in her haste. Her chest was heaving when the soles of her shoes slammed the boathouse stairs.

'Father?' she said. She struck her fist on the door. It swung open on its hinges, releasing the stink of acid and onions. A dim glow spread from a lantern over the workbench and onto the floor, lifting the outline of the trapdoor out of shadow. Between lobster traps and loops of rope, a puddle of drying liquid glistened on the timber planks next to the mattress, where her father kneaded his thigh through a pair of long johns.

'Father,' Else said. 'Pastor Seip is on his way.' She knelt by his side and shook his shoulder until his eyelids parted. 'Do you hear me? Pastor Seip is coming. He'll be here any minute.'

Her father rubbed his mouth with the back of his hand, smudging a trail of saliva over the bristles that studded his chin. He mumbled and struggled to sit up and Else grabbed his wrists and did her best to help him to his feet. His skin smelled of curdled milk and stale tobacco. She held her breath and wrapped an arm around his waist, not letting go until she had supported him outside, past the fishing wire and *Norges* jars scattered on the ground.

Else left him to find his own way across the yard and raced ahead to make the farmhouse ready. After switching on the lights in the hall and dining room, she built a fire in the oven with logs and scraps from the woodbox. Tendrils of smoke floated after her into the kitchen, making her cough as she filled the kettle under the tap. When her father appeared in the doorway, beads of water were snapping on the hob. He considered Else in a squint. His throat was hoarse when he spoke.

'Make some coffee,' he said and lurched towards the sink. He rolled the tap and grappled with his jumper as a stream poured into the basin.

'You should wash in the bathroom,' Else said.

Her father moistened his hands and passed a bar of soap between his palms. He screwed his eyes shut and smeared suds over his face, then lathered his neck and the knots of hair on his chest and under his arms. Else removed herself to the dining room, where she lingered by the window, keeping watch on the hill that led from their property to the road. She saw the outline of Pastor Seip approaching from the milking barn.

'He's here,' Else called. 'Hurry upstairs. Put on something clean.'

Her father emerged from the kitchen trembling and naked. He hobbled into the corridor, marking the floorboards with watery footprints. Else grabbed his clothes from the kitchen counter and stuffed them into her milking pail in the cupboard before finding a rag with which to soak up his tracks. She was on her hands and knees by the sideboard in the dining room when the minister rapped on the door. She stood and hid her rag in the hallway chest before tugging down the waist of her jumper.

She smiled when she invited Pastor Seip in. He glanced past her into the hall. 'There you are,' he said. 'You set off in such a hurry, I've never seen the like. Isn't your mother here?'

'She's at the *bedehus*,' Else said. 'May I take your coat?'

He stepped inside and took off his coat. Else hung it on a peg nailed into the wall.

'And your father? You must have told him I was on my way.'

'He's just coming,' Else said. 'Would you like a cup of coffee?'

She showed him into the Best Room, scolding herself for not thinking to air the space when she had had the chance. The room smelled stuffy in spite of its chill. Its corners gathered dust and cobwebs. Else struck a match to a candle on the bureau, while Pastor Seip settled onto a cushion. She laid the table with onkel Olav's cups and lifted the coffee pot from its shelf.

'I'll just check the water,' she said and slipped into the hall. The minister's hands were folded in his lap when she returned with a full pot.

'I'm sorry,' she said. She placed the pot on the table.

'Well, yes,' said Pastor Seip. 'Where has he got to?'

'The coffee, I mean. I hope chicory will do.'

Pastor Seip's tight lips made room for a sigh. His mouth closed at the sound of footsteps on the stairs before Johann's tread delivered him stooping through the doorway. He lunged forward with an outstretched hand.

'Pastor Seip,' he said. 'How good of you to come.'

The slur in his words sent Else's heart pitching in her chest. A look of disgust creased the minister's forehead. He accepted the handshake without getting up and frowned when his host collapsed into a chair. Johann scratched the fur on his cheeks and chin with fingers stained sepia. His eyes seemed to sink behind puffy lids. They hunted the room for Else.

'Pour some coffee, then,' he said.

Else filled the cups with chicory. The candle's flame chased dribbles of wax onto its pewter candlestick while she waited for someone to speak. Neither man touched his drink.

'Well,' said Pastor Seip. 'I can see my visit today was ill-advised.'

'Not at all,' said Johann. 'Would you like some sugar with your coffee? Else, you forgot the sugar.'

'Perhaps another time would be more convenient.' Pastor Seip plucked at his jumper as if seeking reassurance that he, at least, was in order. He got to his feet.

'You're not leaving?' said Johann.

'Tell Dagny,' said Pastor Seip. 'Tell her I'll see her on Sunday, will you?'

In the hall, Else helped the minister into his coat and saw him out through the front door. She returned to the Best Room, where her father had stayed seated. He stared at his cup in drowsy contemplation. He lifted it to his lips and took a sip, then spat his mouthful onto the table. Johann leapt from his chair and threw back his arm, drenching the furniture and curtains in chicory. A tendon stiffened in his neck when he flung the cup. It smashed against the wall, showering the floor with black and gold.

'Buy some damn coffee,' he said and staggered past Else, following the minister into the yard. He vanished under the branches of the morello cherry tree towards the boathouse. Alone in the Best Room, Else picked the gold leaves off the floor, collecting them in her palm. She recovered the rag she had hidden in the hallway chest and mopped up the chicory.

AT SEVEN O'CLOCK on Friday, Else waited for Lars. There were no coaches due and the forecourt was empty of cars and people. By the locked doors of the bus depot building she watched for him in the dark of a winter deprived of snow, when the cold seems to freeze out the stars.

A single headlight sparked in the gloom before she heard the buzz of a moped. It drove into the car park and slowed to a stop. Its light blinked out.

'Else?' said Lars.

'I'm here.'

Else started towards his voice and their bodies collided. Her laugh was swallowed by a kiss. Lars's teeth snagged her lip, but his mouth was warm.

Once he had led her to the moped she clambered on behind him and locked her arms around his waist, resting her cheek against his coat, snuggling into the down which moulded itself around her jaw. He turned his key in the ignition and spun the handle grips and Else held fast as the moped carried her onto the road. Lars took them up the mountain and onto a narrow path. As they powered uphill, the town fell away below them. The harbour glittered like a treasure chest afloat on an inky sea. They sped by a handful of houses fenced off from the rock face with withered lawns and bright windows. The wind slapped Else's cheeks and mussed up her hair and brought tears to her eyes.

When they swerved onto a track trimmed with fir trees, Else recognised Haakon Reiersen's land. At the end of the path, Lars's home stood in a reservoir of light that spilled from the eaves of the shingled roof. Else had never been here at night. It had been years since she had been here at all, and when Lars cut the engine at the bottom of the drive, she did not move from the bike's saddle, but peered at the house as if dazzled by its brilliance. Lars disentangled himself from her arms and slid off the moped.

'My parents won't be able to hear us out here,' he said, 'but still. It's better to be careful.'

'They're home?' Else asked.

'Don't worry. We're not going in.'

When she had dismounted from the bike, he wheeled it into the shadows behind the garage. Else crept after him up the drive, her eyes on the house, her nerves raw. Lars fixed the kickstand before examining the garage door. He squatted and twisted its handle. With a tug, the door flipped outwards. It skated back on the ceiling rails as he drew up to his full height, lugging the door with him.

His father's Cadillac was parked inside. Its tail bumper glinted under its summer-sky body, so that Else had the sense that it was alive, a noble beast hibernating in an unequal pen. Lars ushered her in before pulling down the door, squeezing the driveway light into a thin line at their heels. There was a jangling, a scrape, then a flame that warmed his smile when he waved it by his chin.

With the lighter raised ahead of him, Lars grasped Else's hand and circled to the front of the car. The door clicked when he eased it open. He lowered himself into the driver's seat and shifted on the leather as he reached down to the floor. He sat up with a lantern hooked on his finger, which he placed on the dashboard before lifting its case. The windshield reflected an orange flush when he held his flame to the candle. Once he had replaced the lantern's cover, he climbed over the centre seat armrest into the back, where at last he opened the door for Else.

'I'm ready for you now,' he said. She ducked inside as he inched along the cushion. Lars rummaged in a plastic bag by his shoes and produced a blanket and a bottle of the Wine Monopoly's six-kroner *Rødvin*.

'Where did you get that?' Else asked.

'Pappa's just been in Kristiansand,' he said. 'He bought a few bottles. Mamma doesn't know.'

'Won't he miss it?'

Lars shrugged. 'I promised we'd be warm, so we're going to need it.'

He had already uncorked the bottle. Lars spread the blanket over their laps before yanking the stopper out with his teeth. He swigged and passed the wine to Else. Liquid flooded her mouth. It burned all the way down.

'That tastes awful,' she said.

'You think so?' he said. 'You should try Rune's moonshine. I'm not sure his uncle is doing it right. The circus men won't know what hit them.'

Else giggled. Lars drank.

'Are you coming tomorrow?' he asked.

'I don't think so,' she said.

'You always say that,' he said, 'and then you come.'

Else accepted the cigarette he gave her, breathing deeply when he lit it. She felt she was sinking into the stuffing of her seat. She puffed out the smoke and stretched a hand for the bottle. She gulped down a long swallow. 'I can't wait to get out of here,' she said.

'God,' said Lars, 'me too. The sooner the better. As soon as school's done, I'm moving to Oslo.'

Else thought of onkel Olav's merchant ship sailing its timber cargo from Canada to Japan. He had been younger than she was now when he signed up as a deckhand on the America Line's DS *Stavangerfjord*. Her grandmother had collected the telegrams he had sent over the years from New York, Melbourne, Trinidad. Else had found them when she was a child, pressed between the pages of an album of family photographs.

'I want to travel,' she said.

'So do I,' said Lars.

'I want to go to America.'

'Me too,' he said. 'We'll go together.'

A tube of ash fell from his cigarette onto the blanket and he brushed it away while Else brought the bottle to her lips. When Lars next kissed her, her head rushed with nicotine and alcohol. She closed her eyes and saw acrobats spinning and flipping in the Big Top's ring.

'Here,' Lars said and took her cigarette. 'I'll put them out.'

He opened the Cadillac's door and melted from sight. When he returned and shut the door behind him, the candle blew out. He stroked Else's knee beneath the blanket. His hand glided up her leg.

It was easy in the dark. As Lars rubbed her thigh Else surrendered to the wine, to the plea of his touch. She felt hot and cold, asleep and awake. He kissed her face and neck and was heavy on top of her. He lifted her jumper. The seat's leather was cool, the blanket rough against her skin. Fingertips skittered over her stomach. She emptied her head. Her senses swam in the garage smells of smoke and petrol.

Afterwards, Lars drove her to the Longpier on his moped. He dropped her off at the corner of Havneveien and Torggata.

'So are you coming tomorrow?'

'I'll try,' she said.

'You should just say yes,' he said and kissed her goodbye.

On her journey to the public dock, Else stood on the ferry's deck for as long as she could bear the wind that tore through the layers of her clothing. She thought about what she and Lars had done and her heart tripped in her chest as she sobered up and spread her arms to air herself out. Once ashore, she recovered her father's bike from behind the oak, but decided not to cycle. She walked it over the frozen mud, her feet uncertain in the dark.

A light was on in the dining room when she arrived home. Else hurried into the farmhouse, her teeth chattering as she hung her coat in the hall. She paused to listen for hints of her mother: the radio's murmur; the thrum of the sewing machine. The house was as silent as church.

In the dining room, her father sat by the oven with his legs stretched towards the fire. A ribbon of smoke wound heavenwards from his cigarette. He picked threads of tobacco from the tip of his tongue.

'You're late,' he said.

Her mother was not in the kitchen. Through the open curtains of the window between the fridge and the stove, the outhouse's red paint appeared muddy around the heart that had been carved out of its door. Else blinked at the black hole to avoid looking at her father, whose face was tense, his hands restless.

'Where have you been?' he asked.

'I had to stay after school. For choir practice. For the Christmas concert. Is Mamma at the *bedehus*?'

'She's gone to bed,' her father said.

'But it's still early.'

'She isn't well.'

'Perhaps I should go up . . .'

'She's damned well asleep,' her father said.

Else flinched and he reached for the mug that he had placed on the floor by his chair. He sipped and swallowed and clasped it in his palms. Else's mouth was sour with Lars's wine.

'You missed dinner,' he said.

'I'm not hungry,' she said, but crossed the room to the kitchen to pour herself a glass of milk. She cut into a loaf of bread and spread the slice with her mother's strawberry jam, thinking all the while that her father knew. Somehow, he knew: he had sniffed it on her, as if her skin had sponged up Lars's smell. Else scrubbed her hands under the tap, working the soap between her fingers, scraping traces of him from under her nails. She dried them on a dishtowel and brought her plate into the dining room, where she sat at the table and nibbled her bread. Each swallow stuck in her throat. Now and then, her father's shoulders quaked with a sticky cough.

'What psalms are you singing?' he wanted to know. 'For the Christmas concert. What are the psalms?'

Else was glad her mouth was full. The only students of the Gymnasium who took part in a Christmas concert were those who belonged to the Youth Choir at the *bedehus*, which performed at the Christmas tree party each year on 26th December. While she chewed, she tried to recall the concert organised by the schoolhouse the previous year.

'*Deilig er den Himmel Blå*,' she said. 'And "A Child is Born in Bethlehem".'

Her father lifted his mug to his lips. Else crept back to the kitchen, where she washed her plate and glass and replaced the loaf on the pantry's middle shelf. She took a moment to collect herself, summoning the words of the first verse of *Deilig er Jorden* from her memory in case he asked for a rendition, though she knew her voice would fail. She stared at her feet as they carried her over the floor to stand in front of him.

'I'm going to bed,' she said.

Her father drank from his mug. His chin drooped to his chest as he glared at the fire.

Else mounted the staircase to her bedroom and closed the door. In the dark, she began to undress. She pulled off her jumper, her roll-necked shirt; she unhooked the bra whose clasp Lars had struggled to unfasten. The simple embroidery of its twin cups ridged under her fingers like filigree. She unzipped her trousers and let them fall around her ankles. Her bare skin turned to gooseflesh in the cold. Outside her window, the branches of the cherry tree swayed in the breeze and tapped the glass.

Else groped for the nightgown folded under her pillow, but paused before slipping it on. Standing next to her bed in her underpants, she leaned forward at the waist and drew a hand between her thighs. She remembered the shock she had felt earlier when Lars had started to whimper into her ear. She put on the nightgown and buried herself under the covers, where she lay blinking into the emptiness above.

Sleep would not come, no matter how she longed for it. Else listened to the fjord, to the cherry tree's knock. She closed her eyes and pressed her lips against her hand, thinking of the taste of Lars's kiss. When a sound filtered through the wall that separated her bedroom from her parents', she thought for a moment she had drifted into a dream. She sat up in bed when a sob tore off in a gulp.

'Mamma?' she whispered.

The tree knocked. The tide washed out to sea.

———

Else expected her mother to be up when she awoke the next morning and went downstairs to the kitchen. She tidied away her plate and glass from the night before and washed the mug that her father had left in the sink, sniffing it first to confirm her suspicions, then erasing the evidence with soap and water.

In the hallway she buttoned her coat and, bucket in hand, set off across the yard to the milking barn, which looked more forlorn in its neglect with each winter it survived. Through the years whole strips of paint had been scrubbed away by rain, sleet and snow, exposing patches of timber that had been warped by the damp. The wind would take it one day, Else was sure. She would come out for milking and the cow would be pawing a pile of splinters.

The barn door screeched when she shoved it over the concrete floor. Inside, the air was ripe with manure. Else lifted the latch that secured the cow's pen and carried her stool to its usual spot before sitting down to begin milking. She could feel the animal's ribs through the scratch of her pelt when she pressed her cheek to her flank. Else's fingers found a rhythm and, as the milk pounded her bucket, the sound of its spurts beat back thoughts of her father, allowing her to remember what had happened in the Cadillac with a sense of awe at her own recklessness.

Her arm was stiff with the burden of her pail as she retraced her steps over the yard. She had come as far as the swede stalks that were the vegetable plot's last crop of the year when she spotted her father emerging from under the boathouse, an oar in hand as he guided the skiff free of its moorings.

Else rushed indoors. In the kitchen, she prepared a tray with a slice of bread and honey and a cup of chicory, which she brought upstairs to her parents' bedroom.

'Mamma?' she said. She balanced the tray on her arm as she rapped her knuckles on the door. When she heard no reply, she dipped its handle with her elbow and nudged it open. 'Aren't you feeling any better?'

Her mother lay in bed facing the wall. The quilt had settled over her like a snowdrift. A pair of tights showed its ankles over the side of the dresser.

'I brought you some food,' Else said. 'You should try to eat.'

'I'm fine,' said her mother. 'It's only a headache.'

Else waited for her to roll over, but her mother did not stir. She placed the tray on the mattress and sat down beside it. She had an urge to stroke the hair that hung limp over the pillow and wondered when grey had triumphed over brown. How strange, she thought, that she had not set it in curlers. Her mother always set her hair in curlers before bed.

'Father's out fishing,' Else said.

The quilt rose with her mother's breath. It sank and rose.

'Is there something you need?'

'No,' her mother said. 'Go and make a start on the morning's chores.'

'The morning's over, Mamma.'

Else smoothed her palms over her trousers and stood and moved to the window to open the curtains. A faint light did little to brighten the room. She looked for her father on the water, but did not see the skiff. With the rowlock missing, he must have used the Johnson motor to zip into the skerry. Her mother's housecoat lay in a heap on the floor. Else picked it up and shook it out and folded it over the arm of the chair.

'Maybe we should fetch Dr Vedvik,' she said.

'No,' said her mother. Then, more calmly, 'No,' she said.

With a sigh, she propped herself up so that Else could see the damage her father had done. The lids of her mother's left eye were swollen, the bruise deepening from purple to black above the cheek-bone. Else felt as though someone was holding her head under water. Her throat closed up. Her mother's face dissolved in salt.

'It's all right, Else.' The words were sodden and slow. 'It isn't as bad as it looks. You mustn't tell anyone. Do you hear me?

Your father will be starting a new job soon. Things will get better then.'

'What job?' Else said.

'At the shipyard,' her mother said. 'I spoke to Karin after luncheon the other day. Haakon has found him a position, though goodness knows it isn't an easy time to be handing out work. We're very lucky. Your father will see that soon.'

Else imagined her mother in Karin Reiersen's parlour trying to phrase the request while her coffee grew cold. She knew what it must have cost her to ask the favour of her old school friend. She sank onto the edge of the bed, sore with the thought of it, just as the idea of her family accepting charity from Lars's parents made her want to scream. She pictured her father, sloppy with drink, handling a welding torch in one of Reiersen's construction sheds. She saw him throwing a fist and slamming her mother to the floor.

'What about the insurance money?' she asked.

'There's no money,' her mother said. 'He hasn't paid the Hull and Machinery insurance in years. It was too expensive, he said.' The corners of her lips quivered in a sad smile. 'We'll be fine, Else, once your father starts work. And Karin has ordered a new dress. That should keep me busy for a while.'

Else wanted to ask where it had happened. Had her mother been in the kitchen peeling potatoes for their dinner? Or sewing in the dining room, or dusting in the Best Room? Was this the first time, or had he hit her before?

'As soon as he starts work,' her mother said, 'everything will be fine, you'll see.'

Else nodded at her mother's bruise. She felt her hand pressed by cold fingers and she squeezed back and said nothing.

Johann returned from his fishing trip having caught two coalfish, which he gutted and cleaned while kneeling on the pier. Dagny pan-fried the fillets and prepared a sauce and the family sat together around the dining table to eat their meal. Else picked at the fish until dinner was done, when she scraped the leftovers into the bin.

She used what was left of the day on her chores and was grateful for a reason to stay busy. After filling a bucket with soft soap diluted in water, she scrubbed the floor and the surfaces of the kitchen. In the Best Room, she flung the windows wide as she dusted and sweated in spite of the wind. She tore the cobwebs with her cloth and thumped the cushions with clenched fists. She polished the furniture until the wood gleamed and her hands ached with the effort.

At half past nine, as she pierced the heel of a sock with a threaded needle she had chosen from her mother's sewing box, Else remembered Lars. He and the boys would be at the paddock by now, sipping moonshine and wondering what had become of her.

THERE WERE NO stars in the December sky on Johann's first morning of work at the Reiersen shipyard. Else lay gazing at the ceiling beams over her bed and waited for the day to begin. Her parents' bedroom door creaked before her mother's clogs click-clacked in the corridor and on the stairs. Pipes groaned. Her father coughed through the wall. Else stayed under the covers for as long as she could.

Once she was up, she milked the cow and returned to find her father in the dining room. His hair had been combed into a side parting. The outbreak of whiskers had been shaved from his jaw. She left him chewing a banana sliced on bread and climbed the stairs to wash in the bathroom. As she brushed her teeth, she studied her face in the mirror and saw nothing pretty in the high forehead and straight nose inherited from him.

The kitchen smelled sweet with roasted chicory when she reappeared, feeling the cold in spite of her long johns and woollen sweater. She buttered a crust of bread, though she had no appetite for breakfast. She ate it on the spot while, beside her, her mother packed two sandwiches in greaseproof paper.

'Can't I pour you a cup?' her mother asked.

Else shook her head at the yellowed remains of the bruise which had been camouflaged with powder. Her mother followed her into the hallway, where her father was searching the closet.

'Where's my coat?' he asked and his wife unhooked it from its peg. Johann pulled it on, then zipped the sandwich that she offered him into his pocket. He drew a hat down over his ears.

'Don't forget your thermos,' Dagny said and handed it to him. 'Good luck today.' Johann trudged outside.

Else dragged herself into the dark that shrouded the lawn and up the hill to the frosted road, trailing after her father at a distance that she hoped would keep her safe from conversation. The earth was frozen stiff all the way to the public dock, its pores plugged with ice and rotting leaves. A crowd had gathered on the pier. The shipyard's labourers outnumbered the passengers who watched for the ferry to town. The workers huddled together as if for warmth, gazing at the shipyard's boat that came for them from across the fjord, its navigation lamps sparking against the black water.

Johann struck a match to the leaking end of a rolled cigarette. He scowled through the fog he exhaled and wiped his nose on his glove. Else licked her chapped lips and anticipated the moment when her father would turn around for home. When the boat put in at the dock, the labourers arranged themselves in a queue and each took their place in the cabin. Johann smoked until the last man had stepped from the pier. He hurled his cigarette into the water.

'Goddamn it,' he said.

He climbed aboard and soon the motorboat was arcing away from the shore. Johann pressed himself into a corner on deck and bowed his head to his tobacco pouch. Else shuffled her feet. The ferry was late; there was still no sign of it. The air smelled of burning logs and she imagined the farmhouses nearby made snug by their blazing ovens. The circus men must be cold in their trailers. She thought all at once of the strong man standing in the manège, of his defiant look as he faced the howling audience. She shivered under her clothes as a wrack of cloud shed the winter's first flurry of snow.

Now

2009

Else waits for Liv to shoulder her rucksack before she gives her the bus ticket.

'So. You know which stop to get off at, right?'

'Don't worry, Mormor,' Liv says. 'I know where I'm going.'

Liv climbs the stairs to the coach and, while the conductor checks her ticket, waves at Else, who swallows the lump in her throat. However often her granddaughter leaves to visit her father, it never gets easier to see her go. This time, Nils has a month off from the North Sea oilrig where he works in the canteen for Statoil employees. Liv will stay with him for two weeks of her summer holiday, before he takes his family away to Cyprus. She does not seem to mind about not having been invited.

'Why would I want to go with them to Cyprus?' she said. 'The baby has colic. It'd just be somewhere else for me not to get any sleep.'

The driver starts the engine and the coach trembles as it reverses out of the depot. Else waves at its rear window's tinted glass, unsure if Liv is watching but carrying on nonetheless. When the bus is out of sight she walks down the hill and through town to Lyngveien, disheartened by the thought of the weeks that lie ahead. She hopes that Liv will call her once in a while, or she will have to rely on updates from Marianne.

Else slips into a side street, where she pushes through a revolving door into Meny. The supermarket smells of chickens roasting. She hangs a basket on her arm and opens a fridge for a pot of yoghurt and another for a carton of semi-skimmed milk. At the rotisserie stands Pastor Hansen, the new minister since Pastor Gonsholt retired to Spain. He nods his thanks when the attendant hands him a wrapped lunch cake and places it in his trolley.

Else prods the oranges and chooses two for her basket, then picks a leek, a courgette, a red bell pepper. Dinner tonight will be for one. Marianne has agreed to work double shifts while Liv is in Stavanger. She is saving up, she says, though goodness knows what for. Since she started waitressing, Else has barely seen her.

But she takes herself in hand as she approaches the cold cuts: she is being petulant, when she should be pleased Marianne has stuck with this job. She has long wished that her daughter would find a vocation she loves as much as Else does her own. Twelve years have passed since Ninni Tenvik's first stroke, when the older woman's physiotherapist volunteered to show her some simple massage techniques. While Else checks the price of frozen shrimp at the fish counter, she remembers what it meant to feel Ninni restored by her touch, as if, during the minutes of their first session together, she had succeeded in unlocking the source of her pain. She began to save up for courses in Oslo, catching a coach there and back, sometimes spending a couple of nights in a hotel. As she collected qualifications, she discovered that her fingers could do more than sew. 'You have healing hands,' Ninni told her once. Before she died, she and Tenvik persuaded Else to accept a loan to set up the spa.

Someday soon, Else hopes that her daughter will experience this kind of fulfilment. Until then, a job is a job. It has been a while since Marianne last had one. In the International Food aisle, Else inspects the jars of sauces arranged on the shelves. Mexican. Indian. Thai. She selects a sachet of oyster sauce to add to her pile, then considers the cellophane packs of noodles as fine as jellyfish tentacles. She lifts one gingerly and skims the instructions on the back.

'Branching out?' says a man's voice close by.

'Petter,' says Else. 'You startled me.'

'I prefer Italian.'

'Well,' she says. 'So do I, if I'm honest.'

She laughs and feels awkward about having laughed. She rereads the noodles' cooking times, leaning away from the arm that Petter reaches in front of her. He grabs a jar and studies the label with its bouquet of tomatoes and herbs before putting it in his basket.

'Are you cooking for the girls?' he asks.

'Not tonight,' Else says. 'Liv's away. She's visiting her father.'

'And Marianne?'

'Working,' she says. 'At the Hong Kong Palace. She's got herself a job.'

'Good for her,' Petter says.

'I thought I'd try something new.' Else shrugs as if admitting to the absurdity of the idea. She replaces the noodles on the shelf and peers into her basket.

'Well,' says Petter. 'I'll be making enough lasagne for two.'

'I've never tried to make lasagne,' Else says. 'Is it difficult?'

'If you'd care to join me?'

'Oh. I wouldn't want to trouble you.'

'It's no trouble,' Petter says.

'I'm sorry, but I can't. I have a pile of paperwork to do.'

'That's too bad,' he says. 'Well, have a good night.'

He walks away, then returns for a box of lasagne sheets. When he is gone, Else stays in the International Food aisle for several minutes longer than she needs to. She decides on a jar of sweet and sour sauce and the bag of rice noodles she had been contemplating earlier. Afterwards, she spies Petter in a queue at the tills and takes a detour through Frozen Foods back to the fish counter.

By the time she pays for her groceries, she has to ask for two plastic bags in addition to the canvas tote she has brought along. She retraces her steps to Torggata, her pace slow with the load of her shopping. A raindrop hits her arm as she nears the Hong Kong Palace. She pauses by its window and steps close to the glass. She has heard that the restaurant is popular. Even so, she is surprised to see it so busy this late in the afternoon.

She spots Marianne waiting on a table, a notepad in one hand, a pencil in the other as a table of diners place their orders in unison. Her hair has been scraped back from her face, showing off the high forehead that screws up in panic. The pencil hangs in the air. An impulse to help her propels Else towards the door, but she stops herself from marching in. Marianne will not thank her for interfering. She continues up the hill that will bring her home.

At six o'clock, she prepares her dinner. In spite of the rain that is falling in the yard, she leaves the door to the garden open, inviting in a damp breeze to escort the smells of her cooking out. She adds the chopped vegetables to a wok and they sizzle while the radio plays. Else hums along to songs she does not know. She pours in the sauce and decides in an act of rebellion to serve her food in a bowl.

At the corner table, she lights a candle before taking a seat and spreading her napkin on her lap. She jabs her fork into a pile of noodles and twirls its handle, wrinkling her nose when they slither off its prongs. Else spears a courgette baton and lifts it dripping to her mouth. She washes the taste away with a gulp of water.

She braves another bite before putting down her fork, standing and crossing the floor to the oven.

The ringed binder is in the cabinet above the hot plate, set against the wall at the end of the spice rack. Else pulls it from the shelf and leafs through the recipes she has collected over the years. When she finds what she is looking for, she slips the plastic folder from the metal hoops and brings it with her to the table. There she sits and empties the folder's contents onto the Formica top.

She examines the brochures one at a time. There is a three-week tour that is high up on her list: 'The Great Wall of China * The Terracotta Warriors * The Three Gorges * The Yangtze River'. Next come the Pyramids – 'Visit the Tomb of Tutankhamun' – and then the waves of the Greek archipelago. Else places a slice of leek in her mouth. While she chews, she smooths the spine of the catalogue flat with her thumb. The water sparkles on the page. How different it looks, the greens and blues and their gentle, clean peaks. It is unlike anything she has seen, though she has spent her life staring at the sea.

A coating of sauce remains on her tongue once she has swallowed the leek. She pushes her plate away and, standing again, switches off the radio. The kitchen's four walls seem to throw back the silence, amplifying her loneliness. Else blows out the candle and tidies away the brochures. She scoops her dinner into the bin and goes into the hall, where she fluffs her hair in the mirror and runs her tongue over her teeth. When she has rubbed at the shadows under her eyes with a licked finger and applied her lipstick, she leaves the house, locking its silence up behind her.

Rain spatters her windscreen as she pulls up outside the yellow house on Gaasestien. For several minutes Else waits in her Golf, keeping the engine running. A lamp is on in the living room. Through the window, she watches Petter settle into an armchair. He points a remote control and colours light up his face. He lifts a mug and sets it down to the scrape of her windshield wipers.

Else jumps when a car drives by. She glances at the houses on either side of Petter's, noting which windows are bright, trying and failing to remember whether she has ever heard about his neighbours. With a frown, she removes her key and reaches for the umbrella in the back seat. She opens her door and steps into a stream that washes pollen pods down the road.

At the top of the drive, she rings the doorbell. A rich smell spills onto the porch when Petter answers.

'Else,' he says.

'You mentioned something about lasagne,' she says.

Petter looks at her with an expression she cannot read. She wonders if he will send her away, but he nods and shifts aside for her to pass. 'So I did,' he says. 'Come in.'

The walls of his hallway are decorated with paintings of seascapes. A potted plant sprouts red buds where it sits on a chest of drawers. When she has taken off her shoes and Petter has hung her jacket, Else follows him down the corridor and into the kitchen. A counter splits the room in two, separating the work surfaces from a spacious eating area. From the TV next door, a woman's voice delivers the evening news.

'Are you driving?' Petter asks.

'Yes,' says Else.

'Then I have water or apple juice.'

Else asks for water and he fills two glasses from the tap, then turns the dial of the oven. While he lays the table, she busies herself with studying the photos of his children stuck with magnets to the fridge. In one of the snaps, they are as she remembers them before they moved with their mother to Oslo. Their grins are missing teeth, their cheeks are freckled from the sun. Brother and sister dangle fishing lines into the water from Petter's sailing boat. In a more recent shot Herman poses in a school photo, his fringe sculpted with gel over a forehead speckled with acne. Siri is wearing eyeliner in the picture beside it. She is trying to hide her braces behind a self-conscious smile.

'They've grown,' Else says.

'They're growing still,' says Petter. 'Herman is almost as tall as I am. I'm beginning to think they'll never stop.'

'How often do you see them?'

'Whenever they'll have me,' he says. 'They're at that age now, you know. They want to be with their friends. So instead of them coming here, I go to Oslo. There's a little hotel not far from where Merete lives. They don't stay over, but I can take them out for dinner.'

Else touches a finger to the mole on Siri's cheek. She imagines ruddy skin under the layer of face powder. 'You must miss them,' she says.

'I do,' Petter says. 'The house is too quiet. Are you ready to eat?'

Else takes her seat as he fetches a tray from the oven. He places it on the table and she blinks at the half-finished lasagne.

'You've already eaten,' she says.

'I've been working up to a second helping,' he says and spoons a generous portion onto Else's dish. He serves himself a smaller square. 'Hope it's edible. *Skål.*'

She raises her glass. Petter sips his water, holding her eye as he does. Else picks up her fork and dips it into the filling that oozes from between the sheets of her lasagne. The combination of tomato and cheese is creamy-sweet. She swallows and cuts herself another bite.

'It's delicious,' she says.

'It's okay,' Petter says. 'Siri's is better. It was Siri who taught me how to make it.'

'She likes to cook?'

'No,' says Petter, 'I wouldn't say that. She didn't like to think of her old dad's arteries after a few too many kebabs. She's a good girl is Siri, though more complicated than her brother. She always was, but now . . . I gather she's giving her mother hell.'

'Daughters do,' says Else. 'That's part of it.'

'But you and Marianne are close. At least, you've always struck me as being close.'

Else smiles, pleased that he thinks so and in no hurry to chronicle the friction between her and her daughter.

'I saw her last week, actually,' says Petter. 'Together with an impressive-looking man on the Longpier. She looked very happy.'

'Is that so?' Else says.

'Is it serious?' he asks. 'Do you think they'll move in together?'

Else is about to tell him not to be ridiculous, that Marianne has just met this impressive-looking man, but a tightening in her chest makes it hard for her to answer. She has not allowed herself to think about what she knows in her heart: that Marianne is doing more than passing time with Mads. She recognises in her something she has not seen since Liv was born. She knows her daughter.

'Maybe,' she says.

Petter nods, though she wonders if he could have heard so small a reply. She inspects the pattern of ropes and anchors on her placemat. They sit for a while without speaking, the silence delicate and interrupted by the scratch of cutlery on their plates.

'When the kids left for Oslo,' Petter says, 'I never imagined. The things I missed.' He shakes his head. 'Herman's video games, for one. He'd got his hands on something hair-raising called *Resident Evil*. All weekend long, you'd hear this eerie music and then be scared out of your skin when the zombie dogs started barking. And Siri needed an hour in the bathroom every morning just to shower and dry her hair. And then there was none of it. Everything was so quiet. But you get used to it. You do. It isn't the worst thing in the world.'

'What did you do?' Else asks. 'How did you get used to it?'

'I learned to sail,' Petter says.

'But you've had your sailing boat for years.'

'That's true,' he says. 'But I never took her out of the skerry. Now I could go to Denmark tomorrow, if I wanted to. I learned to really sail. I can't say I'm sorry for that.'

After the meal, Petter helps Else into her jacket. She zips it up and steps into shoes whose leather is still wet at the toes. Outside, the rain is coming down hard. She pauses on the porch and watches the strings of water falling, listens to the clattering on the roof, the gush of the gutters.

'Drive carefully,' Petter says.

'Thanks for dinner,' says Else.

With the umbrella in hand, she runs down the drive to her parked car. She ducks into the driver's seat and slams the door, resting her palms on the steering wheel as she catches her breath. The fan fogs the windscreen when she starts the engine. Water drips from her jacket onto her thighs while she waits for it to clear and she glances at the house, where Petter stands in the doorway. He lifts a hand to wave goodbye. She pulls her fingers through her hair, rakes wet strands from her face, presses the clutch and drives away.

A WEEK LATER, Else brings a bouquet of picked wild flowers to the cemetery. In the warm chirp of the summer evening, she winds her usual route through the gate and to the rear of the church, past two of the benches that were donated in the Nineties to where the younger plots now claim the soil. The air smells of cut grass and she scans the graveyard until she sees the sexton's tractor by Ole Haugeli's headstone. The gravel crunches under her trainers as she makes her way down the track to the row of marble where her mother lies.

Else spends some minutes beside the grave holding the wild flowers' stems. She eyes the epitaph that does not come close to summing up her loss. 'Dagny Dybdahl. 1932–2008. Beloved mother, grandmother, great-grandmother.' Since the end of winter, a green fuzz has sprung up over the mound of earth that tucks in her ashes. The grass is thinner here than elsewhere, like the fledgling bristles of a pubescent beard. Else kneels to gather the withered irises from the tin at the foot of the plot, chucking out the stale water before refreshing it from the pump and arranging her bluebells and forget-me-nots.

When she has pruned the grave's weeds and browned flower heads, she rises and brushes the mud from her shins. She surveys her handiwork before doubling back towards the church. Else distracts herself from the grief whose scab seems to crack with each visit to the cemetery by thinking of the spring afternoon when she last sat through a service on its pews. By then, Pastor Seip had moved to a parish in Sandnes. Pastor Gonsholt was the minister when Marianne was confirmed. Else remembers her mother beside her in the congregation, wiping proud tears from her eyes as her granddaughter approached the altar. When the minister traced a crucifix on Marianne's forehead, Else forced her lips into a smile although, inside, she felt like weeping.

Instead of continuing to the church gate, she steps onto the path to the Second World War tombs, barely aware of having changed course until she has come as far as the memorial cross. Else checks off the names of the locals who gave their lives to the Resistance – Gregor Sundt, Carl Hansen, Per Henrik Wiig – and wanders past the grave of the English soldier to the north wall, where her father's plot is pressed close to the brick. 'Johann Dybdahl. 1927–1975.' His name is black with algae. Flakes of slate have crumbled from the headstone into grass twisted with weeds and feral blooms.

Else rereads the letters and an unhappy image develops in her mind. Her father sits in the Best Room, his rheumy eyes following Marianne's first roll across the floorboards. Else blinks it away, blocks it out. Johann was dead when Marianne was a little girl. She lowers herself to the ground and sinks a hand into the thatch that sprouts from his plot. Closing her fingers around a stem, she gives it a tug. The weed is sturdier than it looks. Another yank and its roots come loose in a knot of fibres like pale capillaries. Else studies the shoot in her palm. She lets it drop, grasps another. She pulls it free. Lets it drop. *O death, where is thy sting? O grave, where is thy victory?*

Else is out of breath and squatting in a pile of vegetal waste when a voice breaks in on her thoughts.

'I've been wondering when you'd be getting around to that,' Lars says. 'The poor man's grave is in a mess.'

Her head snaps around to where he stands not five feet away. His golden retriever strains against her lead, her tongue lolling pink and plump.

'This is where you walk your dog?' Else says.

'Why not?' says Lars. 'I don't think the dead care.'

He scratches the grooves behind the puppy's ears before dragging her back with a jerk of the wrist.

'Don't let me disturb you,' he says and sits on a bench. Else purses her lips and wipes the sweat from her forehead. She rubs her hands together, showering earth over the weeds she has extracted from her father's grave as she glares at the puppy. The dog wags her tail and sniffs the ground by Lars's shoes. Else retrieves her handbag from a patch of leaves.

'I hear you're seeing Petter,' Lars says. 'I hadn't realised.'

'Is that what you hear?' Else says. She swings the handbag over her shoulder and gets up off the ground, intent on denying him an explanation. As exasperated as she is to learn about the town's gossip, she resents Lars's presumption more.

'The kids are something else, aren't they?' he says. 'Andreas never stops talking about Liv. I think he's in love.'

'Is that right,' Else says.

'Victoria isn't sure it's a good idea. What do you think?'

'They're young,' she says.

'We were young once, too,' he says. His earnest look irritates her enough to keep her from walking away.

'Was there something you wanted?'

'Yes,' he says. 'I want you to sit down.'

Else frowns, wondering what he is up to. Once her eyes have swept the cemetery and she is sure they are alone, she sits on his bench, a tense biceps crushing her handbag against her ribs.

'Do you mind if I smoke?' asks Lars.

'It has nothing to do with me,' she says.

He slides a cigarette from a pack of Marlboro Reds, lights its end and puffs. 'I quit ten years ago,' he says.

'So I see.'

'Don't tell Victoria.'

'Why would we be talking about you?'

Lars's eyebrows shoot up and he smiles and pulls again on his cigarette. 'It's funny,' he says, 'being back here. How is Marianne getting on with her new job?'

'Why do you ask?' Else says.

'She was saying how much she liked it, the last time I saw her.'

'Well, then, you know, don't you?'

'It's good to see she's come into her own. She seems like a great girl.'

Else stares at Lars. She thinks suddenly of what Gro Berge told Janne Haugen, the stories of Lars's family packing up their life in Oslo to escape his infidelities, to start again. There is no hint now of the triumph she felt on hearing the news.

Before she has composed herself enough to answer, the puppy barks and bounds to the end of her lead. Both Else and Lars glance towards the church, where Victoria watches them with her back to the whitewashed wall.

'Shit,' Lars says and tosses his cigarette. Victoria hurries away.

'But, what . . .' Else says to the empty seat beside her. Lars is already up and running after his wife.

'She doesn't,' Else says. 'For goodness' sake, she can't possibly think . . .'

Lars sprints to the church, leaving Else alone and unsettled. She turns to her father's grave, to the mess she has made of his plot. With a dirty hand, she wipes her face and pushes herself off the bench.

Then

1975

A BEDEHUS BAZAAR for the Inner Mission saw the start of the Christmas week that would bring the year to a close. Dagny organised its committee in stringing lengths of clothes line in the hall and pegging up the potholders and knee socks that would go on sale. The chairs were pushed to the walls or carried to the basement storeroom, making space for a long table decorated with gifts for the raffle, including a much-admired tablecloth that Else's form teacher, Geir Paulsen, won, though he had only bought one ticket.

A dollop of strawberry jam oozed over the waffle that Else balanced on a napkin as she climbed to the gallery, leaving the rumours about a deal Haakon Reiersen had struck with the oil fields in the North Sea to circulate in the hall below. She had heard Solveig whispering to her mother about diving bells while they mixed jugs of blackcurrant squash in the kitchen. Esben Omland had asked her father, 'Is it true what they say about a contract with Shell?' but Johann did not know a thing about it.

Haakon Reiersen was a moderate kind of Christian. He drank cognac at the weekends after dinner and allowed his children to play the American rock music records that his sister sent for their birthdays from New York. Neither Haakon nor Karin was involved with the *bedehus*. Instead of attending the Inner Mission bazaar that day, Lars had told Else about their plans to drive to Kristiansand to watch the new James Bond film.

Else had never been to the cinema. Many of those with a stricter faith would disapprove of the Reiersen family outing and, while she ate her waffle, she felt important with the knowledge, as if she were safeguarding another secret, protecting Lars from notoriety. She thought perhaps she might ask him about Shell, but he had been different in the weeks since his liquor smuggling began. He talked of little besides his visits to Tenvik's paddock, where he would deliver the homebrew he brought in canisters for the circus men. The strong man had guzzled a litre of homebrew by himself, while a few sips had sent Petter vomiting onto the bonfire. More than once, while Lars kissed her in the caretaker's shed, Else found herself promising she would join him for the next party. When Saturday arrived, her father's presence at the supper table kept her from meeting his moped in the road.

Else counted the days until the Gymnasium would reopen. She almost looked forward to Pastor Seip's Christmas service as a chance to glimpse Lars during the two weeks without school. While the other children in the gallery ate cake and peered down on the adults milling under the handicrafts, Else daydreamed about stealing through the churchyard to the Second World War graves, where Lars would be waiting for her. She knew it could not happen, even as she imagined the scene. Her family did not stay after worship these days. Once her father had queued to shake the minister's hand, his bad temper shooed them away like seagulls to the sea.

Snow fell in soft lumps that melted into the waves when Else caught the ferry to town alone on the first Saturday of the new year. The boat cut through the fjord to the Longpier, where she lifted her sledge ashore. She lugged it up the harbour and past the shops on Elvebakken, whose doors were shut and whose windows were dark. There were no cars on the road. Their absence reminded her of last year's petrol rationing, when fears of Arab oil sanctions had prompted the King onto public transport.

In their place, cross-country skiers hurtled downhill from the Gymnasium, where a crowd had gathered at the gate. Else looked for Lars among the knot of her classmates who were fixing boots to ski bindings or readying their sledges. Gro Berge told her he had disappeared with Rune and Petter to smoke cigarettes in the school grounds. Their coats glittered with snow when they returned. Lars folded an arm around Else's shoulders.

'There you are,' he said.

Through the afternoon, the boys discussed the various gifts they had received for Christmas. Lars enthused about Roger Moore in *The Man With the Golden Gun*. They laughed about Arne Kvinge, whose snores during Pastor Seip's Christmas sermon had had the minister spitting at the pulpit. Petter showed Else the Zippo lighter that had been a present from his brother with strict instructions not to let their mother know. Else's ears rang with cold when she put a hand on Lars's chest.

'Ready for a race?' she asked.

'Only if you're ready to lose.'

They lined up in the middle of the road, Else between Petter and Rune, all three holding steady for Lars's command.

'*Klar. Ferdig. Gå!*'

Else kicked down the hillside, her feet slamming the ground before she hopped onto the runners. Her sledge plummeted towards the fjord, faster and faster, snow falling away beneath her as flakes flew at her eyes. Petter and Rune lagged behind and she threw her weight forward, swerving to avoid a girl who shouted as she sped by. The wind-whiz hushed as the hill flattened out. Her sledge slowed and stopped and she wiped tears from her cheeks. Up ahead, a tern wheeled in circles over the ice that crusted the shallows.

Lars grinned from the foot of the pier and clapped his hands. 'Second place,' he said. 'Not bad.'

He pulled his sledge to Else's side and kissed her cheek. His nose felt like an icicle against her skin. He led the way to the Gymnasium, past Rune and Petter, who bickered and tagged along behind them. Else's fingers were numb. They throbbed when Lars squeezed them through her gloves. She relished the ache. The day was theirs and the old year was over.

A FRESH SNOWFALL spilled into the barn when Else opened its door, dusting the ground with a shimmering layer that faded to translucence and promptly vanished. The cow was snug in her stall. Else stroked her neck before shovelling the night's dung into the dung pit and spreading new straw and replenishing her supply of hay.

Once seated on the stool, she clasped the cow's udders in her fingers. She had started to milk in a slow, even tempo when a drop of water splashed her head and slid to her right temple. Above her, the ceiling beams sagged under an accretion of snow. As she considered the roof, a new drop landed between her eyes, quickening to a dribble which she blotted with her sleeve.

In the yard, the farmhouse glowed red against the overreaching white that wiped out the vegetable plot and weighed down the branches of the berry bushes. Else carried the pail to the back door and hung her coat in the hallway. A hot breath from the dining-room oven's fire scalded her chill-bitten cheeks. Sitting with his elbows on the table, her father sponged up the egg yolk on his plate with a hunk of old bread.

'The barn roof is leaking,' Else said.

Her mother looked up from the sink as she set her bucket on the kitchen counter. Dagny dried her hands on her apron.

'Did you hear that, Johann? The barn roof is leaking.'

'I heard it,' he said.

'You might clear the snow,' she said, 'before it does real damage.'

'All right,' he said. 'I'll have a look when I get home from work.'

But later that afternoon when he arrived home, Johann made no mention of the barn. He took off his coat and the shipyard smells of metal and sweat unpicked themselves from his jumper. He rubbed at the crusts in the corners of his eyes before bunching his trouser legs to his knees and crouching on the second step to unlace his boots. He kneaded the arch of one foot, then the other.

Dagny served the stew she had made of yesterday's leftover meat and potatoes. The family ate and afterwards, while Else washed the dishes, her mother pulled a chair to the oven and chose a blouse from her sewing pile. She arranged it on her lap so its arms hugged her shins and squinted at the thread she was aiming through the eye of her needle.

'Johann,' she said, 'you won't forget the barn.'

Johann seemed focused on packing tobacco into a rolling paper. He licked its edge and smoothed it down. When the cigarette was lit, he locked the smoke in his lungs.

'I stopped in earlier,' Dagny said. 'The snow is awfully heavy.'

'I've had a hell of a day,' Johann said.

'Maybe you would have a look.'

'It will keep until morning,' he said. 'I'll have a look then.'

The next day, Else woke to the sound of a hammer tapping. It took an act of will to abandon her sheets. Her bare toes curled on the floorboards of the corridor and in the bathroom, where she washed her face with icy water. Her reflection was as pale as the half-moon outside. She combed her hair and doubted she would ever be warm again.

She dressed and crept downstairs. The hammer had been silent for several minutes, but its blows repeated in her head when she greeted her mother in the dining room. Dagny had spread a bundle of bed sheets on the table to protect the wood from being scorched by her iron. She was wearing the nylon housecoat that was spotted with polish stains.

'Good morning,' she said.

Again, the hammer banged.

'Is that Father?' Else asked.

Her mother nodded. She drew a wrist across her forehead, unsticking the wisps of hair that the iron's steam had glued to her skin. Instead of starting directly for the barn, Else decided that, today, she would eat breakfast first. She poured a cup of chicory and topped two slices of bread with Ninni Tenvik's pickled herring. She hoisted herself onto the kitchen counter, where she crossed her ankles and rested the dish on top of them. Through the window, the outhouse appeared to be sinking in snow.

Else prepared to jump down when her father broke from his labour. Her breakfast resumed when the hammering did. She cut a third slice of bread.

'Don't you see what the time is?' called her mother from the dining room.

'I'm going,' Else said.

'See that you do. I don't have time to milk the cow myself.'

Else found a pail in the cupboard and, in the hall, zipped on her winter coat and stepped into her boots. She braced herself for the bitterness of the yard, where the darkness was thinning to a watery light that trickled into her father's tracks. When she pushed into the barn, he glared at her from the top of a ladder.

'It's about time,' he said. 'I wondered if you'd be getting up at all.'

He had raised the ladder in the cow's pen. With his knees braced against a high rung, he stretched towards the wooden planks that he had already nailed into the ceiling. Else studied the beams that still bulged and dripped water onto the sawdust. She turned her attention to the cow pawing the floor in a stall that had stood empty since the horse had gone lame two years before. Her hooves were skittish in the unfamiliar space. Her eyes rolled with the thudding of the hammer. She skipped sideways when Else held out her hand. 'Come now,' she said. 'Come now, good girl.'

Else lifted the stool from its crook and planted it in the sawdust next to the animal. With her back to her father, she settled down to her task. The beat of the hammer muted the gush of milk. It scattered her thoughts, restoring her to herself with every strike. Both she and her father worked to their own rhythm. Neither spoke. She had almost finished when he climbed down the ladder.

'That should do it,' he said. 'Move the cow back when you're done.'

'Shouldn't you clear the snow from the roof?'

'There's the shovel,' he said. 'You're welcome to it.'

Johann replaced the hammer in his toolbox and snapped its lid shut. He collapsed the ladder and leaned its length against the wall, then buttoned his coat and grasped the toolbox's handle. Snow eddied through the door in a rush of wind when he stooped out of the barn.

The roof caved in before the end of the week. Else trudged through the door into a space washed white. Snow had tumbled through a hole in the barn's ceiling and collected on the ground in heaps barbed with splinters and rubble. The stockade that fenced in the cow had been crushed under falling timber and now she grazed across the room, pausing between mouthfuls ripped from a hay bale to nuzzle the prongs of a pitchfork. Mist wafted from her nostrils towards the torn planks that framed a charcoal sky. Else dropped her bucket and ran to the farmhouse to fetch her mother.

That day, she stayed home from school. While her parents took stock of the damage, she tidied the kitchen and bided her time until her father left for the shipyard. She joined her mother in the barn and together they cleared the debris, shovelling snow and clots of sawdust into the garden. Once they had spread straw over the muddy floor of the horse stall, Else opened its gate to the cow.

'We can't keep her here,' her mother said. 'We'll have to take her to Tenvik. Don't be long with the milking.'

When Else's pail was full, she and her mother readied them-selves for the walk to Tenvik's farm. They led the cow outside, where she lowed as her hooves sank into snow. She voided the dung from her bowels and Dagny waved a switch over her haunches. The cow kicked out and lumbered up the hill and down the road slicked with black ice.

When they arrived at Tenvik's farm, snowflakes clotted the air. The roofs of his barns and henhouse pricked a swirling sky, each building rising higher for its white peak. As Else hurried behind her mother and the cow onto the yard, she recalled the stamp and whir of the Big Top band which, a few months ago, had led her down the winding track to the paddock. Remembering the thrill of the circus made the day seem darker, the worry about the barn roof harder to bear. Her gaze fell on the farmhouse leaking wicks of ice from its gutters and she wondered whether she had dreamt the whole thing.

Her mother removed a mitten before knocking on the front door. After some minutes, she began to circle the farmhouse. '*Hallo?*' she called with every few steps. 'Ninni? Knut? Is anyone there?'

Else saw the barn door open before her mother did. With one hand, Knut Tenvik clutched the flaps of his coat.

'Good heavens,' he said, 'you haven't brought the cow?'

'I'm afraid so,' Dagny said. 'The barn roof's fallen in.'

'Come up, come up.' Tenvik threw the door wide and waved them up the ramp. 'Hurry up with you, before the poor beast drops dead in my yard.'

He released the latch of the twin door and the cow trotted inside. Else jogged after her mother into the musky smell. The space was divided into two columns of pens which ran down the length of the room to the far wall, where bags of feed were arranged on the floor beside stacked hay bales. A dozen cows or more swished their tails and chewed their breakfasts and grunted and lowed in a drowsy chorus. Else hesitated when she noticed the strong man in a distant stall. He had been hunched between two cows, but now stood at his full height.

'Oh,' her mother said. 'I . . . You have company.'

'Now what's this about the roof?' asked Tenvik. 'Can't it be fixed?'

'I hope it can,' Dagny said. 'I'm sorry for the bother. Else will come every morning to milk and feed the cow.'

'There's a space free at the end,' Tenvik said. 'Else, bring her along down there, would you? But what about this roof? Will Johann manage himself?'

'Yes,' Dagny said. 'Johann will manage it.'

Else did as Tenvik had asked and steered the cow down the middle aisle to the end of the room. Her eyes widened in alarm when the strong man stepped forward to meet her, placing a palm on the white smudge that marked the cow's muzzle. With his other arm, he gestured at the empty pen. It was the closest that Else had been to him. She could hear the slow draw of breath in his nose. She stood for a moment and watched the gentle manipulations of his hands as he coaxed the cow into the stall. Then, with a start, she hurried back to her mother, who looked on with a pained expression on her face. Else realised that the strong man must recognise her. She thought of her visit to Tenvik's paddock, when she and Lars had discovered the two stranded trailers. She felt caught out. She wanted to leave.

'Be careful he does a proper job of it,' Tenvik said, 'or it'll just go again. You can bet on more snow. You're sure he wouldn't like help? These boys would charge a fair price.'

'Quite sure,' Dagny said.

Without another glance in the strong man's direction, she moved away down the ramp. Else followed after Tenvik, who escorted them as far as the road.

'Don't worry about the cow,' he said. 'Now, Dagny, you'll let me know if you change your mind.'

'I will,' she said.

'Else,' he said, 'we'll see you tomorrow.'

Dagny and Johann argued about the roof late into the night. From her bed, Else listened for the smack of a hand against bone. Instead the quarrel ended with the back door slamming, but the relief she felt was fragile. Her father went on to spend the night in the boathouse – his first since starting the new job at the shipyard.

When she arrived at Tenvik's farm, not even the chill of an early-morning walk had dispelled the groggy feeling that came from lack of sleep. With dulled senses, Else closed the gate behind her and peered at the barn where the cow had passed the night. She half expected the strong man and his companions to come charging down its ramp into the yard. Its doors were shut. She crossed to the farmhouse, her boots snapping the crust that packed in the snow.

Ninni Tenvik answered the door to her knock. She smiled and ushered Else inside. 'Knut told me about the barn,' she said. 'How is your mother? Never mind about your boots, it's washing day.'

Ninni directed her down a corridor whose pine walls showed the grain of the wood and into the dining room, where she pulled a chair out from under the table. 'Have you eaten breakfast?' she asked.

'Yes,' Else said.

'Wait here, then, while I fetch Knut.'

She left the room and Else sat on the chair and folded her hands in her lap. Her eyes wandered from the curtains that were like veils on the windows to the rickety cabinet without doors, whose shelves displayed plates painted with sailing boats. Dried roses were piled on its top ledge, giving off a whiff of summer's decay which Else caught when she turned to study the photographs. On the sideboard, two black-and-white babies were captured in silver frames. She remembered the short graves side by side in the cemetery and looked away.

She jumped up when Tenvik came through the door.

'Else,' he said, 'don't you know where the cow is? You've brought a pail? No need to be so polite tomorrow, just help yourself. The doors aren't locked.'

Tenvik saw her into the yard and she waded through the snow to the barn, her cheeks blooming in the cold after the minutes inside. She climbed the ramp and fiddled with the door's clasp before pushing into the comforting lull of the stables. Apart from the cows, Else was glad to find that the barn was empty. She trod down the aisle to the furthest stall, flanked by Tenvik's cattle with their plump bellies. The Dybdahl cow was feeble by comparison. Her ribs poked through her hide. Her joints bulged like nodes on a sapling's bough.

Else stroked her neck, running her palm over cords of muscle. Someone had left a stool for her in the aisle. She set it on the ground next to the cow and began to milk with her eyes closed, losing herself to the inner workings of the animal's body. Gases fizzed. Juices gurgled. An image of her father crystallised in her mind. She saw the hollows under his cheekbones. His angles had sharpened through the winter as if the cold were shrinking his skin, pinching it tight over his skull. Her mother had pleaded with him the night before. If he did not mend the roof, the barn would crumble. Then what would they do?

'Let it crumble,' he had said.

When she was done Else carried her pail outside, where a miserly light hinted at dawn. Yakov Bezrukov was clearing a path from the farmhouse to the barn. He was some distance from the ramp but, on seeing Else, he let the blade of his shovel rest in the snow. Its handle supported his weight as his eyes took her in.

'Good morning,' he said.

Else scurried down the ramp. She started for the gate, moving faster as he advanced.

'Wait a minute now, I'm not going to bite you.'

She looked for Tenvik in the mute landscape, but she was alone with the circus man. Her heartbeat muffled the crunch of her feet. Yakov grabbed her arm to cut her off. A splash of milk slopped over the rim of her bucket.

'There,' he said. 'We haven't finished talking. I hear your mother is hiring.'

'She isn't,' Else said.

'That's not what I heard. Tenvik was asking Valentin about fixing a roof.'

'She isn't hiring,' Else said.

'Well, Tenvik seems to think so. Who knows, maybe she likes having help? Maybe we all come to live on your farm?' He showed teeth yellowed by tobacco. He let her arm go and the milk swished in her pail. Yakov's scar drooped from his eye like a tear. He spun away when Tenvik rounded the corner of the farmhouse. The strong man followed behind him, his eyes narrowed to the wind.

'Is everything all right here?' Tenvik asked.

'Fine,' Yakov said. He thrust his shovel into the snow.

'You've finished with the cow?'

'Yes,' Else said.

'Now, tell me. How is your father getting on with that roof?'

'Fine,' she said and glanced over her shoulder at the road.

'That's good to hear,' said Tenvik. 'But they've forecast more snow. How much time do you think he'll need before it's mended?'

Else tried to guess how her mother would want her to answer. Before she had settled on a reply, the farmer was talking again.

'I've come to an agreement with Valentin,' he said. 'I'll cover his expenses for fixing the barn – not a full repair job, mind you, but enough to keep it standing until spring.'

'No,' Else said. 'I don't think. Mamma wouldn't . . .'

'She will, though, once she sees the damage is bound to get worse. All she has to do is feed him dinner. He'll get on with the rest. Tell her it's all taken care of.'

Else stared at Tenvik, unsure of what to do next, suddenly reluctant to go home.

'Well,' he said, 'shouldn't you be getting to school? Valentin, maybe you would carry the bucket for her.'

The strong man reached a hand for her bucket and Else let him have it and turned to the gate. In measured strides, he kept pace with her as she hurried down the mountain towards the fjord's mercury drift. Wind whipped the branches of the trees, shaking icicles from their pines which smashed like glass or sank through snow, leaving prints to be plugged with the next blizzard.

Else pulled up her hood when they reached the Bjørndahl property; she could sense the twitching of the curtains in the windows. The strong man gazed at the fjord, where two figures in yellow tossed fishing lines from a rowing boat. When they had passed the spit of rock where the house nestled by the water, Else peeked at his profile, the curve of his ear. She saw his throat working when he swallowed. Long lashes grazed his skin when his black eye blinked. He seemed lost in thought and it occurred to her that he had forgotten she was there. His indifference made her brave. She clenched her hands, squeezing the wool of her mittens in palms clammy in spite of the cold.

'My parents don't know about the paddock,' she said. 'They don't know I've been there with Lars. They wouldn't like it.'

She braced herself for his reaction, but the strong man continued to watch the water. Perhaps he had not understood, he only spoke his own language. Then, 'All right,' he said in a voice that was too soft for such a body. A snow shower fell from the mountain's ridges and Else skipped out of its way. They took the bend in the road where she sometimes met Lars and climbed down the hill lined with birch trees to the farm.

'There it is,' Else said.

She pointed to the barn, which squatted like a sentry to the yard. She pushed open its door, revealing the wintry scene within. Valentin handed her the pail and unbuttoned his coat, then moved to the centre of the room. He kicked a log whose ragged end poked out of the snow.

Else left him contemplating the ceiling and plodded to the farmhouse. Since she had set out earlier that morning, her mother had swept a path from the barn, a narrow trench with collapsing walls. She found her at the sewing machine in the dining room. Steam rose from a mug she had prepared. She smiled when Else carried the bucket through to the kitchen.

'How's the cow?' she asked.

'Somebody's here,' Else said.

'Oh?'

'One of Tenvik's workers. He's in the barn.'

'Whatever can you mean?' her mother said. The pulse of the sewing machine's needle failed and then Dagny was on her feet and darting into the kitchen. 'Are you saying that one of those foreigners is here?'

'Yes,' Else said.

'But why on earth . . .'

'The big one,' she said. 'He has an agreement with Tenvik.'

Her mother's face was grey as she swept through the dining room into the hallway. 'We'll just see about that,' Else heard through the wall. She crept to the window to watch her mother swoop over the yard, her coat flying behind her. At least, she thought, her father had already left for the shipyard.

Else changed into her school clothes in her bedroom and lifted her satchel from the floor. She shouldered it to the bottom of the stairs, where she pulled on the coat whose lining still bore her heat. Her mother stood in the doorway of the barn, her arms folded as she shouted over the sound of Valentin's spade.

'I will not pay you an *øre*,' she was saying as Else approached. 'Tenvik must have lost his mind this time!'

'I'm leaving,' Else said.

'Hurry up with you, then,' her mother said, 'before you miss another ferry.'

The scoop of the shovel faded as Else tramped to the top of the hill. She hooked her thumbs under the satchel's shoulder straps and bowed her head to the wind that chased the snow over the road.

Else missed the ferry. The day's German class was underway when she took her seat.

'Else,' Paulsen said. 'Thanks and praise, you've decided to join us.' He invited her to list the prepositions that require the *accusativ*. She stumbled through *bis, gegen, um,* while he scowled and shook his head at the class.

During lunch, Else sprang over the grit that studded the schoolyard's ice to meet Lars at the shed.

'Is it true?' he called when he saw her. 'Is the strong man working on your barn?'

'Since this morning,' Else said.

Lars whooped where he waited with Rune and Petter in a scrap of sun. He kissed her when she stopped beside him. She was too pleased to care who saw.

'How long is he staying?' Petter asked.

'I don't know,' Else said. 'Until the roof is fixed.'

'Ask him what he lifts,' Rune said. 'I'd bet he could lift three hundred kilos.'

For the first time in months, Else felt the private thrill that united the boys in their dealings with the circus men. It had Lars twisting around during New Norwegian to share surreptitious smiles with her from his desk. At the end of History he walked her to the Longpier, suggesting questions she might ask the strong man if she had the chance. His approval soothed the worry that scratched behind her breastbone, distracting her from her mother's distress, from fears of what her father would do.

When she arrived home, Valentin was still in the barn. She descended the hill towards the rasp of his saw. Her mother had abandoned her post by the door, though the snow told of countless trips she had made across the yard. Else tracked her footprints to the farmhouse, where she began to shed her layers in the corridor.

'Else,' called her mother from the kitchen, 'is that you? Wait a minute there. Don't take off your boots.'

Her mother bore a tray when she stepped into the hall and frowned at the puddle Else had dripped onto the floorboards.

'Take this out to him,' she said. 'He can eat in the barn.'

She gave the tray to Else, who brought it outside. She took care not to let the meatballs roll off the plate as the water glass bumped a mug of chicory, releasing a gentle tinkling into the air. A lantern's light seeped under the barn's door in a weak challenge to the dusk. Else tapped the wood with her toe.

'*Hallo?*' she said. 'I have your dinner.'

When the strong man opened the door, his brow was moist with sweat. He stood aside to make room for her to pass. He returned to his work while she stepped around the ladder he had raised in the cow's pen and placed the tray on the milking stool. Valentin touched his saw to a log that balanced between two benches her mother had been saving for firewood. The lopped-off remains of a tree were piled in a corner of the horse's stall. Pine needles and wet sawdust covered the ground in a prickly mulch.

Valentin sliced a strip of wood from the log with as much effort as Else used to carve the morning loaf. Chips sprinkled the leather of his shoes like snow. A streak of perspiration stained the spine of his shirt. Rings darkened his armpits and collar band. The space smelled briny and bovine, of bogs and sap and, now, of chicory.

'Aren't you going to eat?' Else asked.

He cut another plank from his log before he lay down his saw. Once he had wiped his palms on his trouser legs, he looked around for the tray and moved over to the stool. Else edged away until her back pressed against the wall. He lowered himself to the floor and lifted the tray onto his lap. She wondered if she should go, but stayed where she was as he began to eat. Valentin picked up the knife and split a meatball in two. While he chewed, his eyes flicked from his plate to where she watched him from the shadows of the room.

'How was school?' he asked.

Else shrugged. She heard the water in his gullet as he sipped from his glass. 'When are you leaving?' she asked.

'We'll see,' he said. 'There's a lot of damage. It'll take a few days.'

'I meant,' Else said, 'when do you go back to the circus?'

'In the spring,' he said. 'The season starts in Haugesund.'

Else nodded as if that meant something to her. She made a note of the detail to tell Lars tomorrow.

When he had finished his meal and drunk the chicory, Valentin cleaned the grease from his lips on his hand. He stood and offered the tray to Else, then took up the lantern that hung from a nail sticking out of the wall. He held it high to brighten the snow once he had opened the door.

'Thank your mother,' he said.

Else ducked under his arm. A candle shone in the dining-room window, guiding her to the farmhouse through the dark while, behind her, Valentin's saw left the peace of the night in tatters.

The strong man left in good time before Johann was due home from the shipyard. In the kitchen Dagny fried more meatballs and peeled the skins from boiled potatoes, scraping the shavings that curled on her knife into the bucket under the sink. Else unscrewed the lid from a pot of lingonberry jam and put it next to her father's plate on the table. She saw him through the window, a shape in the dark that could easily have been mistaken for a deer.

The front door opened and shut and she hurried to the kitchen to carry the potatoes through. She judged her father's movements according to the corridor's protests: the groan of the bottom step when he removed his boots, the floorboards that creaked when he crossed to hang his coat, the quiet when he paused to crack the tension from his back. By the time he arrived in the dining room, she and her mother had finished preparing the dinner table. They took their seats while he washed his hands and splashed his face in the kitchen.

His jumper was spattered with water when he joined them and heaped food onto his dish and mashed his potatoes with the tines of his fork. He poured the sauce and helped himself to several spoonfuls of lingonberry jam. Else watched him chew and thought of Valentin eating his dinner in the barn, sitting in sawdust as he swallowed meatballs without gravy. Her mother watched, too. Her jaw was hard, her knife and fork idle in her fingers. She blinked and seemed surprised to discover that nothing was on her plate.

'About the barn,' she said.

'Now I'm tired,' said Johann. 'I don't want to hear more about the barn tonight.'

'Tenvik has loaned us a worker. He's been here today. He's made some progress.'

Johann's eyes moved slowly. He spoke through a mouthful of potato. 'A worker?' he said. 'What the hell do you mean, he's loaned us a worker?'

'One of the men from his farm.'

'The circus apes? He's brought one here? And who's paying for that? Hm? Who's paying for that?' He gulped down his food. 'Send him away,' he said.

'The barn needs fixing.'

'Send him away,' he said. 'I don't need Tenvik's goddamned charity.'

Johann speared a lump of meatball, raised it midway to his lips, then flung his fork onto his dish. He slammed a palm on the table top, sending a shiver through the crockery. Dagny flinched and shrank back in her chair. Fear froze Else's breath to splinters of ice that numbed her lungs and pricked her throat. Through the window, the sky was moonless. The night gobbled the stars.

Her father was up and headed for the boathouse without another word about the barn. Else stayed where she sat and did not dare to look at her mother. After some minutes, Dagny stood and carried the plates into the kitchen. She moved to the oven to add a log to the fire.

'I might go and lie down,' she said and padded from the room, leaving Else to clear the rest from the table. She washed the dishes, dried them, dried the pots and glasses and put each piece in its place on the shelf.

HER MOTHER DID not send Valentin away. Each morning when Else passed him on the road to Tenvik's farm, she would nod her greeting and his eyes would skip from the fjord to acknowledge her. When she returned, her bucket full and her hand sore with lugging it, his saw would be grating in the barn, a hammer pounding. She never knew if her father had seen him in her absence, if, face to face in the yard where the snow crushed itself in its thaw, they exchanged words. What would her father say? Whatever it might be, Valentin did not leave.

In the afternoons when Else came home from school, her mother would dispatch her with his dinner tray. She would wait until Valentin had eaten his meal, always arranging himself on the floor as he had that first night, blowing on a spongy cube of fishcake or dipping his bread into a stew. From her seat on the milking stool, Else would marvel at the barn's transformation. A network of planks boarded up the ceiling. Three posts seemed to grow out of the ground to support the roof. She watched one evening as he manoeuvred a fourth into the sawdust and hoisted its other end to the swelling above, the tendons popping in his neck as he heaved without uttering so much as a grunt.

For some reason, she felt comfortable in the strong man's company – perhaps because she seemed to concern him so little. He left her in peace, only speaking to answer her questions about the circus, or about his travels. He had driven through Europe, through Germany, East and West, seen Denmark and Sweden, the northern lights. The winters were too long up north, he said. Someday he would go south, he would settle in the sun.

Else parcelled up these trifles to present to Lars in the caretaker's shed, where he would kiss her for her troubles.

'Find out more,' he would say. 'Find out if he needs anything. How much homebrew can he handle, anyway?'

A blizzard swept in from the northeast, wiping out the mud a milder temperature in recent weeks had laid bare between cakes of ice. On Else's journey home from town, snow clouded the ferry's windows, mottling the view of the coastline to the shipyard. She stepped onto the pier at the public dock and battled her way to the farmhouse through whirling flakes, her legs plunging into powder, pulling her in as far as her calves.

Else's eyes were streaming when she arrived at the yard. Wind scoured her cheeks as she struggled past the barn, where Valentin's hammer thudded softly under the howl of the weather. She thought of him there in the lantern's light, warming his hands in his own steamed breath. His coat was not thick enough for this cold. His toes would be frost-bitten in his boots.

Else did not go straight to the farmhouse for his dinner but instead stole to the edge of the garden, hiding behind the bowed branches of the redcurrant bushes in case her mother should happen to glance from the dining room. On the fjord, the pier jutted out of the ice, a bleached gangplank into the storm. She mounted the boathouse stairs and shoved its door until it yielded. The snow shrugged a grey light onto the room, onto the ropes and nets and the rectangle of the trapdoor, onto fenders that hung from hooks in the wall over *Norges* jars and cans of oil. Else climbed over the rowing boat's oars splayed on the floor and set down her satchel beside her father's makeshift bed. With the mute distillery as her witness, she unbuckled the straps of the satchel.

She fished out the flask she had used that day to carry Ninni Tenvik's blackcurrant squash to school for her lunch. She took off her gloves, rubbing the worst of the chill from her fingers before she unscrewed the flask's cap. From her father's *Norges* jars, she chose one that was three-quarters full of his clear, stinking liquid and decanted three centimetres of homebrew into the dregs of her drink.

The flask sloshed its contents in her coat pocket as Else ploughed to the farmhouse under the white crown of the morello cherry tree and through the back door into a heat that scalded her skin. She shook her hat and brushed the snow from her arms.

'Mamma?' she called.

'I'll be right there,' her mother said.

Else stamped her boots on the doormat. Her mother laughed when she saw her.

'Go on,' she said, passing her Valentin's tray, 'stop soaking my floor and get back outside with you.'

Else carried the tray to the barn, her eyes slits against the snow. Valentin opened the door when she knocked, letting her in to melt a stream into the sawdust. The space was bitter with a draught that seeped in from the window and through the cracks between the door and its frame. A new fence closed off the cow's stall. Else deposited the tray on the milking stool.

While Valentin finished up with his hammer, she poured a measure of homebrew into the mug of chicory. Her fingertips tingled as she tightened the flask's top. She had placed it back in her pocket before he stopped his work to eat.

'It looks good,' Else said, pointing at the fence as he sank to the ground and reached for the tray. He clasped the mug in his palms and she waited for him to drink but, after some moments, he put it down and considered his dish. Dinner tonight was a vegetable casserole – a recipe Solveig had given her mother after the last *bedehus* meeting. Valentin extracted a carrot chunk from a pool of white sauce and popped it into his mouth.

'I suppose,' Else said, 'you're almost done with the barn.' Valentin nodded, his focus still on his meal. 'How much longer will you need?'

'Two days,' he said, 'no more.'

Else thought of the cow snug in Tenvik's barn. Poor animal, she thought, to be forced from relative comfort to return to her old quarters. For her part she would not miss the morning walk, especially now with the fresh snowfall, although, in truth, she had not minded it so much, had not minded coming home to the scrape of Valentin's tools. Yakov had left her alone the few times she had seen him shuffling in or out of the pig barn. Once she had glimpsed him running from the henhouse, his hands nests for what she assumed must be pilfered eggs.

Valentin shovelled the last of the casserole between his lips and sighed at his empty plate. He picked up the water glass and drained it in a series of short gulps. Again he lifted the mug, cradling it in his palms, resting the curve of the porcelain against his chest as if to warm his heart. He closed his eyes and breathed the vapour through his nose. His eyes opened and found Else's face.

He tasted the brew and his jaw softened as the liquid slipped down his throat. He raised the mug and took another mouthful. Else looked away, ashamed to feel so pleased.

'I thought you might be cold,' she said.

'So I was,' Valentin said. He drank again and relinquished the mug to Else. 'You look cold yourself.'

She hesitated, but accepted the mug. She sipped and a firework went off in her gullet. She swallowed air whose scent of damp pine and woodchip she had come to associate with Valentin. With a shy smile, she handed him the chicory and pulled the flask from her pocket. She refilled the mug with the remaining liquid, then waited for the strong man to drink it down.

By the time she left the barn, the tracks that testified to her expedition to the boathouse had almost vanished. The snow had filled them in like cement. Still it was the snow that gave her away.

That afternoon's dinner was punctuated by a faint pattering that came from the barn. Through the meal, Johann's eyes snapped up from his vegetables to glower at the flakes that danced in the sweating window. In spite of the moonshine that warmed Else's belly, her nerves were pricked. She was restless in her chair. She stopped herself from jumping each time her father barked at her mother from the head of the table.

'When will that ape be done out there?' he said. 'I'm sick of listening to his damned hammering.'

'Soon,' Dagny said. 'In a couple of days.'

'What in hell is this I'm eating? Why haven't you cooked any meat?'

Johann picked his way through half a portion of Solveig's casserole before stalking outside to the boathouse. Else was sitting by the oven reviewing the sewing pile when he burst through the front door, his coat still buttoned to his chin. Her mother leapt from her seat as he barged into the dining room.

'That circus ape,' he said, 'is a thief. He's been in the boathouse.'

'I don't think so,' Dagny said. 'He's been in the barn all day.'

'There are puddles on the floor. He's been in there, all right. Someone has.'

Else's heart lurched. Her fingers pinched her needle.

'Unless it was you?' her father said. 'Why would you go in there?'

'I haven't,' said her mother.

Johann moved into the room. His stare pinned itself on Dagny, who backed away.

'I didn't,' she said, 'I swear.'

'Father,' said Else.

'Why would you go in there?'

'Johann, no.'

His teeth were bared when he lowered his face to his wife's. She screamed when he grabbed her hair and struck her head against the wall.

'What were you doing in there?' he said. 'Were you checking on me?'

'Johann, please!'

He knocked her head harder. 'Spying on me in my own house?'

'Father,' Else said and was on her feet.

'Why were you there?'

'Father, stop! It was me!'

Before Else knew it her father had her by the throat, his fingers pressing her windpipe. He lifted her off the ground and she was sailing across the room and falling and crashing to the floor. A wild cry erupted from somewhere behind the pain that shot from her ribs and up and down her side. She could not breathe. Her mother shrieked, her father closed in. Then a banging behind her startled his charge.

Valentin was at the window, his face visible through the glass that rattled when he thumped it with his fist. A vein bulged under the skin at his temple. He pointed a finger at Johann.

'You,' he said.

Johann ran from the room. His footsteps pounded the stairs and then came the smack of a door through the ceiling. Else tried to sit up, but the ache in her side sent her back to the floor. Her mother was next to her.

'Else,' she said.

She felt hands on her shoulders, her mother's palm on her cheek. She let her terror melt to tears and buried her face in her mother's lap.

'Oh, Else,' she said, 'what have you done?'

Else touched her fingers to her neck. Only then did she remember the needle whose line had imprinted her thumb. When she looked at the window, Valentin was gone. The snow spun and billowed and flitted away.

VALENTIN NEVER RETURNED to the Dybdahl farm. It fell to Dagny to settle matters with Tenvik. She arrived on Tuesday morning to collect the cow and explain that the circus man's services would no longer be needed. Tenvik nodded without argument and she led the cow home through the snowbank, gripping the forelock of the head which swayed from side to side. There would be no getting rid of the draught in the barn but, even with it, the conditions for the animal had far improved.

Johann shut himself up in the boathouse, where he remained for several days. In the mornings, Else would leave her mother staring at its door from the window and set out for the public dock, longing for the ferry's deliverance from the strain that had her wincing with every crackle of the oven's fire. She ignored the shipyard workers, who threw her wondering glances before they climbed aboard the shipyard's boat. On her journey home from school, she stationed herself on the ferry deck and willed the wind to numb her, to empty her out.

Sunday's sermon told her to embrace suffering. '"Blessed is the man whom thou chastenest, O Lord,"' the minister said. After the service, while the parishioners huddled together for warmth and news in the churchyard, Reiersen broke away from his wife in her mink to cut off the Dybdahl family's retreat.

'Johann,' he called and Else felt her mother stiffen and all the eyes in the cemetery turn on them. 'A word, a quick word.'

Her mother touched her father's elbow. He halted by the gate, a hand resting on its post.

'This week,' Reiersen said. 'Well, I hear you've been missed. Are you ill?'

'No,' said Johann.

'A fever,' Dagny said.

'Well. I'm glad to see you're better. I'll tell Syvertsen to expect you tomorrow, then, unless there's a reason not to?'

While they spoke Lars watched from under the horse chestnut tree, not far from the church steps where Pastor Seip had paused in his blessings to observe the exchange. Lars studied his father taking a labourer to task with an expression that seemed to say he was learning a hard lesson. With his arms crossed, he chewed the inside of his cheeks. Else knew it had been a mistake to find him in the crowd. Their eyes met and he held hers for a moment before looking away.

Neither mentioned what had happened during school the following week, nor the week after that, once it had happened again. This time when Reiersen challenged Johann about his absences, his tone was hostile, his dissatisfaction clear. Even within the shelter of their silence, Else could sense the splitting open of a still-healing wound which, not long ago, her and Lars's shared interest in the strong man had stitched up. She worried the spot, prodded it, made it throb just as surely as the marks left on her neck by her father's fingers and hidden by a scarf that she refused to unwind, no matter how Lars urged.

'Can't you meet me tomorrow?' he asked her more than once. 'The Cadillac will be free. I could pick you up at five.'

'I can't,' Else said.

'You managed before.'

'I can't get away.'

'But you managed before.'

Else counted time by the fading of those marks, the dulling of black to plum and yellow. They had almost disappeared when, one afternoon, Lars did not come to find her during the break. Else waited alone in the shadow of the caretaker's shed, sliding the sole of her boot over the ground, dislodging the studs of grit from where their points had tacked them to the ice. Now and again, she would peer around the wall across the schoolyard, her gaze searching the asphalt. She shivered in her coat. She raised her hood over her hair and packed her hands into her coat sleeves.

Through the afternoon's classes, Lars sat in his seat between Petter and Gro Berge and did not turn around. Else caught herself staring at the back of his head and forced herself to look elsewhere. In the schoolyard outside, the snow reflected winter sunlight so bright that its glare stunned her. The fjord glimmered at the bottom of the hill as if its ripples had been stitched with circus sequins. Else remembered how, on the night under the Big Top, Lars had lain beside her at the edge of the manège. The riders' costumes had sparkled molten white under the lights. Lars had held her hand until the strong man took his bow.

They were surprised the letter from Reiersen did not come sooner. Johann brought it home after having spent the best part of three weeks in the boathouse, on some days only emerging to scavenge for food or to use the toilet or to revive himself with a cup of chicory. His thermos was in the kitchen when Else arrived home from school and joined her mother from the hall.

'I thought he went in this morning,' she said.

'He did,' said her mother.

The fat in Dagny's skillet spat and cooked two fillets of coalfish. She jabbed their flesh with a fork while her other hand pressed her stomach, its fingers curled above a limp wrist. Her profile glowed with hints of fresh bruising.

'What happened?' Else asked.

'I fell on the ice,' her mother said.

On the kitchen counter, next to a pile of carrot peel, Else saw an envelope addressed to her father.

'It's from the shipyard,' said her mother. She put down her fork and rubbed an eye. She opened the refrigerator door and checked its contents for something she did not find. 'He's been fired,' she said. 'They've finally got round to firing him.'

'Where is he now?' Else asked.

'Where you'd expect,' her mother said.

'Will you speak to Karin?'

Her mother gripped her fork. A fillet of fish broke apart in her pan when she tried to turn it. Slivers stuck to the metal, browning and crisping while she jabbed at them. 'Set the table, will you?' she said. 'Dinner is almost ready.'

———

On a Saturday at the end of March Else stepped off the ferry at the Longpier and, with her chin tucked behind her scarf, walked under the branches of the ash trees that shaded the harbour to Elvebakken. The worst of the snow had melted from the roads; what remained was hard-packed and black with exhaust fumes, or else soft and wet enough to trickle through her boots and moisten her toes.

Today a group had gathered at the bottom of the hill, where the Elvebakken pier cut a slab out of the ice that extended like a sheet of brushed metal over the water. A handful of boys swung sticks at a hockey puck, lobbing it back and forth and hollering if it flew too far. They took turns to feel their way, testing the surface of the ice before returning, puck in hand, each a hero come home.

Else found Lars with Rune, Petter and Gro Berge, whose smile dug dimples into her cheeks. They loitered on the pier and shared a cigarette. Else slipped into a gap at Lars's side.

'I didn't think you would come,' he said.

She closed her eyes when he kissed her, blocking out the sight of Gro's buckling smile and embracing the relief that soothed her heartache, trying to catch it in her arms.

For the next half-hour Else stayed on the pier together with Lars, his hand in hers while the boys played hockey and Stine Wiig engraved patterns on the ice with the skates she had strapped to her shoes. In a loud voice that drew the attention of their peers, Rune dared Petter to a race. They bounded from land and glided on their boot soles towards the brink where the ice began to thin into the fjord.

'Come on,' said Lars. His breath was hot on Else's ear. She shadowed him through the crowd which closed up in their wake. They climbed Elvebakken, picking over the filthy patches of snow that spotted the pavement. Behind them, shouts from the ice dwindled to the occasional, high-pitched shriek. Else looked over her shoulder to the bottom of the hill, where the race had its winner, though she could not make out who it was. She thought of her mother insisting she take the trip to town. 'A bit of fun will do you good,' she had said.

Lars led Else through the schoolyard to the caretaker's shed. He grinned as he pushed open its door. Inside he cleared a space on the ground, lifting the shovel and rake to the grit box before spreading his coat on a corner of the concrete. He pressed himself to Else.

'I've missed you,' he said.

She knelt beside him on the coat.

'No one will find us here,' he said.

He kissed her again and Else stretched out on the floor, which was hard and cold against her spine. Lars tasted of the cigarette he had smoked with Gro. He pulled off his gloves and unbuttoned her coat. His hands found her skin and her eyes were wide with the icy nip of his fingertips. She remembered the last time in the Cadillac, the fug of the wine and the lull of darkness. She breathed in the damp, mineral smell of the shed and searched his face, hoping to hold his eyes. He buried his nose in her hair and fumbled with her trouser button.

When it was over, he rolled onto his back and zipped himself up. He propped himself on his elbows and seemed to focus on the grit box until his breath was steady once more. He started to laugh. He shook his head. 'We should get back,' he said, 'before they miss us.'

'Can't we stay for a while?' Else asked.

'I'm freezing,' he said. 'I should put on my coat.'

Lars got to his feet and brushed down his clothes while Else rearranged herself, her bra and jumper, the elastic of her underpants and her trousers. As soon as she stood, he scooped up his coat and shook the filth from its wool. He restored the shovel and rake to their original places, then opened the door and passed into the day. The sun was bright after their time in the shed, the sky clear, its blue surprising. Else squinted as she stepped outside. She caught his hand.

'Lars,' she said.

She wanted to say something that would make him stop but, before she knew what, he had snatched back his hand. Else followed the line of his gaze to where Pastor Seip watched them from the gate. He waited, a figure in mourning, his black coat, his black hair. Her pulse was a stampede in her head, its rush as painful as hooves. She cowered behind Lars as he tramped across the schoolyard to confront the minister.

'What were you doing in there?' asked Pastor Seip.

'Nothing,' said Lars. 'We were talking.'

'Talking,' he said.

Else's face was hot. She recognised the reproach that narrowed the minister's eyes, that same sneer that he had trained on her father when he had discovered him drunk at home. In a weak gesture, she lifted a palm to smooth her coat. Pastor Seip continued up the hill to the grocery. Else looked to Lars, who had already begun his descent to the fjord.

'The Lord teaches us,' said Pastor Seip, 'to trust in Him, to put our faith in His judgement. For who of us can truly know another man's heart? We are wretched beasts, racked by lusts and desires that we must strive daily to conquer. But the Devil is cunning and we, in our weakness, succumb too readily to his trickery. Is it not so that, every day, we stare the Devil in the face and mistake what we see for innocence?'

Else had not slept the previous night. She had remained awake while the cherry tree's branches rapped the window, replaying in her mind the moment when she had emerged from the caretaker's shed to see Pastor Seip at the school gate. The horror of discovery filled her up; she felt overstuffed, her stomach aching and sour. As she sat on the bench between her parents and endured the sermon, she did her best to direct her thoughts elsewhere. She remembered the Big Top rising in a fog of white light in the middle of Tenvik's paddock. Try as she might, she could not hold the image. She glanced at Lars in the nave's first pew. Fair curls skimmed the collar of his suit jacket.

'For three years under His ministry,' said Pastor Seip, his voice seething from the pulpit, 'Jesus loved Judas as He loved His other disciples, as He loves all men. Yet Judas betrayed Him for thirty pieces of silver. He gave himself freely to the Devil, just as Jesus knew he would. Many here would do the same. For who remembers the promise of heaven's bounty when pleasure offers itself here and now? Who has a faith strong enough to turn away when the Devil leads them to commit wicked deeds in secret places?

'God's mercy is great, but so, too, is his wrath. So says the first chapter of Paul's Epistle to the Romans. "For the wrath of God is revealed from heaven against all ungodliness and unrighteousness of men." We will answer to God for our sins, and He will punish us as a father punishes his wayward child. Do you imagine Almighty God cannot see into secret places? Did not Jesus know that Judas would betray Him? After He had washed His disciples' feet, He dipped the sop and gave it to Judas. And Judas rejected His love and Satan entered into him.

'It is written in the Book of Jeremiah, "Can any hide himself in secret places that I shall not see him? saith the Lord. Do not I fill heaven and earth? saith the Lord." No place is secret from God. The Lord sees all.'

After the service Else shuffled down the aisle towards Pastor Seip, whose slight build blocked the doorway. As she approached, fear goaded her guilt. Beside her, her mother's face was empty. She nodded when Solveig Haugeli wished her a good day. Her father cleared his throat, a soft shifting of mucus that repeated until he offered his hand to the minister.

Pastor Seip considered Johann's fingers as if studying his nails for dirt. He relented to a limp handshake.

'It was a fine sermon,' Dagny said.

He pinched his lips and his eyes glossed over Else, who tripped outside and breathed in the mist that had drifted up from the fjord. It coiled around the headstones in celestial wreaths, winding and unfurling and wafting away. She hurried after her parents through the churchyard to Dronning Mauds gate.

In the days that followed, Else helped her mother. She dusted and wrung cloths in buckets frothing with suds and peeled the potatoes that she carried up from the cellar. In the evenings after dinner, she attended to the sewing pile. A family of mice had made their nest over her bed. They scratched behind the ceiling beams throughout the night, when she would track their progress by the click of scampering feet and each second would hang like a threat in the air.

On Friday afternoon when school was done, Else caught the ferry from town to the public dock. A sliver of colour wedged open the view to the horizon. The path home was slippery with slush which washed into new shoots sprouting in the mud at the roadside. Here and there a bootprint was moulded in ice, the grooves of its sole immortalised until spring.

Else almost knocked into Pastor Seip when she took the bend by the Aaby farm. The minister blew his nose into a handkerchief, which he bunched and stuffed into his coat pocket. He drew himself up when he recognised her and marched purposefully on. She caught a whiff of chicory as he brushed by.

Else stared at the dull rock of the mountain, at the frozen pebbles caught in its cracks, and wondered what Sigrid Aaby would do if she tapped on her door. How much time would she let her stay before sending Atle to fetch her mother? Down on the water, the Aaby boathouse straddled the ice that had shattered their pier during the winter. The Reiersen shipyard's graving dock was still deserted on the opposite shore. Else's eyes climbed the beams of its cranes and she remembered Valentin pointing at her father through the window. 'You,' he had said. The image grew dim. She walked home.

The farmhouse was quiet when she snuck into the hallway, where she set down her satchel and unzipped her coat. The lights were off in the dining room. A pile of embers cooked in the oven. In the kitchen, unequal amounts of chicory cooled in three of onkel Olav's cups. They stood on the counter waiting to be washed. Their porcelain was warm to the touch.

Else sat in a chair by the dining table and searched her mother's sewing basket for a needle. She managed to compose herself for long enough to pass a thread through its eye. She chose a sock from the pile and pushed the point of her needle into the wool at its heel, while a twist of smoke unwound from the oven to a stain on the ceiling the colour of burnt sugar.

Winter flounced into the house when the front door opened, dispersing the smoke and the fire's meagre heat. Else followed the tread of her father's boots: three strides before he appeared in the dining room. His hair was dishevelled. His clothes hid muscles that years of seafaring had tacked to his bones. Her mother was at his elbow. Her eyes met Else's and she knew what was to come.

'There she is,' Johann said. 'We've been looking for you. You'll never guess who's been visiting.'

He swayed on his feet. Else could smell him from where she sat.

'Pastor Seip was glad to see us while you were out, was what he said. He wanted a word while you were out of the way.'

He took a step forward.

'Johann, no,' Dagny said. She gripped his arm and he wheeled around. He smashed her cheek and she hit the wall and crumpled to the ground.

Else sprang to her feet. 'Mamma,' she said, but she shrank when her father turned on her. He launched himself across the room. His palm closed over her throat.

'In a shed,' he said, 'with the Reiersen boy. What were the two of you doing?'

'Please,' her mother said.

His fingers squeezed. Else clawed at his wrists. Blood rolled between her ears. 'Whore,' he said.

He let her go and she spluttered and gulped the stink of liquor into her lungs. Flames seared her throat. Hands tugged her hair and she cried out. The room was spinning; it whirled as he dragged her into the hall. Hair ripped from her skull. Her scalp was ablaze.

'Stop it, stop it!' screamed her mother. Her father threw a fist and she crashed into the sideboard and fell. Else stumbled beside him, the stairs beating her ankles as he hauled her up, his arm crushing her ribs. He shoved her down the corridor and into her bedroom, grabbed her shoulders and shook her until the walls rocked. Sobs spilled from her mouth when he dropped her on the floorboards. She crawled to a corner on her hands and knees and drew her limbs in and covered her ears with her hands.

The door slammed. There was a grating in the keyhole.

'No,' Else said. She forced herself to stand. She staggered to the door. Its handle rattled in her fingers.

'No,' she said.

On the bedroom floor, she folded herself up and turned her face to the wall. She heard her father on the stairs and then her mother started to scream.

Now

2009

ELSE GRASPS THE edges of the cake tin in her hands, pressing white dents into her thumbs as she climbs the drive to Lars and Victoria Reiersen's home. Two columns of fir trees bow their crowns over the road on either side, blotting out the stripes of a mackerel sky. The track is wider than it used to be. A smooth swathe of asphalt steamrollers the dirt and gravel of her memory. She recalls zipping up this path long ago on the back of Lars's moped. It is the last thing she should be thinking about now. With every step, the flutter of trespass almost sends her home.

The house is smaller than she remembers. Else stops in the shade of a lilac tree and takes a moment to reacquaint herself with the building. Her eyes follow the vines up the gables to the roof, whose tiles gleam silver-black in the sun. Where Lars's mother planted rhododendrons, he and his wife have a trimmed box tree. Potted hydrangeas lead the way up the slate steps to the front door. The garage is open. Bicycles and children's scooters spill onto the tarmac, blocking the path of the Audi parked in the drive. The car must belong to Victoria. Lars's BMW is nowhere to be seen. Rearranging her grip on the cake tin, Else carries on to the top of the stairs.

She has rung the bell twice before Victoria answers the door. Victoria's face lifts in surprise before falling in dismay. She stands with the nozzle of a Dyson forgotten in one hand as she gapes at her visitor.

'Else,' she says.

For the first time all summer, Else notices the dark stains under her eyes. Her nails are bitten, her hair greasy at the roots. Victoria is childlike in a pair of tartan pyjama bottoms and an oversized T-shirt. The word 'GIANTS' is printed in green letters across her breasts, which prod the cotton in two sharp nubs.

Else holds out the cake tin. 'I brought a *kringle*,' she says. 'It's a welcome gift.'

'We've been here since June,' Victoria says.

'I know. I should have come earlier. Are you free for half an hour?'

'All right,' Victoria says.

In a foyer that smells of antiques and old rainwear, Else leaves her shawl folded on top of her shoes. Victoria shows her into a hallway, whose brass chandelier is switched off and whose rug is thick under her bare feet. Ahead, the dining room is just as Else remembers it from the days when she would follow Lars through to the basement stairwell, stroking the brocade chair backs with her fingers, all the while looking about her in hushed awe. Now, with his wife in front of her, it is the hush that returns. Each silver bowl and crystal figurine on display in the glass cabinets warns against being touched. Her memories of youthful capers are nudged off-kilter: they seem as out of place in this house as Victoria does. The younger woman pads in her socks over the floorboards. Her T-shirt swamps her frame down to her thighs.

At least the kitchen is bright. Sunlight streams through the windows when they enter, melting the shadows from the buttercup walls. Liv had a hand in this. Else thinks of the paint splattered on her granddaughter's miniskirt and is ashamed of the resentment she felt. She imagines Victoria withdrawing from the stuffiness of the house, gathering herself up on the kitchen bench and resting her chin in the pocket of her palms as she gazes at the fjord.

Victoria fills the kettle and flips its switch once she has set it on its stand. She turns to Else and crosses her arms.

'All I have is instant,' she says.

'That's fine,' Else says.

'So. What can I do for you?'

'I wanted to clear the air,' Else says.

Victoria blinks at her. She squints and Else has the impression she is weighing her words, deciding whether or not to say something. Why has she come here? Damage control. That is the real reason for this visit. Else has planned it on an afternoon when she knows Andreas and Thea have their weekly sailing lesson. Lars should be at the office for some hours yet – the national summer holiday ended on Monday. For her part, her time is her own until Eva Lund's facial at three.

Victoria reaches for two mugs from the corner cupboard and scoops a teaspoon of coffee granules into each. She tops them up with boiling water and opens the fridge for a carton of milk. 'How do you take your coffee?'

'Black,' Else says.

Her host carries the mugs to the kitchen table and invites Else to sit while she finds plates. Else chooses a chair, then watches her sink a blade into the cake she woke early this morning to bake.

'Now that the air is clear,' Victoria says, 'what shall we talk about?'

'How do you feel you're settling in?'

'Not as well as I'd hoped,' Victoria says. 'Of course, when you move to your husband's hometown, you expect that you'll run into one or two ghosts. But there are some things you can't prepare yourself for.'

'I can see how it might be difficult,' Else says.

'Can you?'

'In the cemetery,' she says and fiddles with the handle of her mug, 'I wonder if you may have got the wrong idea.'

'Oh?' Victoria says.

'Lars and I were only talking.'

'Is that so?' she says. 'What were you talking about?'

Else makes an effort not to frown when she thinks of Lars asking her about Marianne. 'Our children.'

'What about them?' asks Victoria.

'Lars wanted to know how Marianne likes her new job. It was as innocent as that.'

An odd smile screws up a corner of Victoria's mouth. She snatches at a crumb from the raisin-and-walnut filling that has leaked from the cake slice onto her plate, raising it to her lips and sucking the sugar from her fingers. Else is unnerved by her reaction. She wonders if she has misjudged the shape of her hurt. The image of her cowering in her kitchen breaks apart.

'What about Liv and Andreas?' Victoria says. 'They seem to be getting on well, don't you think?'

'It seems so,' Else says.

'You don't think that's inappropriate?'

'They're eleven years old.'

'For now,' Victoria says. She stirs her coffee into a vortex, sets down her spoon, pinches the bridge of her nose. 'What's going on here?'

'I'm not sure I know what you mean.'

'No,' Victoria says. 'No, of course you don't.' Her stare is firm, though her hands are trembling. Else is the first to look away.

'The reason I came to see you,' she says, 'is to say that if Lars and I bump into each other from time to time – and we will, because this is a small town – then it's neither my choice, nor is it my doing. If we can be clear on that point, then it's as far as we have to agree.'

'We'll see,' Victoria says. Her lips twitch. All at once, her tone changes to one of saccharine sweetness. She glances around the room, waving a hand at the walls. 'How do you like what we've done with the place? I gather you've been here plenty of times before.'

'Not for many years,' Else says.

'Oh, that's right,' says Victoria. 'Not since Marianne was born.'

Else pushes back her chair and stretches for her handbag on the floor. As she bends over, a rush of blood makes her head swim. She braces herself against her knees until the dizziness passes. When she sits up, she is stunned to see Victoria's eyes are glossy with tears.

Else stands and shoulders her handbag. 'I'll let myself out,' she says.

'Why not?' says Victoria. 'You know the way.'

THE HOUSE IS quiet when Else arrives home after work. She hangs her shawl in the hallway and changes into her slippers, her ears straining as she does, though there is nothing to hear. Liv will not be back from her father's until the weekend. She misses the buzz of the television set, the clop of Marianne's heels on the stairs. With a shiver in spite of the balmy evening air, she makes her way into the kitchen and turns the radio on. She carries it with her to her bedroom and, setting it down beside the bathroom sink, begins to run herself a bath. While she waits for it to fill, she fumbles her mobile phone from her pocket and finds her granddaughter's number on speed dial. It rings five times and segues into a pre-recorded response.

'This is Liv's phone. Leave a message.'

'It's me,' Else says. 'Ring me tonight before bed. Okay? I want to hear about your day.'

Else hangs up but remains staring at the buttons, considering whether to try again. She leaves the phone by the radio and undresses for her bath.

Afterwards, when she is dry and the radio has played Dire Straits for the second time that hour, she creeps in her bathrobe down the corridor to Liv's bedroom. The door is open and she steps inside, wondering if it is possible to intrude on an eleven-year-old's privacy. She stoops to rescue a pair of shorts from the floor as she passes, folding them and laying them at the foot of the bed. Once seated at the desk, she has an urge to rifle through its drawers for a diary, but stops herself. She presses the 'On' button at the corner of the computer. The machine whirs to life.

Else guides the mouse's arrow to the compass icon on the desktop and clicks it awake. 'Google' appears in a box on the screen. She hesitates, though it is not the first time she has given in to curiosity since Marianne convinced her to buy a computer three years ago. Even so, she types the letters of the strong man's name with a sense of apprehension. She has been unable to put the meeting with Victoria out of her mind. *What's going on here?* The challenge ricochets between her ears, bruising the soft tissue of her self-preservation.

Valentin Popov.

She has never forgotten. She pushes 'Return' and waits for the results.

There are 134,000 hits.

Else scans the listings on the first page. She proceeds to the second, then to the third. Towards the bottom of the screen on page four, she finds the entry she is looking for.

'Bienvenido a Circo Valentino!'

The mouse's arrow transforms to a pointing finger that hovers over the title. Else clicks. The website starts to load.

From the top corners of the screen, two cartoon elephants trumpet the proclamation *'Bienvenido a Circo Valentino!'* from their trunks. The letters dance between them, bold and golden against a dark, starlit sky. Under their bubble ears, other animals smile in cramped columns that run down the margins of the page. Lions, puppies, chimpanzees. A Big Top rises out of the ground at the centre of the pack, its mast crossing the poles of a handful of flags. Else clicks on a Union Jack and the title transforms to 'Welcome to Circus Valentino!' A menu presented in boxes along the bottom of the display directs her around the website: 'Touring route', 'Ticket information', 'This year's programme'. She chooses 'About us' and a fresh panel opens. Black-and-white pixels gain definition. With a hand pressed over her heart, Else peers at the image as it refines.

Valentin stares out at her from an ochre-tinted photograph. He is young – younger, she thinks, than when he visited her town. His hair curls away from a face as wide and smooth as a pie dish. One shoe rests on a dumb-bell, which lies idle on the ground while he grins and holds a medal in the palm of his hand. With the other, he clutches a flag that is wrapped around his shoulders. The tallest of the men beside him only reaches his chin.

Else begins to read the text that runs down the left side of the window:

Born in 1948 in Sofia, Bulgaria, Valentin Popov showed himself to be a weightlifter of promise early in life. At the age of 16, he made his debut in the Light-heavyweight weight class at the European Weightlifting Championships. He took gold at the same event the following year.

In 1967, Valentin joined the Moscow Circus and toured Europe as the troupe's strong man. At the end of the season, he seized an opportunity to stay in the West, defecting from the Eastern bloc and joining a circus that was headed north. The next ten of more than twenty years performing as a strong man were spent travelling throughout Scandinavia. In total, he appeared in the manège in twelve countries with five different circuses.

His experiences fuelled a dream of one day starting a circus of his own. In 1989, together with his wife, Flaviana, Valentin began hiring acts for a breathtaking, breakthrough programme. The now famous yellow-and-red Big Top was erected in Bari on opening night and, for the very first time, Valentin stepped into the manège as ringmaster. The audience's response to the show was overwhelming and Circus Valentino was born.

Every year since, Valentin, Flaviana and their children, Patrizia and Paolo, have taken Circus Valentino on tour, to the delight of the viewing public. With a reputation built through critical acclaim and commercial success, it has become Italy's favourite circus . . .

An image among several arranged alongside the text catches Else's eye. She stops reading. The purple and red swirls of the circus poster are faded with age. From the centre of the placard, a clown seems ready to burst from the display. His eyebrows glance off his hairline in two arched bows; his teeth are railway tracks that split and meet again on the other side of his nose. In the top left-hand corner, the declaration 'Circus Leona Is Coming!' shoots a chill up Else's spine. Next to the clown, a man in a loincloth lifts a horse over his head.

Else blinks at the caricature of the strong man before continuing to scroll down the page, taking in the rest of the scanned memorabilia that Valentin must have collected throughout his travels. In one photograph he straddles the midpoint of a teeterboard, sporting a costume that complements those of the women he balances on his shoulders. In another, a circus troupe glitters against a Big Top backdrop. Valentin smiles next to a stilt-walker, who looms out of the shot.

The final picture shows the strong man – now Circus Director – posing proudly with his family. They stand together in the manège: three generations of dark, foreign beauty. Valentin is buttoned into a spangled coat and a shirt whose frills bloom at his chin. Helices of hair poke out from under the brim of his top hat. His moustache has been shaved clean. One arm encircles his wife, who is striking in a peacock-feathered dress and an emerald dusting of make-up. Their son and daughter beam on the couple's either side with their spouses, who each hug a baby to their chests. Between Valentin and Patrizia, a child volunteers a shy, milk-toothed grin. She holds her grandfather's hand close to her cheek.

Else clicks the 'X' at the top left corner of the display box. The circus's blaze snuffs out, clearing the way for a different photo saved to the desktop. It shows three generations of her own: Else, Marianne and Liv, so alike, all of them, with their uncertain smiles and hair a shade of summer gold. Her eyes find Marianne's, which share her colouring, a pale grey that Liv, too, has inherited. Else presses the computer's 'Off' button. The desktop goes black.

She is asleep in front of the TV when the snap of the lock startles her awake. She props herself up as Marianne enters the sitting room. Tonight her uniform is rumpled. Her hair is bunched in a knot at the back of her head and her make-up has lost its lustre, though a trace of kohl is still smudged under her eyes. Marianne drops onto the sofa by her mother's feet. For the first time that evening, Else is restored to a fragile calm.

'How was work?' she asks.

'Busy,' says Marianne.

'More than usual?'

'Kjersti Nydahl had a birthday party,' she says. 'Twenty people, and all of them ordered sweet and sour pork. I think the manager had to go out back to slaughter another pig. What are you watching?'

'I don't know,' Else says.

'Why don't you go to bed?'

'Are you staying tonight?'

Marianne shakes her head. 'Mads is picking me up in half an hour.'

'You look tired,' Else says.

'We'll take it easy,' she says, 'don't worry.'

The glow from the TV bleaches Marianne's features, but still Else sees the hardening of her jaw. 'That sounds like a good idea,' she says and rubs her eyes. She has had a long day herself.

'Did you talk to Liv?' Marianne asks.

'She's fine. She says she's having a nice time. They went to the Oil Museum earlier.'

'Sounds like a blast.'

'You should ask Mads over for dinner.'

The crackle of gunshot pulls Else's attention back to the television set. A wild man sprints across the screen. Another follows, as unflustered as the first was panicked. Else senses Marianne searching her face. She keeps her look even. She will manage this.

'If you want,' she says. 'Whenever you want.'

'You're inviting him for dinner?'

'It's up to you, Marianne.'

Else pushes herself off the sofa and stoops to kiss her daughter's forehead like she used to do when she was a child. A wayward curl tickles her chin.

'It would be nice to meet him,' she says.

'You know he's not going anywhere, Mamma.'

'I know,' she says.

Else shuffles away. At the top of the stairs, she flips on a switch to light her path down the corridor. She shuts the door behind her when she reaches her bedroom and leans against the wood. It is cool through her T-shirt. Tinny sounds from the TV filter in through the walls, their threat neutralised with distance. Else closes her eyes. She folds her arms across her chest and presses, trying to smother the familiar ache. In the darkness, she sees Victoria as she left her, crying alone in her yellow kitchen. She sees the strong man hoisting a horse above his head.

Then

1975

ELSE FLINCHED WHEN she heard the knock at the door, but did not look when her mother stepped into her bedroom. Her legs, arms, back, neck throbbed from having spent hours folded up in this spot, her forehead pressed against the window-pane as she peered into the night. Now, the darkness had dulled to a flat, grey morning.

'How did you sleep?' her mother asked.

She did not answer. Her eyes strayed to the spring buds that blistered the bark of the morello cherry tree. If she were to stand and open the window and stretch out her arms as far as she could reach, her fingers would almost touch the tips of its branches. She knew, because she had tried it. They were still too far away to be of any use to her. The three-metre drop from the window ledge to the ground put paid to any ideas she had of jumping.

'You haven't spent the night on the chair, have you?' Dagny said. Crockery clacked as a breakfast tray was set down on the bed.

'I hope you're hungry,' Dagny said. 'I opened another jar of strawberry jam. The last one is already finished.'

Else's eyelids were heavy as she blinked and shifted her position to rest her forehead on a new patch of window. Behind her, the springs of the bed announced the lowering of her mother's body onto the mattress.

'Else,' she said. 'Please, you have to eat something. Are you listening?'

They sat in silence for a minute, then another, before Else's tongue came unstuck from the roof of her mouth. Her throat was dry and so she swallowed, realising that more than a day must have passed since she last spoke.

'Has he said when he will let me out?' she asked.

'I am doing what I can,' her mother said.

Else nodded. Her gaze drifted to the fjord. The islets of ice that had deadened its surface during the winter months were all but gone, licked away from underneath by the steel-coloured waves. She would have missed the last of the skating at Elvebakken by now. Any frozen strips left on the water could not be trusted to take her weight. Else imagined gliding out too far and the ice splitting around her, one fracture giving way to the next in the shape of a trawler's net. She closed her eyes and relented to sinking.

Her mother cleared her throat. 'You'll never guess who I saw at the market yesterday?' The bed creaked. Else heard careful footsteps. 'Lars Reiersen was buying sugar peas. He was asking after you. I told him you were feeling better.'

Her mother put an arm around her shoulder. When she felt fingers in her hair, she did not pull away. She opened her eyes and they settled again on the water. Lars had been at the market, asking after her. Lars had bought sugar peas with no idea of what was happening.

'Your father can't keep this up,' Dagny said, 'and I am trying. I promise I am.'

Her voice cracked and Else looked at her face. There were no new bruises, as far as she could tell. A scarf knotted at her mother's throat hid the fingerprints on her neck and, under the knobbly yarn of her jumper sleeve, a bandage swaddled the spot where her father had held the kettle two weeks before. Tricks and camouflage to hide her slow ruin; perhaps there were other injuries that Else could not see? She took her mother's hand. Side by side, they contemplated the cherry tree through the window. Its branches waved in the murky morning.

The front door banged shut and her mother leapt to her feet. 'There is your father,' she said. 'I'll be back soon. Please, eat something.'

She left the breakfast tray on the quilt and hurried out of the room. Else stared after her before turning again to the window.

Lars at the market.

Lars buying sugar peas.

Lars asking after her, but not coming to her rescue.

Two weeks had passed and he had not come. He would not come for her now.

At the edge of the waterfront, the snow that remained was packed as tight as stone. Else wondered if she would still be here when it disappeared altogether. In the time she had been shut in her room, she had witnessed the shrinking, hardening, blackening of all of that white, exposing more and more of the smothered earth underneath. It stretched brown and barren from the farmhouse to the pier. Twice, she had imagined seeing the *Frøya* floating there, anchored fast and bobbing on the water, but when she blinked, the boat was gone.

Now, in the empty space, an eider duck beat its wings before settling on the water's surface and propelling itself into the fjord. A light rain was starting. Its drops trickled in crooked lines down the windowpane, sketching a senseless blueprint on the other side of the glass.

———

It was night when the first pebble hit the window and Else was startled awake. She opened her eyes to a clear sky pricked with stars. From the next room, her father's snores shook the walls of the house. Each intake of breath devoured the silence.

'Else!'

Her name came from outside and she scrambled to her feet. She undid the window latch and peered over the sill, but saw no one.

'Over here!'

The voice was closer than she had anticipated. Else looked across to the branches of the cherry tree, still visible in the moonlight. They sagged under her visitor's weight. Without the cover of leaves to hide behind, his outline was plain to see. He clutched the tree trunk with one arm and waved his free hand at her.

'Lars?'

'It's Petter.'

In spite of herself, Else's heart sank. 'Petter,' she said, 'what are you doing here?'

'Oh, you know. Just felt like a chat.'

'A chat? Are you mad?'

She heard a giggle. 'Not as mad as all that. There's a party at the paddock. I thought tonight you should come.'

It was not what she expected. Else wanted to laugh, but her relief was fleeting. She glanced down at the ground for what might have been the hundredth time that day.

'I can't get out,' she said. 'My bedroom door is locked.'

'Your door is locked? Why's it locked?'

'It's too high for me to get down from here,' she said.

Petter was quiet. Else strained to see the details of his face but all she could make out were his eyes, glittering in the half-light like two pots of oil.

'You'll have to jump,' he said finally. 'Not down. Across to me.'

'If I could have done that, I would have done it already.'

'But now I'm here to catch you,' Petter said.

'You *are* mad,' she said.

'Maybe. But I'm a decent catch, too.'

Else shook her head and withdrew into her room. She sat on the bed beside the food tray that her mother had left for her earlier that evening. She had not touched the stew. It had congealed in its bowl and now its flavours mixed in the air with traces from her chamber pot, settling on her skin and weaving themselves with the fibres of her clothing. She blinked at the cold vegetables and a jolt of fury shocked her muscles awake. Her eyes skipped from the washbasin in one corner, still filled with dirty water, to the basket of knitting that her mother had brought for her distraction. Each object screamed of her captivity. Else imagined feeling the cold wind in her hair, slapping her cheeks, scouring her lungs, rinsing out her mouth as she bolted through darkness.

She listened for her father's snores, then hurried back to the window.

'Yes,' she said. 'Yes, I'm coming. Just give me a minute.'

As quietly as she could, she pulled open the drawers of her dresser and grabbed the warmest clothes she had, tugging one jumper after another over her head until her trunk was stiff with wool. Her boots were downstairs in the hall. She cast about the room for something to wear on her feet and chose a pair of shag socks and some summer plimsolls: they would have to do. Before returning to the window, she snatched the bedspread that a great-aunt had crocheted and rolled it into a scarf.

Petter remained crouched on his perch. 'What are you doing?' he hissed.

'Just getting some things.'

'What, are you packing a case? Come on, let's go.'

Else placed one foot on the windowsill and drew herself onto the ledge. Her hands gripped the sides of the window frame for balance. She looked across to Petter, now straddling a branch with both of his arms outstretched.

'Are you ready?' he asked.

'Ready,' she said. Else's pulse knocked like a fist in her skull. She took a deep breath before she dropped into the night.

Falling, flying, sinking, sinking. The black sky closed over her head like water. A snap, a crack; a solid something struck her chest. A cry from somewhere she could not fathom. Scrabbling for a hold, legs kicking the air. Petter's eyes, his fingers clamped above her elbows. Pinching her skin. His hands dragging her up and up.

'I have you,' he said.

'Don't let go.'

'I told you I was a good catch.'

Else gripped his arm. With his help, she managed to tuck her body over the branch on which he sat. She lifted one leg, twisting up and around until she had hauled herself into a sitting position.

'I left my moped parked off the road,' Petter said.

Else nodded at her parents' window. 'Come on. We have to hurry.'

She tried to listen again for her father's snores, but her heartbeat muffled all other sound. She gripped the branch with hands that shook and, as quickly as she could, shinned down the tree trunk.

By the time her shoes touched the ground, Petter was halfway across the yard. She raced after him, sliding through the mud beside the vegetable plot. An animal smell wafted from the crumbling barn, accompanied by the sound of the cow's sleepy huff. Else's own breath panted as she ran. Her socks and plimsolls sucked up spring melt. The cold water swamped her toes, icing her flesh to the bone.

At the edge of the property Else scrambled up the hill to the road, rocks crunching underfoot with every step. The branches of the birch trees on either side of the path blotted out the moonlight, stretching and joining like fingers clasped in prayer. Else had the sense that they were advancing on her, that the trees were closing ranks, a holy army bent on thwarting her escape. It was a relief when the hill plateaued and she was able to outrun them.

She found Petter waiting for her on his moped. She could make out his smile and his hand fumbling for the key.

'Not here,' Else whispered. 'Let's push the bike further down the road.'

'Wooohoooo!' Petter howled.

'Shut up! What are you doing?'

'We made it, didn't we?'

'They could still wake up. The engine's too loud. Let's just . . .'

But he was already turning the key. The engine snarled to life. 'How's that for a daring rescue?'

Else hurried forward and swung her leg over the saddle behind him before lacing her arms around his waist. Her chest was still heaving from the effort of her run. She was aware of his back pressing against her and she did her best to calm her breathing.

'So where have you been? They said at school you were ill. What did you do to get locked in your room?'

When she did not answer, Petter snorted.

'Suit yourself,' he said and nudged the pedal with his foot.

The moped jerked and took off down the road, while his question hummed in her ears. What had she done? Else knew what she had done. She had been careless. Stupid. Sneaking off with Lars to the caretaker's shed – of course her father had found them out. For the first time since Petter's arrival, she let herself feel her disappointment: it should have been Lars, not him. But Lars had not come. He had been at the market buying sugar peas; he had carried on with life as normal. It was Petter who had climbed the morello tree.

Else squeezed her arms tighter around his stomach. If she could convince him to drive her to town, then someone would help her – either that, or she would catch the first coach out. She brought her lips close to his ear and shouted over the motor.

'I need to get into town! Do you hear me, Petter? I said I need to get into town!'

Petter lifted a hand from the handlebar and batted his ear. The moped zipped on and desperation tied a knot in her throat. But she would bide her time. She would make him see. As soon as they stopped, she would explain and he would do as she asked.

The wind was savage, stinging her eyes. Else ducked her head, but it found her behind the shelter of Petter's shoulder. It buzzed in her ears, a murmuring swarm that pricked her nose and throat with every breath. Her toes curled with the cold, but the air smelled of sea salt, of wet manure and early spring. She drew it deep into her lungs, ignoring the bite. She had escaped.

For some moments, she let herself go to a wild, bouncing joy. She raised her face to meet the wind. Freedom rushed at her in a blur of shadows.

Petter pressed the brakes of his moped. Its engine became shrill and, with a yank of the handlebars, he swerved headlong into the gloom at the side of the road. A jagged track opened under the moped's wheels. They bumped over rocks embedded in the earth and raised tree roots which slowed their progress almost to a standstill.

'Where are we?' she asked.

'Don't you know? Tenvik's paddock is ahead.'

'But why have we come here?'

'I told you. It's a party.'

'But I have to get into town,' Else said.

Petter released the pedal and the moped came to a stop. The engine sputtered and was silent. He fixed the kickstand with his boot.

'Don't you hear me?' Else said. 'I have to get into town.'

He clambered off the saddle, pulling himself from her arms. 'But it's the middle of the night.'

'You have to listen . . .'

'Else, what's wrong? Why do you have to get into town?'

Petter waited for an explanation, which melted like snowflakes on her tongue. She understood suddenly how hopeless it was. Even if he agreed, what good would it do? Who would believe her? Perhaps they already knew. Everyone knew about her father's drinking. She thought of the townspeople whispering in the churchyard, of how they watched her parents hurry off every Sunday to catch the ferry. Her mother's make-up did a poor job of covering the welts on her cheeks. Certainly, they knew. They shook their heads over the beatings, but did nothing to intervene. Why would they now? If she went to them for help, they would deliver her to her father. She had no choice: she would have to run away. But she had no money. She had nothing but the clothes on her back. What coach driver would take her if she could not pay for her ticket? If she spent all night begging, they would send her away, each one in turn.

'Well?' Petter said.

'Please,' she said, no longer sure of what she was asking.

He fished his Zippo lighter from his pocket and rolled its flint with his thumb. It flared in a puny flame that burned a patch out of the darkness.

'If you want to go to town,' he said, 'you can walk. I'm going to the party.'

Petter strode down the track, leaving Else alone on the moped. She watched him go, her heart a dead weight in her chest. An image of her mother, battered and bloody, flickered behind her eyes. She blinked it away; she must not think about that now.

The light that bobbed with Petter's movements began to dwindle. Else dismounted from the bike and ran to catch him up.

The forest closed around them. The trees threaded their branches into a net which collected the moonlight overhead, spilling chilly streams through isolated holes of sky. Under her boots, the ground was frozen and littered with sloughed-off branches. Petter swore each time he tripped over one. Else pushed deeper into the night, leaving footprints of cracked ice in her wake. Her socks squelched with mud and water. She wrapped the bedspread around her shoulders, but it did little to ease the cold. Her teeth rattled in her mouth. Blood cooled in her body; she felt it sluggish in her veins.

She paused when a twig snapped nearby. She heard grunting, the lope of hooves. She grabbed Petter's arm and the Zippo's flame blew out.

'What's that?' Else asked.

'Deer,' he whispered.

A shadow charged the darkness. Then silence settled over them. Petter sparked his lighter. He held it close to his cheek.

'Will Lars be there?' Else asked.

Petter sniffed. 'Sure,' he said. 'It's the last party. The circus men are leaving tomorrow.'

'They're leaving?' she said.

'They're going back to the circus. The new season is starting.'

She did not hear his second sentence. His words repeated in her ears.

The circus men were leaving.

First thing tomorrow, the trio of men who had stayed behind to find work for the winter would hitch up their trailers and travel north to rejoin the circus. To Haugesund. That was where Valentin had told her the new season would begin. Else thought of their costumes on the night when she had followed Lars under the curtain of the Big Top. She remembered the colours, the sparkle and shine under the lights.

And then there was Valentin.

She cleared her throat and blinked at Petter. 'We should get going,' she said.

'Now you want to go to the party?'

'Why not? That's why we're here.'

Else stumbled after him through the wood, dismissing the heaviness of her legs and allowing herself to think only of the strong man. Instead of the circus giant in the Big Top's ring, she saw the man who had shared his chicory with her in the barn. She remembered the last time she had seen him, when he had knocked on the dining-room window and pointed a finger at her father. 'You,' he had said. Valentin had stopped him. No one else ever had.

'Petter,' she said. She laid a hand on his arm and he paused. His eyes looked wounded in the Zippo's thin light.

'What is it?' he said.

'Thank you,' she said, 'for springing me.'

He smiled at that. 'It was something else, wasn't it? And that jump of yours, God, don't you know anything about athletics?'

He prattled on while Else tried to formulate a plan. Again and again, she arrived at the one thing that had changed.

The strong man was leaving.

A LOW RUMBLE of laughter brought her out of her thoughts. She saw the smudge of light in the darkness just as Petter pointed towards it.

'Almost there,' he said.

He hurried on and Else struggled to keep up. The glow spread as they drew nearer, tinting the night little by little and revealing the pine needles that laid a blanket under her feet. Clumps of rotting weeds were dotted in the earth, frozen and tangled like balls of knitting. Frost twinkled on the tree trunks, crusting the bark with a snowflake skin.

Else stopped at the edge of the forest. The bonfire crackled beyond the cover of the trees, releasing wisps of wood smoke into the air. Its light caught on the faces of the circus men who lolled on upturned crates, toasting themselves and punctuating their language with the laughter she had heard. Else recognised Yakov by his crooked eyelid, Oleg by the ponytail that hung over his shoulder. A petrol can sat between them in the mud. There was no sign of Valentin.

Behind the men, the two trailers were parked at the mouth of the track that led to Tenvik's farm. Else saw a silhouette dance across their walls. She took a step forward and the trees on either side of her fell away. Another couple sat further along the fire's perimeter. Lars was with Rune: the captain and his first mate. He was tipping the contents of a petrol can into a mug that he steadied between his boots. When he took a sip, his mouth screwed sideways. He wiped his eyes. His shoulders began to bounce in the easy laugh she knew so well.

Lars at the market. Lars buying sugar peas. Lars drinking moonshine without a care in the world.

'Are you coming?' Petter asked.

He was already clear of the trees when she followed him onto the field. The bonfire had made short work of the residual snow. The ground was sodden and her feet sank into it. Else's toes recoiled from a fresh gush of water as she looked again to the trailers, which loomed like whales beached in the mud. Nothing moved there but the darting shadow and light.

'Else!'

Lars's shout echoed in the darkness. Else pursed her lips and glared at the fire.

'Else! Petter! Over here!'

She stood her ground when Petter broke away from her to join the others. She was not about to jump to Lars's call – not a chance. Without so much as a glimpse in his direction, she began to pick her way over to the circus men. She did not get far. Yakov was watching her from under his half-mast eyelid. He lifted a mug to his lips and his gaze dipped the length of her body. Else crossed her arms over her chest when his tongue flicked the corner of his mouth. She yanked the bedspread tighter around her shoulders.

'Else!' Lars said.

This time, she went to him.

'There you are,' he said. His voice slurred in a way that reminded her of her father. Rune's face was loose, his nose running. Petter had taken his place with them next to the fire.

'Do you want some?' Lars asked.

'No,' Else said.

'It's bloody rancid. You know how we got it here?'

'Petrol cans,' she said.

'Petrol cans!' he said. 'Pretty clever, eh?' His cheeks plumped in a smile. Else wanted to hit him.

'Your father's going to skin you alive,' she said.

'*Skål*,' he said and raised his mug to her.

Rune cheered while he drank and Else peeked at Yakov. He had resumed his conversation with Oleg, but still he watched her.

'Where have you been?' Lars asked. 'I heard you were ill.'

'Yes,' Else said.

'Fucking hell. But you're better now?'

'Yes,' she said.

'Fucking hell. *Skål!*'

Lars drank again and Petter and Rune did the same. Else's eyes swept the field for Valentin. When she did not find him, she sank onto a corner of Petter's crate.

'Don't you want a drink?' Lars asked.

'No,' she said. She held her hands out to the fire, grateful at least for the heat that stroked her body and thawed the night's chill. She shut her eyes. The glow beat the inside of her eyelids.

'Go on,' said Lars. 'Have a drink.' He thrust a mug into Else's palm. With a sigh, she swirled the liquid that was as clear as water. It burned her throat when she swallowed, making her gasp.

She saw Valentin then. He sat some distance from the others, alone on one of the rocks that bordered the north end of the paddock. He was almost out of the firelight's reach, but she could still distinguish the broad heft of his shoulders. She remembered him as he had been on that first night in the circus ring, when he had hoisted the animal towards the ceiling of the Big Top. His veins had stood clear of his skin like a pattern of ropes that spanned from arm to arm, winding around his neck and over the muscles of his stomach.

'*Skål!*' said Lars and sipped. His forehead creased when Else refused to drink. She passed her mug to Petter.

'Have two,' she said and got to her feet.

'Where are you going?' asked Lars.

She set off along the edge of the bonfire, heading the long way round so as to avoid Yakov.

'Else!' shouted Petter. 'Where are you going?'

'*Skål!*'

'Else!'

'*Skål!*'

'*Skål!*'

The boys' voices merged into a single, drunken bleat. Else retreated to the trees at the paddock's rim. Their needles brushed the fingers of her outstretched hand as she trudged through the mud. She cried out when Yakov pounced on her from the shadows. He snatched her up in his arms.

'Dance with me,' he said.

His mug spilled onto her chest, dousing her in homebrew. The smell filled her nose and mouth.

'Get off!' she said and kicked his shin.

Yakov stumbled back. He laughed. He lifted his mug, shaking it at her in a question. His lips peeled away from his teeth in a leer. Else plunged into the murky light between the forest and the fire, her blood loud in her ears as she fled. With every step, she braced herself for the moment when he would tackle her into the mud. Instead, his laughter faded behind her.

On the other side of the meadow, she found Valentin on his rock. He looked up when she stopped in front of him.

'Else,' he said.

His gaze settled again on the bonfire. While Else worked to catch her breath, he raised his cup and sipped. The corners of his eyes crumpled like paper. He sucked air through his teeth.

'I didn't think we would see you again,' he said.

She lowered herself onto the rock next to his. 'Please,' she said. 'I need your help.'

A shout exploded behind the trailers. Valentin glanced towards it and turned back to the fire. 'You shouldn't be here,' he said.

'I can't go home. You know why. You've seen what my father is like.'

He said nothing. The line of his jaw was tight.

'When you leave,' she said, 'take me with you.'

'Else,' he said.

'Please, Valentin.'

'Else . . .'

'I can't stay here. I'll cook and clean . . .'

'Else,' he said. 'Enough!'

The rest of her sentence snapped off between her teeth.

'I'm going to a circus,' Valentin said. 'Do you know what that means? It's no place for you.'

'I'll do anything,' Else said.

'I'm sorry,' he said, 'but it's too difficult.'

A barrage of cheers fell about them from the sky. Else felt panic tear loose in her chest. She saw her father again in the moments before he had shut her in her bedroom, the whites of his eyes shot through with colour like cracked eggshells leaking their yolks. She remembered the pain that rose in bruises to the surface of her skin, the sour smell that tainted the air even after he had left. She heard the key in the lock, remembered the walls pressing down, closing her in, burying her alive.

'I can't go back,' she said and meant to continue, but instead closed her mouth and bent her head to hide her tears. A touch made her start. Her hand had vanished under three long fingers. Valentin was peering at her. His dark eyes were fierce.

'Take me with you,' Else said. 'I'll do whatever you say.'

His nostrils flared. He blew a heavy breath. 'All right,' he said. 'Here, have a drink.'

Valentin passed her his mug and turned back to the fire, but he did not let go of her hand.

Else sat with him long after pins and needles had begun to nip at her feet. She did not stamp them away, but focused instead on staying quiet. She matched the rhythm of her breathing to his. She blinked with trepidation, fearing a reversal of his good will if she appeared too nervous, or too impatient. If she displeased him he might decide that she was more trouble than she was worth, so Else strove not to draw attention to herself. The prickle travelled from her toes up to her calves, but she would not move to slap the life back into them. Meanwhile, the bonfire popped and fizzed across the paddock. Its heat washed over her in gentle ripples that did nothing to relieve the cold.

When his mug had been drained, Valentin pushed himself off his rock, pulling her to her sleeping feet as he did.

'Come,' he said.

He was still holding her hand when he lumbered off towards his trailer. Else hurried along beside him, her eyes darting around the clearing. She searched for faces in the dark even as she prayed that they would get by unnoticed. She saw Yakov first. He had returned to his crate. When he spotted Else with Valentin, his lips distorted in a sneer. He jabbed Oleg with his elbow as, one after another, the boys came to meet them from their side of the fire.

Rune swayed like a sailor, his knees locking and unlocking underneath him.

'What in hell?' he said. 'Would you look at that? Else and the strong man. Do you see that? They're *holding hands*! Lars, do you see that?'

Petter followed. He looked from Else to Valentin and his jaw dropped. Else knew how it must look. She knew what they would think – what they would say. It was all she could do not to wrest back her hand. She gritted her teeth and carried on walking. Valentin was going to help her. She could not risk unsettling him now.

Lars limped into sight at the rear of the group. 'What are you doing?' he called and ran to cut them off. 'Else, what in hell are you doing with him?'

He stopped in front of her, his hands on his hips. Else felt her insides scooped hollow.

'Lars, don't.'

'What's going on?'

She shook her head. 'Please,' she said, 'just go away.'

He flinched as if she had struck him. He grabbed her arm. His body tensed when Valentin's hand settled on his shoulder. The strong man leaned towards him, stooping low until their foreheads were parallel. The blood in Lars's face turned to milk.

'It's none of your business,' Valentin said and steered Lars out of his way. He resumed his walk to the trailer with Else in tow. She told herself not to think. She closed her eyes and her feet carried her over the mud. Valentin climbed the stairs to her new home, yanking open the door before stepping inside. Here, Else resisted. She spun around to look at Lars one last time.

In the orange firelight, his face was puckered with hurt. He stared at her, hands clenched, lips thin. Else tried not to think about kissing those lips. She saw him pressed against her that first time behind the bus depot, his eyes skimming shut as his mouth found hers.

Lars at the market. Lars buying sugar peas. Lars being Lars, even though she had disappeared.

Else pressed her lips together. She turned her back on her friends and followed Valentin into the caravan. As the door swung shut, Yakov fired a cheer into the night.

For several moments she remained by the entrance, listening to the noise that leaked through the walls of the trailer from outside. The smell of paraffin pervaded the darkness like fumes from a paint tin. Else's head felt thick. She reached out a hand to steady herself, recoiling when her fingertips dipped into something cold and wet.

A spark showed Valentin crouched on his haunches beside a table, almost within touching distance. He shook out a match with one hand while the other replaced the cover of an oil lamp. It cast a dim light over the space between them. Apart from the table, there was precious little in it: a bench, a neat stack of crockery, carrots and potatoes in a crate. On the shelf in front of her, an empty drying rack kept company with an upturned washbasin and a single-hob gas cooker. A water barrel stood on the floor. Else saw the ladle hooked to the top and wiped her fingers on her trousers.

'It's late,' Valentin said.

She nodded. She tried to smile but her mouth was dry. Her eyes pulled away from the oil lamp's reach to the opposite corner of the room, where she could make out a bed. It was smaller than her bed at home; surely this would never bear Valentin's bulk. She imagined a leg hanging over the side, a mighty arm falling to the floor, slack in sleep. She saw herself wedged between his body and the wall and looked away.

'Shall I make us some coffee?' she said. Her hand wobbled when she reached for the water ladle. Then Valentin was beside her. He stood as near to his full height as the roof would allow. His palm brushed her arm.

'I'm tired,' he said.

He drifted off and Else caught the ledge of the kitchen counter with her fingers. A new light glimmered by the bed and Valentin's shadow waltzed over the ceiling and walls. She could sense him moving. His body was too close. Her hands gripped tighter and she blinked at her whitening knuckles.

'Else.' This time, his voice was impatient. 'Come on. It's time for bed.'

She joined him where he waited for her at the other end of the kitchen shelf. The ceiling bore down like a free weight on his neck and shoulders. Else stepped into him. She tilted her head, bringing her lips to rest against his jawbone. His skin was rough. His muscles twitched. She dropped her eyes and hoped that it would be over quickly.

'Is that what you thought?' Valentin murmured. He pushed her gently away. He shifted to the side, revealing a mound of clothes on the ground by his feet. It had been placed at one end of a blanket. He gestured to the bed.

'You sleep there. I'll stay here. That's all,' he said and eased himself to the floor.

Valentin knelt beside the blanket, smoothing out its wrinkles before lying down and gathering his limbs inside its borders. With his back to the bed, he closed his eyes. A stream of conversation trickled in through the walls while Else watched him from the middle of the room. His breathing grew dense, but a scratch of his armpit told her that he was not yet asleep. In the distance, she heard the sound of engines. She knew what it meant: Lars was gone. So, too, were Petter and Rune.

Else slipped off her plimsolls in an effort to keep her tread light and ventured towards the bed. She crawled onto the mattress, where she rolled off the wet socks that had marked the floor behind her with footprints. She pulled the sheet over her clothes as far as her chin. When she faced the wall, she saw a handful of photographs had been pinned to the padding. A woman smiled next to her pillow. Her edges were blurred, as if she were a ghost trapped inside the square. Else imagined Valentin lying in her place, falling asleep each night haunted by that smile.

The next picture was of Valentin himself. He was younger here, but Else had no trouble recognising him. There was his face, the size of a tree stump, his hair like wood shavings curling away from his scalp. He beamed at her from behind the photo's gloss and held out a medal in the palm of his hand. One foot was cocked on a dumb-bell on the ground. A flag was draped around his shoulders.

Else glanced to where Valentin lay on the floor. He was looking at her. She unpicked the picture from the wall and showed it to him.

'What did you win?' she asked.

'I didn't win,' he said. 'Try to sleep. We'll talk in the morning.'

He turned onto his side once again and Else considered the last photo, where a church stood at a slant, its stone carved and topped with angels. It was strange to her, too elaborate to be a church but a church nonetheless – the cross above its entrance left her in no doubt. She reached out a finger to trace the two converging lines before closing her eyes. Pastor Seip lurched at her from out of the darkness. Else snatched back her finger and blinked. The oil lamp spluttered, sending a shiver through the glow that it threw onto the ceiling. When she looked again at the church, she did not need to close her eyes to picture the minister. She saw him standing on his pulpit, palms clasped, his voice dripping over the congregation.

'Our Lord in heaven' – she heard the words as if they were whispered into her ear – '*we pray for the soul of Else Dybdahl, that she may not have strayed too far for redemption.*'

The families in the first pews muttered to each other in a rising grumble of disapproval. Behind them sat her mother, her face collapsing under a burden of humiliation. Her father chewed his teeth beside her, biding his time until the moment they arrived home, when he would be free to vent the full extent of his fury.

Else replayed the scene in her mind and felt her body wilting with exhaustion as the last of her strength drained away. The image of her mother stayed with her now: she could no longer defeat her nervous look, nor dismiss the memory of her neck mottled with bruises. Else prodded her arms where her father had squeezed them black on the night he had locked her in her bedroom. In the days that had passed since, she had sat by her window and monitored their recovery. Had her mother's bruises healed just as well?

She lay motionless, imagining unspeakable deeds until, all at once, she realised the chatter outside had stopped. Only the hiss of burning paraffin disturbed the silence. Else sat up in Valentin's bed. She kicked off the sheet and slid to the end of the mattress, retrieving her socks and shoes and folding herself up in the bedspread from home before retracing her steps to the caravan's exit. Behind her, Valentin adjusted his position on the floor. He did not speak when she pushed the door open.

The embers of the bonfire simmered in the field. Otherwise, all was still. Else stayed in the doorway. She watched as the colours of dawn bled into the sky.

A COLD, CLEAR morning had chased off the night before Else stirred from the trailer's top step. Leaving the door ajar, she retreated into the caravan's kitchen and, as quietly as she could, lifted a pot from a hook knocked into the wall. She scooped three ladlefuls into it from the water barrel and fumbled with a pack of matches that she found on the shelf by the drying rack, scratching one along the length of the box and holding it between the prongs of the cooker's hob. With a soft rush, the gas took up the flame. She set the pot to boil and began searching for coffee.

When the coffee had brewed, Else filled a mug and carried it to the cot. She perched on the edge of the mattress and waited for Valentin to roll onto his back. He supported his head on an arm and dug the middle finger of his free hand into his eyes. Else set the cup on the floor.

'Did you sleep?' she asked.

'Some,' he said.

'I can't leave,' Else said. 'My mother. I have to go back.'

Valentin nodded. He sat up, rested his back against the wall. He reached for the coffee, sniffing it before taking a sip.

'It's hot,' Else said.

'It's fine,' he said.

He glanced at the mire of the paddock through the open door. After swallowing another mouthful, he offered the mug to Else. She smiled: it would be the last thing they ever shared.

'Don't walk home,' Valentin said. 'Ask Tenvik to take you.'

'I don't think my father . . .'

'You'll be safe if someone else is there.'

She understood what he meant. If Tenvik escorted her, she would buy herself time. Perhaps he was right. The towns-people would learn of their night together anyway. In an hour or two, Lars, Petter and Rune would wake in their beds and shake the sleep from their senses. How long would they need to realise they had not dreamt her following Valentin into his caravan? How long before they told?

Else dipped her nose to the coffee. It was rich and strong, without any trace of chicory. She let the flavour rinse the sour taste from her mouth before drinking it down and passing the cup back to Valentin. They took their time to polish it off. After finishing the dregs, Else peered into the bottom of the mug. She stood and returned it to the kitchen shelf.

'When will you leave?' she asked.

'Soon,' said Valentin. 'Tenvik has settled up with us already. We'll go when the others wake up.'

Else imagined Valentin helping to pitch the circus tent in a new field, while camels and horses stamped their hooves in the animal tents and their riders bartered with farmers delivering hay bales by the wagonload. The ringmaster directed roustabouts, his sideburns quivering as the stripes of the Big Top unfurled. Else could picture it exactly. She saw herself there, observing the bustle from Valentin's trailer. Her longing sharpened with the fantasy. She looked at the meadow outside.

'Do you think you'll come back next year?' she asked.

'I don't know,' Valentin said.

'I hope you do.'

'Take care of yourself,' he said.

With a parting smile, she ducked into the sting of early morning. Behind the hillock at the paddock's distant border, the roof of one of Tenvik's barns prodded the sky. The trailer's steps were slippery with the frost that Else had watched layering through the night, like threads of cobweb spinning into a single, lethal lace. As she began to creep away, the door to the second trailer opened. Yakov rubbed his eyes at the top of the stairs. His shoulders dropped when he noticed her.

'Still here?' he said. 'Did you get what you came for, or will you stick around for more?' He nudged the door with his boot as if to invite her in. 'We still have time.'

Yakov picked his way down the stairs and tramped over the paddock towards her. Else took a step back before Valentin appeared in the doorway, his frame damming up the way into his caravan.

'Yakov,' he said.

Yakov held up his hands. 'I'm just going to water the potatoes.'

'The potatoes are that way.'

Yakov sighed. He shrugged at Else. 'Sorry, treasure. Maybe next year.'

He changed direction and loped off. Valentin climbed down to stand with Else in the field.

'He won't bother you,' he said. Then, in a raised voice, 'Oleg? Let's load the trailers. It's time to go.'

He placed a hand on Else's arm and, with a gentle squeeze, nodded his farewell. Then the strong man turned away.

Else started up the path that had brought her from the farmhouse to the paddock on the night of the circus. It snaked off from the campsite around a cluster of fir trees, its mud still set by winter. On either side of the track spring buds fattened, apple green on the bark of a petrified thicket. She hugged the flaps of the bedspread to her chest and wondered what her father would do when she and Tenvik arrived.

Ninni answered the door to the farmhouse. 'Else,' she said, 'is it you? Is everything all right?' She ushered her in. 'Dear girl, what are you wearing? Why have you come out dressed like that? Where is your coat? And your boots? Knut? Knut! It's Else Dybdahl who's come!'

'Else?' Tenvik said as he strode through from the dining room, brushing crumbs from the creases of his lips. 'Is there a problem with the barn? Valentin is leaving today.'

'I know,' Else said. 'He told me.'

The farmer exchanged glances with his wife, then looked past Else as if expecting the entire circus troupe to follow. His eyes were wide when they found her again. Else tried to silence the chatter of teeth in her head. After some moments, Ninni reached for the closet and slid a coat from its hanger. She waited for Else to unwind the bedspread before fussing it around her shoulders and buttoning it up over her ash-smudged jumper.

'There, now,' Tenvik said, 'it's all right.' He spoke as though to one of his livestock, his manner soothing and even.

'Will you take me home?' Else asked.

'I'll take you home,' he said. 'Everything's all right. Wait here, I'll be right back.'

He mounted the stairs two at a time while Ninni carried on rummaging through the closet. She pulled open drawers, rooted out a hat, a pair of mittens.

'Your hands are ice cold! Here, these will warm you up.'

Else accepted each item that she offered, grateful for the wool that scratched her skin and for the kindness that she knew she did not deserve. She watched for Tenvik on the stairs, hoping he would hurry before his wife's concern withered her resolve and she changed her mind and failed her mother for good.

Tenvik drove her home in his Volvo. Else sat beside him in the passenger seat, studying the countryside that slipped away and trying to commit to memory the colours of the land, their promise of spring. Now and again, the farmer drew a breath as if preparing to ask for an explanation, but he kept his questions to himself. The black boil of Else's fear seemed to infect him as they neared her family's property: she could sense his nervousness when he manoeuvred the gear stick, which jarred as his arm yanked and jerked.

Tenvik touched the brake before he steered them off the road and onto the hill. He parked next to the barn.

'Here we are,' he said.

He glanced at Else, who let her eyes take in the farmhouse, the boathouse and the pier. A pair of crows picked around a puddle in the yard. One spread its wings and lifted off into the sky. With the weary effort of an old woman, Else pushed the car door open and lowered her feet into the mud. Tenvik heaved himself outside and they set off towards the farmhouse with their heads bowed.

They had passed the old well when her father opened the door to the farmhouse. Else fell back, taking cover behind Tenvik.

She followed him to where her father waited for them on the step.

'Johann,' Tenvik said. He scratched his head and tossed a wistful look at his car. He gestured at Else. 'I think you may have mislaid somebody.'

His chuckle died in his throat when Johann's eyes thinned. Tenvik tugged at his ear.

'She's a good girl,' he said. 'There's no harm done. I have a bit of a fascination with the circus myself. Is Dagny home?'

'She's at the *bedehus*,' Johann said.

'Is she? Well. In any event, they're leaving. Back to the circus. I dare say they must have set off by now. How have you been finding the barn? Maybe we could take a look. I'd like to see it. I grew quite attached to that cow of yours.'

'Else, go inside,' her father said.

'That's right, Else, go in and get yourself warm. I'll come for the coat another day.'

Else shuffled inside, while her father unhooked his coat from a peg and thrust his arms into its sleeves. He joined Tenvik on the step and shut the door behind him before the men moved away to the barn. In their absence, Else checked the dining room and the kitchen. Her mother was not there. She hurried up the stairs to the second floor. The door to her bedroom was closed – only now, when she tried the handle, it opened without difficulty.

The room looked the same as it had the night before, when Petter had climbed the cherry tree. There was the knitting basket, the washbasin, the stew stiff on its plate under a skin of clotted juices. A draught blew in through the open window, bulleting between the four walls before shooting out again. On the dresser, a breakfast tray told her that her mother had been the one to discover her escape. How long ago? And where was she now?

Else tiptoed down the hall to her parents' bedroom. The house was as silent as the bottom of the sea. The quilt her parents shared lay in a heap at the end of the mattress. Her father's long johns stretched their legs across the floor. Else skirted around the bed to the closet. Her pulse knocked when she tested the door.

'Mamma?' she said.

The latch was unbolted. Inside hung her mother's Sunday dress, her father's Sunday suit, an ironed shirt, a few blouses. She made her way to the bathroom, whispering for her mother as she went. Through a square window, Else saw Tenvik's Volvo still parked in front of the barn. She went down the staircase.

'Mamma?' she said into the stark chill of the Best Room. Its chairs cast a shadow onto the inky walls. She withdrew into the hallway, where she lifted the lid of the wooden trunk and pulled open the door to the cellar.

'Mamma,' she called, 'are you there?'

There was only one place left to look, though Else baulked at the thought of it. She pictured her mother beaten and helpless and ran into the yard.

The door to the boathouse grated open, revealing an undulating light that bounced off the water and slipped into the room through the seams between the wall planks. The sluice of the fjord soaked up through the floorboards and the layer of detritus spread out on top. Her father's *Norges* jars poked out of the wasteland of fishing tackle. The room was grimier than it had been when Else had come to measure out a drop of homebrew for Valentin. Remembering what had followed, she tapped her heels against the threshold, taking care to kick off the snow that clung to her soles before venturing inside.

Else felt cramped under the low roof. Her fear danced shivers up and down her spine. The walls seemed to ripple as she moved across the floor, watching out for loose fishhooks in the mess. The oars for the rowing boat lay crossed at the handles, like a single limb whose bone had snapped at an awkward angle.

'Mamma,' she called, 'where are you? Are you there?'

The answer came from the fjord lapping under her feet. Else brushed against a net suspended from a hook that was screwed into the ceiling, releasing a shower of salt and dust and desiccated seaweed. The mattress was bare, its flower-print sheet bundled into a ball on the ground. She ducked for a view underneath the workbench but saw only the idle distillery. At the end of the room, she pulled up the trapdoor. The rock ledge was deserted at the bottom of the ladder. The skiff was empty.

Where was her mother? Perhaps her father had been telling the truth and she was safe at the *bedehus*. Or perhaps this morning, when she learned that Else had run away, she had done the same. Her mother was on a coach on her way out of town and Else had come back to face her father alone. The thought punctured her. Her breath left her in a wheeze.

A sound made her jump. She turned to see a silhouette that filled the doorway, blocking out the sky. Else recognised the line of her father's body. She looked past him for Tenvik, though she already knew that he must have gone. With the sun at her father's back, she could not see his face. She did not need to. He stepped into the room.

'Father, I didn't . . .'

Her toes caught on a net snarled on the ground. Else tripped on its yarn and belly-flopped, landing on an arm that failed to break her fall. In the next moment, her father was standing over her. His hand closed on her elbow. She tried to wrench it free.

'Where is Mamma?' she said. 'What have you done to her?'

He grabbed her then, his fingers crushing her wrists. He dragged her up only to knock her to the ground. Else collapsed over the shell of a lobster trap. Her mouth and ribs throbbed.

'First the Reiersen boy. Then the circus freaks.'

Her father picked her up. He shook her and she screamed. His fist hooked her jaw. Cowering by his boots, Else curved her back into an absurd shield. Needles drove into her skull when he pulled her up by a fistful of hair.

'The Devil is in you.'

He made a cage of his arms. His stink plugged her nose, tickling her throat until she retched. Her father spun her around and bowed her over the workbench. One hand gripped her head, mashing her cheek into its surface. Else's fear stunned her. The walls billowed. The floor seemed to list under her feet.

'The Devil is in you,' he said and tore at her trousers. Johann fumbled behind her at his waist. His body curled around her, pinning her under him. His skin was hot on her skin, his breath in her ear. Else's howl was driven from the pit of her heart when he pushed into her. The force of it rammed her stomach into the workbench. Splinters bit her cheek, dripping runnels of blood onto the wood. Her father folded an arm around her waist, a brace to hold her still.

'Little whore,' he said.

He grunted and lunged as if to stab right through her. She felt herself splitting apart. Her muscles slackened. She stared at the light that wrinkled the walls and became limp. She listened to the murmur of the fjord, saw its waves wash her away.

When he had finished, Johann pulled back. The clink of his belt. His labouring lungs. He stumbled to the open trapdoor to relieve himself. His piss purled into the water below. Else drew up her underpants and trousers. Her legs buckled and she slumped to the floor. She folded herself under the workbench, pressing her pulped cheek to her knee. She hardly registered the figure stepping into the doorway. Johann's back was to them both when he crouched to pick up a *Norges* jar. He gave it a shake before unfastening its top.

'What have you done?'

Else closed her eyes at the sound of her mother's voice. She dug her knee into her cheek, felt the blood hot and slippery on her skin. Her body shuddered with a rush of nausea.

'Johann, what have you done?'

Her eyes blinked open to a vision of her mother clutching an oar, wielding it at her father. Johann laughed when he stood, but his nostrils flared with rage. Dagny tightened her grip on the oar.

'So help me God,' she said.

Johann kicked aside an oil can and charged at his wife. Dagny brought the oar swinging round. A moan slipped from her lips when it connected with his skull. She dropped the oar. Else saw her father tipping backwards. Arms flailing, boots skittering, his heel came down on a *Norges* jar that shot out from under him. His eyes flickered with panic. He teetered and tumbled through the trapdoor's open hatch with a shriek.

A thud, then a splash. Then nothing. Else waited for the roar that would signal her father's resurrection. None came. She looked at her mother, who stood as if set in plaster. She crawled out from under the workbench and to the hole in the floor, peeking down at the skiff's moorings. Her father lay a foot from the barbed rock ledge, spine twisted, arms and legs spread at his sides. The fjord's skin had sealed above him. It twinkled in prisms of sunlight, placing jewels in his mouth, in eyes that seemed to stare through her to something terrible. Coils of blood melted from his temple into seaweed that fluttered in the tide. A jellyfish trailed its tentacles over his throat. At his temple, a rock appeared to sprout from the bone into the silt, taking root and fusing him with the seabed.

A touch made Else gasp. Her exhalation came in a low, anguished cry.

'Else. My Else.' Her mother's fingertips spread nettles over her cheek. She wrapped Else up into a bosom heaving with sobs.

'Is he dead?' Else whispered.

Her mother followed her gaze into the water. Johann's lips were parted in mid-scream.

'Let's go inside,' she said.

She put her arm around Else's shoulders and began to lead her to the door. On their way out of the boathouse, she paused to wipe the blood from the oar's blade with an oil rag that she reclaimed from the floor. She clutched it in her fist as she helped her daughter down the stairs. Together, they staggered across the yard.

Now

2009

ELSE CARRIES A tray of dishes, cutlery and wine glasses through the back door and begins to lay the table for four in the garden. She wipes down the wood, shakes out the blue trim of a freshly ironed tablecloth and anchors the napkins under the forks. Once she has arranged the tea lights in clusters, she pauses at a rosebush and chooses a stalk for the centrepiece. Two sunset blooms spread their petals under a third, tight bud. She snips the stem with a pair of scissors and brings it with her into the kitchen.

Music from Marianne's stereo pounds through the ceiling. Her footsteps jar with the bass as she flusters about her bedroom. She has not shown her face since she arrived home from the Hong Kong Palace earlier that afternoon and disappeared upstairs. Else knows she is dreading dinner. As she models outfit after outfit in her mirror, she is anticipating the evening's awkwardness and wondering if Mads cares, if he loves her enough to endure it.

Else loves her enough. She will behave. Whoever Marianne

leads through the door later on – whatever he looks like, whatever he says – she will be civil. She will not ask difficult questions. She fills a cream jug with water for the flowers and tries not to think about whether Mads will be staying the night.

She is whisking the ingredients for a marinade when Liv wanders into the room.

'What's for dinner?' she asks.

'We're having salmon,' Else says.

'Do you need help?'

'There's not a lot left to do,' Else says. 'The salad still needs to be made.'

'Anything else?'

'How about decorating the cake?'

While Else seasons the salmon fillets, Liv shakes a punnet of raspberries under the tap before setting them out to dry on a sheet of paper towel. She turns the cake onto a platter under Else's supervision. A whiff of chocolate rises from the dark sponge.

Marianne sails into the kitchen. 'Have you seen my sandals? The gold ones. You know, the gold ones?'

'They're in the hall with your other shoes,' Else says.

'You made a cake?'

'We have to have dessert,' Else says. 'It's a special occasion.'

'It's a quick dinner before Mads and I go out,' says Marianne.

Without missing a beat, Else stirs the rice bubbling in a pot on the cooker. She replaces the lid and reduces the heat, then flips the salmon in its marinade. Beside her, Liv interrupts her job of ordering the berries in a pattern on the cake to consider her mother.

'You look nice,' she says.

Else studies her daughter, whose skirt barely covers her under-pants. Under her inspection, Marianne draws herself up. Else bites her bottom lip. She washes her hands at the sink and wipes them on her apron.

'You do look nice,' she says and carries the roses outside.

She is sitting in the garden nursing a glass of wine with her eyes hooded against the sun when she hears the doorbell. Her eyelids flick open. Her body tenses, but she forces herself to stay put. Else examines the table, smoothing a crease from the cloth with the flat of her hand. She wipes the lipstick from the rim of her glass with her thumb. Takes another sip. Wipes it clean once more.

Liv bolts from the kitchen and down the steps onto the lawn. A magazine is rolled in her fist. She throws herself into a chair and props her bare feet against the wicker of its twin beside her. Small shrugs betray her excitement with each breath. She grins at her grandmother and pretends to read.

Marianne appears in the doorway holding a stranger's hand. A tattoo sprouts from out of his shirt collar and up the side of his neck. Orange, yellow, red. Else thinks she spots a beak, or perhaps it is a talon. A similar style of penmanship leaks from his sleeves down both forearms. Mads flashes his teeth at Else and Liv and takes in the garden scene with a slow sweep of the eyes. Else dislikes him at first sight.

But she will behave.

She watches him swagger down the stairs with the confidence of someone expecting an easy victory. She gets to her feet. Her lips part in what is designed to be a benevolent smile.

'My,' she says, 'isn't that an interesting tattoo.'

Marianne's face seems to crack. Liv jumps out of her seat.

'Mormor . . .' she says.

But Mads is laughing. 'Glad you noticed it,' he says.

'How far does it go?'

'All the way,' he says. He thrusts a bottle of wine into

Else's outstretched hand. 'I hope white's okay. Where do you want me?'

Mads rubs his palms against the T-shirt stretched over his chest and turns to the table. Else gestures at a chair. There is a hole in his earlobe the size of a nostril. Her lips part, but Marianne cuts her off.

'We can't stay long,' she says.

'What are you talking about?' says Mads. 'The Manhattan will wait for us all night if we want it to.'

'How wonderful,' says Else. 'I'll be right back.'

Liv follows her into the kitchen. 'Mormor,' she says, 'what was that?'

'Hm?' Else slots Mads's bottle between two cartons of milk in the fridge and pulls another from the middle shelf. 'Will you pour the wine? Water for you.'

'Be nice,' says Liv and returns to the garden.

Else fluffs the rice in its pot with a fork before scooping it into a serving bowl. A cloud of steam escapes the oven when she opens its door, scorching her cheeks. As the haze clears, she reaches for the casserole dish with her oven-mitted hands. The tops of the salmon fillets are golden. The sprigs of thyme laid out on each one are shrivelled and crisp.

Her tray is loaded with the fish, the rice and a bowl of salad when she rejoins the others. The discussion dies as she approaches the table. She frowns.

'Well,' she says. 'I hope you like salmon.'

'Smells great,' says Mads.

He lifts his glass once Else has found her seat and tips it to her.

'*Skål* to the cook,' he says.

The meal begins in silence. The smacking of lips, gulping of wine and children's cries from a neighbouring garden only emphasise the absence of conversation. Else picks at her food and peeks at Mads, who shovels heaped forkfuls into his mouth. Marianne looks miserably at her watch. Else clears her throat.

'So, Mads,' she says. 'I hear you're a dancer.'

'Sure,' he says. 'When I can afford to be.'

'And when is that?'

'When it pays,' he says.

Else arches an eyebrow and fusses with the pepper grinder.

'Most of the time I work in the garden centre,' he says.

'Does that pay?'

'Mamma,' hisses Marianne and Else shrugs. Mads's eyes remain bright with his smile. He finishes chewing and wipes his mouth on his napkin.

'It's all right for now,' he says. 'I'll have to find something else come winter. If you hear of any jobs going, let me know, all right?'

From where Else sits, she has a better view of the artwork on his neck. An eagle's beak gapes at his jawline, as if the bird is preparing to swallow his head.

'What about you?' Mads asks. 'Marianne said you own a shop.'

'A spa,' Else says.

'Does that pay?' asks Mads.

'I don't think you'd be right for the place.'

'More wine anyone?' says Marianne and fills her own glass to the brim. Mads reaches for her free hand. He gives it a squeeze and does not let go and something slips behind Else's ribs. She watches him lift Marianne's fingers and brush them gently with his lips before their hands tie a knot across the table. Else feels her eyes prick and is not sure why. She wants to protect her. That is all she has ever wanted since Marianne was born.

She loves her enough.

Before Else speaks, she makes an effort to soften her tone. 'What sort of dancing do you do?'

'All sorts,' says Mads.

'You must have a speciality, though.'

'He's a flamenco dancer,' says Marianne.

'Well,' says Else. 'That doesn't sound very Swedish.'

'My mother's Spanish,' Mads says. 'My grandmother came to live with us when I was six. I used to watch her dancing in the kitchen after school. She'd try to teach me the steps. She taught me everything I know.'

'What's flamenco?' asks Liv.

'It comes from the gypsies,' Mads says. 'Flamenco was a way for them to express their suffering. No one wanted them. They were persecuted. They used dance to show their anger and pain at what was being done to them. But it's not just about sorrow. That's why I like it. It makes room for every passion, also love and joy.'

'That sounds sensible,' says Else.

'I wish I could have met your grandmother,' says Marianne.

'So do I,' says Mads. 'You would have liked each other.'

The second bottle is empty by the end of the main course. Else and Liv take in the dirty plates, leaving Marianne and Mads to a moment of privacy.

'It's going well,' whispers Liv.

Else scrapes the fish bones into the bin under the sink. 'Mm,' she says. 'She seems to be calming down.'

'No, I mean, you're doing well,' says Liv. She kisses her grandmother's cheek and disappears through the door with the dessert bowls and spoons. Else stays behind to load the dishwasher. When that is done she adds the finishing touches to the cake, sprinkling powdered sugar over the sponge and the raspberries. Before carrying it into the garden, she checks her mobile phone. She has two missed calls: one from Petter, one from Lars. Else contemplates the display until its light dims.

'Mormor, are you coming?' calls Liv.

'Coming,' she says.

Without listening to her messages, she puts down the phone. She lifts the cake platter and steps outside.

ELSE LIES STILL, staring into the nothingness above her. The house seems to tick in the darkness, though there is no one left to wait for. Liv is home, safe in her room. Marianne and Mads are further down the hall. Marianne and Mads. Else tests the union of their names again and again. Marianne and Mads, lying together in her bed. She imagines their limbs twined in sleep, their breath soft, simultaneous, while Marianne presses her nose to his tattoo.

Else twists and turns, wringing her unrest into the sheets, flopping from her side onto her back. She stretches her arms to the edges of the mattress and arranges her spine down its middle. She flexes her toes, points, flexes. The bones in her feet give off a satisfying crack. As the digits of her alarm clock count off the minutes, she broods on the tender looks that her daughter shared with Mads through dinner. With her own eyes, she has seen that Marianne loves him and, what's more, that Mads loves her in return. What happens now if he changes his mind and leaves? What will happen to Else if he stays?

She is ashamed as soon as the thought arrives, but still tries to conceive of the life that Marianne, Mads and Liv could build away from the home that she has held together for so many years. Else listens to the house, to its overbearing silence, and repeats Petter's assurance that loneliness can be borne. She summons a picture of him standing on the deck of his sailing boat, wind-blown behind the wheel as he steers a course into the sea.

A grey morning light sneaks around the edges of the curtains, coaxing objects in her bedroom from out of the shadows. The brass handles of her wardrobe doors. The vase of cut peonies on her dresser. The clock reads 04:46.

04:47.

04:48.

She knows that daybreak has been and gone. She reaches for the glass on her bedside table and takes a sip of water.

04:50. It is late enough.

Else slides her feet from under the duvet and into the slippers parked on the floor beside her bed. She shuffles to the window and yanks open the curtains. Her body is bathed in light.

The day looks clear, the sky as blue as she imagines the Mediterranean to be, but the air will be chilly at this time. She chooses a pair of jeans from a pile of laundry waiting to be sorted on her armchair, zipping them up before pulling a jumper over the loose sway of her breasts. From the bottom drawer of her dresser, she finds the shawl that used to belong to her mother. She blankets her shoulders and breathes in deeply, hoping for a trace of a scent that has long since faded.

Else tiptoes up the corridor, past Liv, past Marianne and Mads, Mads and Marianne, and down the stairs. Once she has retrieved her phone from the kitchen counter she steals into the hallway, where she straps on her clogs and lets herself out into the street. No one is up. She has the morning to herself. She strolls by her neighbours' houses, glancing at window boxes as she goes. Peder Wiig's clematis is doing well. Janne Haugen's roses less so. The bugs have been at them; they are beyond saving now. Else draws the shawl closer across her chest to quell a shiver while the soles of her shoes slap the asphalt. She turns onto Torggata, where hot-dog boxes clog the gutters.

At the bottom of the hill the fjord spreads out like the night sky, the ripples of water twinkling in the light. Else is out of breath when she reaches the harbour. She places a hand on her chest to steady her heart. The waves nudge the concrete of the Longpier. A breeze pinches her cheeks, ruffles her hair, soothes the headache behind her eyes. She recovers her mobile phone and dials the numbers for her voicemail.

'*You have two new messages*,' says the automated voice.

'Else. Petter calling. I hope you've received my messages. I won't bother you again if you'd rather not see me, but ring me if you would.'

A beep, then Lars's voice replaces the first. He sounds agitated after Petter's formal tone.

'It's me,' he says. 'We have to talk. It's important. Call me as soon as you get this.'

Else hangs up the line. Her hand drops to her stomach, her fingers rigid around the phone's plastic. She looks out across the fjord to the islands that shelter the town from the sea. The rock is weather-beaten and stubbled with lichen. Three hundred years ago, before the harbour was equipped to receive merchant ships, crews would offload their cargo there. Rumour has it that brothels serviced the sailors while rowing boats ferried goods to the mainland. Else does not know whether the stories are true.

The port is gone now. No one lives on the islands. Whatever buildings were once there have been razed to the ground. Still people wonder. Still the whisperers whisper.

Else types a message with her thumbs:

Free at 1600. I'll wait for you in the cemetery.

She punches the 'send' button. An envelope flies across her screen. She pockets the phone and sits on a bench to wait for the trawlers.

THE WIND IS up when Else arrives at the churchyard. Throughout the afternoon, massing clouds have merged into a single, interminable strip and now the sky is dark and dense with unshed rain. A storm is coming. Else can smell it like a damp animal running rings, closing in.

Lars sits on the bench near her father's grave. He has not brought his dog with him today. He stares over the tops of the tombstones at Else as she approaches, his head bowed, eyes unblinking. He leans forward to rest his arms on his thighs and clasp his hands. Is he praying? Else is glad they are alone.

She takes a seat beside him and waits for him to begin. In the silence, she reads the lettering on her father's headstone. 'Johann Dybdahl. 1927–1975.' It occurs to her that she is older now than he was when he died.

Lars clears his throat. 'What a weather,' he says.

'What a weather,' says Else. 'You could say that.'

The saliva is audible when he swallows. He licks his lips. 'It's Victoria,' he says. 'She won't let it go.'

Else nods and her chest seems to shrink-wrap her heart.

'I never thought . . .' says Lars. 'We only did it twice.'

Did it, Else thinks. As if they were still kids.

'And all of that time, you were with the circus man. When did you start things up with him? When he was working on your barn? I used to wonder.'

Else remembers. She remembers Lars wondering aloud at the Gymnasium, holding court in front of the caretaker's shed.

'They had their spot right there in the cow shit. Her parents next door . . .'

'. . . the size of a tree, like doing it with an animal . . .'

'You don't have to tell me,' Lars tells her now. 'It's none of my business any more. But I need to know if Marianne could be mine.'

Else closes her eyes. If Lars were Marianne's father . . . She thinks of the weeks spent locked in her bedroom before Johann's death, when she stared through the window at the cherry tree praying for Lars to rescue her, praying that the worst of her fears would not come true. She checked the cotton of her underpants several times a day and thanked God when finally her period started.

'Look, Else,' says Lars. 'I don't see how she can be, but Victoria has this idea. I suppose it's possible. We'd have to do a test.'

'A test,' Else says.

'A paternity test. I could arrange it.'

'There won't be any test,' she says.

'But we'd have to be sure. Think about it. If Liv and Andreas, someday . . .' He grapples with the word. Hisses it through his teeth. 'It would be *incest*. You realise that, right?'

'There's no need for a test. I know who Marianne's father is.'

Else forces herself to meet Lars's eyes. Her heart hammers her breastbone with each pump of blood.

'It isn't you,' she says.

'It isn't me,' says Lars.

'Marianne's father is the strong man.'

A strangled sound escapes Lars's lips. He drags his fingers through his hair.

'Thank God,' he says.

He slumps in his seat as if the air has been let out of his muscles. Else half expects him to slide into the grass. An image winks across her retina of Valentin cradling a baby in his arms. It shores her up. She could almost believe that it was true.

Lars's eyes are wet when they next find hers. She thinks he might take her hand, but he keeps his to himself. 'The strong man,' he says. 'I knew it. I knew it was. I mean, I wondered, you know, back then. But you would have said if it were me, wouldn't you? But Victoria's been so sure. She said it didn't make sense. People would've found out. She said there was no way you could have kept your affair with him a secret.'

'I didn't,' says Else. 'Everyone knows.'

'That's right. That's right.'

He shakes his head and rubs his eyes. In the distance, the cloud flickers with lightning. Both Else and Lars glance at it. He wipes his palms on his jeans as thunder murmurs.

'I have to go,' he says.

Else nods. She fondles the tassels at the ends of her shawl, curling one tightly around her finger until the tip goes white. Lars stands.

'Are you all right?' he asks.

'And why not?' Else says.

'I'm sorry,' he says and turns to leave.

She almost stops him. *What for?* she wonders, but sees no point in asking. What difference would it make?

Lars hurries across the cemetery the way she arrived. He picks up his pace as he nears the church, no doubt anxious to put the scene behind him. Else does not blame him. She stays on the bench and feels the dread of discovery seep through the soles of her trainers into the soil. Marianne must never know.

'Johann Dybdahl. 1927–1975.'

Else reads. She rereads while the thunder grumbles, closer this time. She waits for the first raindrops to spatter her jeans before setting off home.

Then

1975

THE CHURCH BELL'S lament carried on in an echo that wailed even after the ringing had stopped. It cancelled out the scuff of shoes, the rustle of Sunday suits, the congregation's whispering. When it died away, only the beat of the rain disturbed the hush of flattened sound. Mist obscured the graveyard beyond the windows. The building was cold, but Else's armpits prickled with heat. She sat alone with her mother on the first pew. Behind their backs, she could sense the mourners' restlessness.

The organ's prelude began. Soft and sombre, its notes dripped over the congregation before setting in a chord. A collective breath signalled the start of the opening hymn and Else's gaze fell from the model schooner to her father's casket, which stretched like a barrier to the altar. While her neighbours sang, Pastor Seip rose to his feet. His face was grim as he climbed down into the nave to take her mother's hand. He moved on to Else and his fingers skimmed her palm, flaccid and watery as a jellyfish.

The minister returned to his place on the altar and leafed through his Bible until the end of the hymn. He allowed some moments of silence to build before lifting his head.

'May the Lord bless you, and grant you mercy,' he said. 'Today we gather to mourn the passing of Johann Dybdahl. I know I speak for Dagny and Else both when I thank you for joining them in grief. Johann's presence among us will be missed. "For none of us liveth to himself, and no man dieth to himself." So says Paul's Epistle to the Romans, chapter fourteen. Johann has left his mark on those who survive him. He will not be forgotten. In death, he will live on in you.'

A trickle of sweat leaked from Else's neck down her spine, gluing her blouse to the skin between her shoulder blades. Her mother touched a handkerchief to her nose. With the other hand, she squeezed Else's wrist under the cuff of her sleeve.

'Johann was born to Roy and Julianna Dybdahl on the thirteenth of September, 1927. The youngest of two children, he survived Berit, who died in infancy. He was a boy when he began work on the shrimp trawler that would be his livelihood until last October's storm. He married Dagny Solvang from Lindesnes in 1955. Three years later, the Lord blessed them with Else, their only daughter.

'Johann was born, lived, worked and died among us. He did not live to be an old man. The sea that sustained him for most of his forty-seven years, providing him and his family with their daily bread, saw him drowned in a terrible accident on the fourteenth of April. A tragedy, certainly, but a blessing, too, for the sorrows of the flesh are as nothing next to the bounties of heaven. It is not for us to question the workings of the Lord, but rather to give thanks that Johann has been delivered from his trials on earth. "For God so loved the world, that He gave His only begotten Son, that whosoever believeth in Him should not perish, but have everlasting life." So says the Gospel according to John, chapter three, verse sixteen.'

From the choir gallery, a loud sneeze sent a twitch through the mourners. Pastor Seip shot a glare at its perpetrator, then turned his back on the congregation and raised his hands at his sides.

'Oh Lord,' he called, 'please welcome Johann Dybdahl to your bosom. Forgive his sins and grant him everlasting life. Help his loved ones take solace in the hope that they will one day be reunited with him in your kingdom.'

He continued to pray. Else peered at the coffin, her folded hands squeezing the shake from her fingers. *Everlasting life.* Pastor Seip must be mistaken. And yet, judging by the crowd at his funeral, it did seem that the town had put her father's catalogue of failings to rest. The pews were crowded with mourners, whose contributions had turned his casket into a flowerbed. A wreath of roses had been arranged over the spot where his chest lay frozen behind the buttons of his suit jacket. 'From Haakon Reiersen with family', read the ribbon. Else had seen it before the service, when she and her mother had first arrived. Thinking of it now she had to close her eyes, to rein in her anger. What right did she have? She had as good as killed her father. In the eyes of the Lord, she was as guilty as he.

Pastor Seip stopped speaking and, again, the pipes of the organ wheezed. Lips parted for the second hymn, while the candles' flames shimmered like holy tears on the altar.

'*Fold your wide wings, o Jesus, over me . . .*'

The sheriff's office had returned the verdict of death by drowning.

'Aggravated by several knocks to the head sustained during his fall,' Alv Knudsen had said. Else had watched the men arrive from her bedroom window. First Tenvik, who trailed after her weeping mother, and, later, Ole Haugeli. By the time Knudsen responded to Tenvik's call, her father must have grown quite used to the mulch of the boathouse's berth. Dagny fortified the trio with cake and chicory to ease the shock of what they had found.

Then they fished the body out of the water. Else had sat on her chair, her forehead pressed to the glass as they hoisted her father off the property. He hung limp between Knudsen and Ole, his chin sagging to his chest like a drunk's.

The final strains of the hymn faded. In the quiet that followed, Pastor Seip surveyed his flock. Else lowered her eyes to her knees and blinked away the nightmare vision of her father's underwater scream. He could not hurt her now. She was glad he was dead.

'Jesus said, "I am the way, the truth, and the life: no man cometh unto the Father, but by me." Jesus is the way. The path to heaven is through Him, and through Him alone will we arrive at our salvation. Let us pray for the soul of Johann Dybdahl,' said Pastor Seip, 'that he find rest and peace in death. Let us pray for comfort in this, our time of sorrow, and for the strength and humility to accept the wisdom of the Lord. "Our father, who art in heaven, hallowed be thy name. Thy kingdom come, thy will be done, on earth as it is in heaven . . ."'

Beside Else, her mother wiped the tip of her nose. Her lips moved over the invocation without making a sound.

They buried him in the cemetery. When Pastor Seip had finished preaching, six men strode forward from the nave – among them Knut Tenvik, Ole Haugeli and Tom Ivar Lund – and shared the weight of the casket between them. Pastor Seip followed the coffin down the aisle, while Else fell into step with her mother behind the minister. Pew by pew, the mourners joined them to see Johann out of the church.

The cemetery smelled of the thawed and rotting seaweed that the wind blew up from the harbour. Spring rain collected in puddles on the path which left a gritty film over Else's patent leather shoes. She held an umbrella over her and her mother's heads as they walked with arms linked to her father's plot. The hole looked too small for his coffin. Even so, the pallbearers laid it in the straps of the pulley and, with a yank of the winch, the casket began to drop. It scraped the grave's sides, screeching in protest as it went. Else half expected the noise to wake her father up.

'O death, where is thy sting?' said Pastor Seip. 'O grave, where is thy victory?'

After the burial, they served coffee and cake. Tenvik drove Else and her mother the short distance to the *bedehus*, where Ninni and Solveig helped them bring the sugar cake and raisin Bundt from the kitchen up to the hall. The mourners filled their cups with real coffee and cream, while Else and her mother accepted commiserations from whosever hands were free.

'Condolences,' said Trygve Christensen.

'A fine man,' Esben Omland said.

Else tried to smile while her palm was pinched and shaken. Pastor Seip sat at the table beside her, wearing a pained expression as he nodded his acknowledgement of the well-wishers.

'A tragedy,' said Ingrid Bull.

'Such a waste,' said Gjertrud Sundt.

The women lingered for a moment, their eyes searching Else's face. The scabs on her cheek itched where her mother's needle had picked out the splinters. She felt exposed, stripped naked and turned out for all to see. She knew the rumours about the strong man had already started. Upstairs in the gallery, Lars had found a seat with Rune behind the rail. Petter had not come to the funeral.

Else stared at the coffee cup on the table in front of her and sucked a mouthful of air through her teeth. She burped behind her hand.

'Are you all right?' asked her mother across Pastor Seip. Else dabbed a handkerchief over the sweat that beaded her forehead. She swallowed her nausea and let the next mourner take her hand.

By four o'clock, most of those present had offered their sympathies to Dagny and Else. The rest hovered close to their table, waiting their turn to fulfil their Christian duty before going home. Else's coffee had grown cold. She had not eaten her cake. She felt sick and hot under the layers of her clothing, her skin rubbed raw by buttons and seams and wool made tight by perspiration. She thanked the people whose hands rattled the bones in her arm. When Haakon and Karin Reiersen stepped forward, the room began to spin.

'Dagny,' Reiersen said. His fingers closed on her mother's palm. 'Our condolences, once again.'

'Thank you,' Dagny said.

'How are you bearing up?'

'As well as can be expected,' she said.

'A sad business,' said Reiersen. 'If there is anything we can do . . .'

He glanced at his wife, who blushed and leaned forward to kiss Dagny's cheek.

'Condolences,' she said. She did not look at Else. Behind her, Lars stood with his hands in his pockets. He blinked at the floor. He followed his parents to the other side of the room.

'Condolences,' said Randy Fodstad.

'Condolences,' said Arne Kvinge.

The Reiersen family withdrew into the rain. Through the window, Else saw the Cadillac backing into the road.

THE NEWS OF her romance with the strong man began in a whisper, like the rustle of leaves in a mounting wind. Else had been sneaking to the circus man's trailer for weeks. She had contrived to have her parents hire him for their barn work; some said she had sabotaged the roof herself. More details emerged with the passing days to be exchanged at the fish market, at Berge's bakery, in the churchyard after the Sunday service. Pastor Seip no longer spared a nod for her in the street. Twice, Lars's mother crossed the road to avoid her.

Else waited for the ferry each morning as before, looking at the shipyard from the public dock while steeling herself to the other passengers' stares and murmurs. Once aboard she stayed on deck where, as often as not, the weather would preserve her isolation. She stowed herself in a corner by the guardrail, welcoming the rain that pattered the canvas of her raised hood. At the Longpier, she disembarked. Hands shielded mouths; heads inclined to lips. *The Devil is in her.* She hurried along the harbour, her eyes on her boots all the way to school.

Lars wasted no time in taking up with Gro Berge. They met at the caretaker's shed at the start of the school break and reappeared at its end with rumpled clothes and sheepish grins. Else paced alone around the Gymnasium and kept her focus turned inwards. Sometimes Petter would desert Rune by the gate and join her for a round, ignoring the taunts that were aimed at his back. She wished that he wouldn't. She greeted him with silence, wary of the fresh speculations his company would bring. Their classmates giggled when they walked by. Petter endured their ridicule, though she had not asked him to.

The snow had all but melted by May. At the edge of the schoolyard, the last of the ice clung like lichen to the asphalt. Else sat in Paulsen's classroom and peered out of the window. Along the road, new leaves filled out the branches of the trees. Paulsen's monotone dwindled to a hum in her ear, while her eyes strayed to a fragment of sun by the caretaker's shed. The light seemed to seep into her vision, bleaching foliage and bark the colour of ageing paper. She felt her brain cooking, then her stomach wrenched. Someone had eaten herring for breakfast. She could smell vinegar, onions and fish. She clamped her hand over her mouth.

'Else! Where in the world are you going?'

Paulsen shouted after her when she ran from the room. At the end of the corridor, she burst into the girls' toilets and dropped to her knees in the first cubicle. Tears dripped from her eyes into the cistern as she retched up that morning's bread and jam. A new bout of nausea stirred her gut. She heaved and heaved.

She flushed the toilet when she had finished. She blew her nose and wiped her lips and rested her forehead on her arms until she was herself again. Her legs were leaden underneath her when she ventured from the cubicle. She moved to the sink and let the water chase the heat from her palms. Else splashed her face, rinsed her mouth and rubbed her neck with wet fingers. Her eyes glared back at her from the mirror, their whites tinged pink around the irises. Her skin was sallow, as pale as her father's had been when they pulled him from the fjord.

At ten minutes past twelve, the Gymnasium's students poured from their classrooms into the hallway. Else listened through the door to the current of footsteps that carried them into the yard. When the building's hush had been restored, she crept from her hiding place to Paulsen's classroom. He was liberating a packed lunch from a sheet of greaseproof paper. He looked up from his desk when she knocked.

'I'm sorry for leaving in the middle of class,' she said.

Paulsen pursed his lips at the goat cheese on his bread slice. Else remembered the squeeze of his hand after her father's funeral.

'I think I'm getting the flu,' she said.

'Get out with you,' he said.

She turned away and drifted down the corridor, feeling dazed and unsteady on her feet. A blast of sun met her full in the face when she opened the door to the schoolyard. She shielded her eyes until her vision cleared and the caretaker's shed came into focus. Else crossed into the shadow that stretched over the ground on the other side of the Gymnasium. At the rear of the building, she sank onto the steps by the staff entrance. The stone was cold through the cloth of her trousers. She kneaded her belly as she gazed down Elvebakken to the fjord. It was the second time that week she had vomited.

Else stiffened when she saw Petter, who approached and sat on her step. He leaned his back against the door and rested his hands on his knees.

'Were you sick?' he asked.

He scratched his chin and started again.

'I heard you were sick,' he said.

'I'm fine,' Else said.

'You should have seen Paulsen's face when you bolted.' His laugh was thin on his lips. He bounced his heels in a frantic rhythm.

'I've been meaning to say.' His knees grazed his palms. 'That night, when I came for you at your house. I guess your parents must have known about the strong man. They found out, didn't they? That's why they locked you in your room.'

Petter touched her arm when she did not answer.

'You said you wanted to go into town, but I took you straight to him. I made things worse, didn't I? I shouldn't have interfered.'

'No,' Else said. 'You shouldn't have.'

His body sagged as if she had elbowed him in the gut. She felt better at once and then she felt worse. Petter stood and walked away, finally leaving her alone.

In those days, her mother prayed with the urgency of a convert, as if she were making up for lost time. She kept the radio on and turned it up for the morning's Bible reading, often opening her own Bible to examine the verse in its entirety. Else would wake to the sound of her bumping in the bathroom and would picture her bent over the laundry, sorting through her clothes and gnawing her cheeks as she checked the gussets of her daughter's underpants. When Else was alone, she pounded her stomach with her fists. Still the bleeding did not start.

She stayed at home on the Sunday when the new class of confirmands was due to answer to the minister in church. She milked the cow and marvelled at the thought that, only two years ago, it had been her turn. Dressed in a white gown with a crucifix stitched over her breast, Else had stood at the altar while her parents watched from their pew. Afterwards, there had been a party at the *bedehus*. Rune had eaten a piece of each of the six cakes donated to the cake table.

May slipped into June. Apart from her journey into school, Else did not venture far from the farmhouse. She confined her walks to the fields nearby, where bluebells and buttercups sprang from the grass and the air was warm with the smell of horses. Daylight hours won out over the night, flushing the horizon in vivid colours that yielded to darkness for a few hours and no more. Else and her mother hung summer curtains in their bedrooms. In the yard, the green tops of onions and carrots nudged through the earth. Stacks of tinder – worn-out traps, used-up tables and chairs, sawn-off branches and hacked-up tree roots – appeared on rock flats that dipped into the water as their neighbours prepared for Midsummer bonfires. Else picked redcurrants from the bushes in the garden, looping her belt through the handle of her pail while she worked. The juices stained her fingers and she sucked them clean with a hunger that surprised and terrified her.

On Midsummer's Eve, she rowed the skiff into the fjord and pulled a coalfish from out of the water. It was a fine weight, a good two kilos, she guessed. She laid it down in the hull and rinsed her fingers and rowed home.

In the kitchen she tied an apron around her waist and, after retrieving a knife from the cutlery drawer, sliced off the fish's head and poked its belly with her blade, jerking it downward to the creature's vent. Her tonsils burned with bile as she slid her fingers into the gash. She wound them in its entrails, which plopped pink and brown onto the counter. When she held up her hands, they were shiny with blood. The smell hit her, doubled her over. She fled into the garden through the back door.

Her mother found her in the grass on her hands and knees. She had not made it to the outhouse in time. Dagny knelt on the ground at Else's side and combed the hair away from her face. She held it in a bunch at the nape of her neck while she rubbed circles over her daughter's back. Else groaned and gagged and sobbed until the nausea subsided.

Afterwards, her mother brought a cup of chicory to settle her stomach. They had carried two chairs from the dining room into the garden, where they sat by the vegetable plot, which smelled spicy and rich in the sun. A seagull perched on the roof of the boathouse like a weathervane in the windless air. The knock of the skiff on the tide drifted up from the water. Else swallowed her chicory in quick sips.

'We'll pick the blackcurrants next week,' her mother said. 'There are so many this year, we'll have squash and jam to last through the winter. How are you feeling?'

'Better,' Else said.

Her mother nodded at the shipyard. The glare of the sun sharpened the new wrinkles around her mouth. 'Ninni Tenvik has asked if I'll sew her a dress.'

'That's good,' Else said.

'Yes,' she said. 'It is good.'

Else lifted her cup and choked on the fish stink that came off her fingers. No matter how she scrubbed them, it would not wash away.

'I could do with your help,' her mother said. 'It's just as well that school has finished for the year.'

'Yes,' Else said.

'And next year. Well. We'll be busy with other things then, won't we?'

The seagull spread its wings and took off from the boathouse roof. Else watched it fly until it disappeared. 'I don't want it,' she said.

'Hush,' said her mother. 'A baby is a blessing.'

When their chicory had been drunk Else carried the cups into the kitchen, where she washed them and put them away. Her mother changed her clothes and finished cleaning the coalfish before returning outside. From her seat in the cool of the dining room, Else glimpsed her moving through the window, scurrying back and forth in front of the pier. She tried to concentrate on the sewing. She chose a pair of trousers from the pile and considered the hems her mother had pinned up. She threaded her needle with dark blue cotton and pierced the wool with its tip. In and out she sewed, though the garment was old and shabby and beyond rescue.

She was going to have a baby. Her father's child.

She caught her breath when her mother opened the front door. Else heard her on the stairs, her footsteps overhead.

'What are you doing out there?' she called from the dining room.

'Preparing the bonfire,' her mother said.

She left the way she had come in and again the house was quiet. Else closed the circle around the first ankle, tied a knot in the thread and snipped it loose with her teeth. She imagined the quiet broken by a scream. A baby's scream. Its clinging hands, its greedy mouth. What did a baby have to do with her? She sensed an aching in her breasts and poked her thumb with the needle, pushing it deeper until the pain was all she felt.

The first bonfire was lit later that evening, after her mother had boiled the coalfish and they had eaten supper. The sun had yet to set when a coil of black smoke rose on the other side of the fjord, dirtying the pink rinse of the sky. Before long, flames dotted the shoreline. Else carried two buckets across the yard behind her mother, who bore two of her own. To the left of the pier, Dagny's kindling was heaped on a slip of rock between the lawn and the fjord. Else was able to distinguish solitary objects as she drew closer: crab traps, a lobster pot, twists of rope, a single oar. A sponge mattress leaned against the rubble, displaying its mildewed bottom through the holes of a fishing net.

At the sight of the boathouse's contents piled up and ready to burn, Else felt a sore opening in her chest. She hesitated at the foot of the pier, while her mother moved to its edge and crouched to dip her buckets into the fjord.

'Come, Else,' she said.

She beckoned to her daughter and Else did as she was told. They took turns to pour a ring around the stack, isolating it from the pier and the lawn. When the rock base was slick with salt water, Dagny hurried to the boathouse, leaving Else to refill the buckets. Her mother reappeared with a *Norges* jar in each hand. She unfastened the lid of the first and tipped it over the traps. The stink of moonshine soaked the air. Else placed her bucket on the grass along with the others, ready to use in case a wind swept the fire out of control. She watched her mother splash the mattress, saw the flower-print sheet tucked amid a snarl of fishing wire darken with liquid. The hose from her father's distillery curled around the sheet like an octopus's arm. Its rubber dripped with homebrew.

'Stand back,' her mother said.

Else covered her face when the match landed on the pile. The fire leapt with a roar and a shimmer of air. Wood snapped and split and fishing wire melted. The crab traps' metal prongs glowed a vicious red. Against the disintegrating backdrop of the mattress the flames scuttled up the net, eating away its diamond threads. The distillery's hose bubbled and spat. The fumes made Else's eyes water. She stuffed her sleeve into her mouth while her mother fumbled something from her pocket. When Else looked, she saw the oil cloth blotted black with her father's blood. Her mother tossed it onto the fire and, side by side, they watched it shrivel to ash.

They stayed by the pier until late into the night, holding vigil over the bonfire. Its heat singed the grass at the lawn's rim, but there was no need to use the buckets of water they had prepared. When the flames began to dwindle, Dagny stalked off to the boathouse and returned with another *Norges* jar. The homebrew kept Johann's belongings burning as the sky dimmed over the shipyard across the fjord.

THE SUMMER HAD cooled by the time Else returned to Tenvik's paddock at the end of August. Her mother had spent the morning running errands in town and was not due home from the *bedehus* until later. In her absence, Else had milked the cow, dug up the potatoes and laid them out to dry in the sun. Now she sat at the dining table rubbing the ache from her spine. She felt a flutter in her stomach and rested her hand against the spot. This was a new sensation, one that she was beginning to recognise.

'The baby is moving,' her mother had said when she had asked her about it.

Else imagined a foot stamping the lining of her womb and pressed back gently with her palm. Again there was the feeling, like bubbles popping. She stroked the swell of her belly through her blouse. Her clothes were getting tight. Her mother had already tacked fabric panels into the waistband of her trousers. The rest would have to be let out soon. In the two months since the end of the school year, she had measured the changes of her body with dread and wonder. Irresistible bouts of drowsiness had sent her dozing through July. She had awoken one morning to find a seam stitched from her diaphragm to her navel, an uneven line that had not been there the night before.

Only her mother witnessed this metamorphosis. Else continued to shy away from public places and, at certain times of day, from fields and tracks where she risked running into their neighbours. Now and then Ninni Tenvik would call, bringing with her a jar of honey or a basket of eggs. Else would wait out her visits in her bedroom and listen through the floorboards while she and her mother exchanged news of the town. Sometimes their conversation would turn to fresh reports of the oil tankers docked in bays and fjords along the coast. More than once, they wondered whether anything would come of the shipyard's talks with the oil fields.

When she had rested her legs, she stood and crossed into the kitchen, where she sawed off two slices of bread and fetched the cheese from the fridge. As far as she knew, Ninni had never asked her mother about her father's death. Still they must wonder what had happened that morning after Johann had showed Tenvik the barn and he had driven away in his Volvo. A sudden spasm had Else clutching her side. To calm herself, she thought about the paddock. She remembered Valentin on the floor of his caravan, his head propped against the wall between sips of coffee. She had not been back since the day he left. She had decided to go home.

Else pushed away the plate with its slices of bread and cheese. She needed some air. A little air would do her good. She found a pail in the cupboard and headed outside into the yard and behind the barn to collect her father's bicycle. She brushed the cobwebs from its frame and checked its wheels before walking it up the hill. On the road, she placed her foot on the pedal and kicked off, swinging onto the saddle while the bike rolled underneath her.

Else cycled past the Aaby farm to the deserted public dock, where she rose in her saddle to meet the upcoming slope. The fjord fell away behind her, taking the shipyard with it as she followed the track inland. She pumped her legs and the pail swayed from left to right on the handlebar. She was sweating when the woodland appeared at the roadside. Up ahead, she saw the familiar gap in the trees.

Once she had turned off the road and onto the path gnarled with roots, she dismounted from her bike. The forest thrummed with insects. Bees and midges collided with her as she pushed deeper into the trees. Leaves carpeted the earth, hiding the ground between tufts of heather and pine cones and mushroom caps. Among the stinging nettles, she saw the waxy green of blueberry bushes. She did not pause to check for fruit, though she gripped the handle of her pail. Instead she listened for the brook that would tell her the meadow was close.

The light had already changed when she heard it. Else waded through high weeds and over beds of moss. At the forest's edge, she arrived at the field where once Circus Leona's Big Top had sprung from the mud. It was unrecognisable. A temporary fence taped off the perimeter, enclosing an expanse of cropped grass. A handful of horses grazed on the spot where the strong man's caravan had spent the winter. By the mouth of the track that curled away to his farm, Tenvik was keeping watch over his animals with his hands on his hips. He straightened up when he saw Else. He waved and ducked under the tape and she smothered the urge to flee back into the woods.

'Else!' he called.

He strode over the paddock and she scolded herself for being foolish enough to come here. The circus had left months ago. So, too, had Valentin.

'Else,' Tenvik said. He stopped in front of her on the other side of the fence. 'How nice to see you. It's been a while, hasn't it? How are you feeling?'

'Fine,' Else said.

She was barely aware of her hand on her belly, stroking as if to smooth out its curve. Tenvik smiled at the bulge and her arm fell to her side.

'I'm glad to hear it,' he said. 'So will Ninni be.' He nodded at the paddock. 'It looks different, wouldn't you say?'

'Yes,' Else said.

'We can't afford not to use it. Not now, with the economy being what it is. It's hard to say if we're catching up or if we're being left behind.'

Tenvik shook his head and turned his face to the sun. Else breathed in the smell of toasted earth. A wasp buzzed by her ear and she swatted it away, thinking of when Lars had brought her here last summer. They had lain in the grass where a piebald pony now wandered from the herd to rip a mouthful from the soil. A dandelion hung from its jaws. It flicked a gadfly with its tail. She knew that the circus would never return.

'It's good grazing land,' Tenvik said. 'It isn't good for much else, but it will do for grazing land.'

'The horses seem to like it,' Else said.

'You should come by to see us,' Tenvik said. 'With the little one, too. Ninni would be so pleased. We haven't had any new life there for, oh. It feels like a long time now.'

Else nodded. She thought of the graves in the churchyard and felt the popping in her stomach. 'I'll visit you,' she said.

'That's good,' Tenvik said.

'I'd better get started,' she said, 'if I'm going to find any.' She lifted her pail, gave it a shake in the air.

'Are you picking blueberries?' Tenvik asked. 'There are plenty along the brook. Ninni picked a few tubfuls there last weekend.'

Else thanked him and backed away from the paddock. She trod into the shadows that fell under the trees and followed the burble of the brook past crawling anthills and over leaves that covered the earth. The gurgling grew louder and then she was upon it. On either side of the water, blueberry bushes spread their stems. Else squatted and began to pick the fruits. Her hands moved quickly between the branches and her pail. She was surprised when she looked up, her knees and back aching, to find that her bucket was almost full.

The first oil tanker arrived in the fjord later that day. Else saw it on her ride from the paddock to the farmhouse when she rounded the corner by the public dock, which was busy now with ferry passengers. No one seemed to notice her skidding to a halt on the road. She joined them in staring at the ship that had dropped its anchor across the fjord, not far from the shipyard and its empty graving dock. The tanker's broad deck soared in a tower taller than any building in town. Taut lines secured its stern to the shore.

Over the course of the next weeks and months, more tankers appeared from the Skagerrak to moor up beside the first. They formed a neat row, two ships, then three, then four bound together with ropes and hawsers. With each new arrival, the locals rowed out their skiffs or steered their motorboats in for a closer look. They bobbed along the length of each hull, back and forth, staggered by their size. Dagny took to scowling at the tankers from the dining-room window and muttering about a spoiled view. Tenvik discussed them with his wife whenever Else visited. She listened with one hand on her belly, the other holding a cup of tea.

Ninni was knitting a cardigan for the baby: a *lusekofte* in white and blue, to be finished with tin buttons.

'I think it will be a boy,' Ninni liked to say. 'Have you thought of names? Klaus is nice. Or Marianne, if it's a girl.'

Else knew from the headstones in the cemetery that these had been the names of the Tenvik children. She was not ready to think about what she would call the baby. She tried not to think about the baby at all. She sewed the clothes her mother brought home by the armload, pausing now and again to gaze at the tankers across the fjord, a beached herd robbed of its promise, forced to deny the pull of the sea.

The sun set earlier every day. Dawn arrived later in a gloomy sky. Else realised that autumn had passed and winter was upon them.

ELSE WAS FIVE days late when, on a Thursday morning in January, her contractions started. She had been working at the table in the dining room, which had been spread with blankets and sheets to protect the wood from her iron. Her arms were stretched long, but still she was forced to stoop to reach the surface beyond the obstacle of her belly. The cramp came in a ripple, a slow spreading of pain. She set down the iron and pulled out its plug.

Her mother arrived from the barn carrying a pail of milk. She shook the snow from her hair as she stepped into the dining room.

'I think it's started,' Else said.

'Sit down,' said her mother. 'I'll bring you a glass of water.'

Else sat in a chair by the oven, gritting her teeth against a new stirring of pain. She pressed the floor with the balls of her feet until it had passed.

That afternoon, Dagny hurried from the farmhouse. Else watched her through the window, a black speck against an unbroken plain of snow. The glass rattled with wind as she marched past the barn and onto the hill, the hem of her coat fluttering behind her. The trees swallowed her up and Else was alone. She hoped it would not take her mother long. She had promised she would ask Tenvik to drive her home as soon as she had finished with his telephone. The hospital would send a car once she had rung. It would not take long.

Else stood to feed a log into the oven. She paced the floorboards, stopping to clutch the table ledge whenever the pain flared. She swallowed air into her lungs, breathed out and in and tried not to think about what was to come. But fear had grown solid inside of her, gaining substance and form with the expanding of her belly. She would not allow herself to think about the baby. There was only this moment, and the next, and that was all.

A band of flames had erupted across her lower back by the time her mother returned. Else bit down hard on a moan as the front door opened and the wind burst into the farmhouse.

'Tenvik wasn't there,' called Dagny from the hallway. 'I'd hoped he would drive me, but only Ninni was home. I've rung the hospital. The midwife is on her way. We'll stay in the dining room so you won't have to use the stairs.'

She was halfway into the room and struggling out of her coat when she saw her daughter. The coat dropped to the floor.

'Else,' she said. She rushed to her side. She laid one hand between her shoulders and the other on her forehead. Else lifted her face to her mother's touch. It stung with a cold that cut the fever. The rest of her stayed bent over the dining table, her chest pressed flat on the pile of sheets and blankets.

'It hurts,' Else said through clenched teeth.

'I know,' said her mother. 'Wait here.'

'Don't leave me,' she said.

'I'm right here. I'm in the kitchen.'

'It hurts,' said Else. 'It hurts, it hurts.'

Her mother set the kettle to boil. She filled a bowl with water from the tap and brought it into the dining room together with a clean kitchen cloth.

'Come now,' she said and supported Else while she helped her out of her jumper. The wool was clammy over her head. It cut off the air. Then the jumper was off. Else clawed at the buttons of her blouse with slippery fingers. Its cotton stuck in the creases of her armpits. Her face and throat were slick with sweat that ran between her breasts.

A new contraction kicked her in the back, folding her again over the table. She groaned and wept.

'The car is coming,' said her mother. 'Just hold on.'

Hands smoothed away the hair that clung to her neck and cheeks. A damp cloth stroked her skin, dripping water onto the table. Else exhaled slowly and the tension released. As weak as her body was, she pushed herself up and started pacing again.

She lost track of the minutes, of the distance she walked before each new contraction winded her. She knew only that the pain was getting worse and that the midwife had yet to arrive. Again and again, her stomach squeezed. Her womb turned to stone and she cried out for help. Her mother crept back and forth to the window.

'It will be here any minute,' she said.

But the car did not come, however much she looked for it. She left the room and returned with towels that smelled of carbolic soap. After freeing Else from her clothing, easing the blouse and bra and trousers from her limbs one at a time, she slipped a nightshirt over her head and rubbed a hand along the base of her spine as if trying to snuff out the wildfire. Else screamed with the spasm of her guts. She clutched her belly.

'No no no!' she shouted.

Her body surrendered to trembling. A cold gush of sweat poured down her back and she shook and her insides beat like a butter churn.

'Breathe,' said her mother, 'breathe, breathe.'

Her throat and mouth filled with vomit. She spat it onto the floor.

'Breathe breathe breathe.'

She felt a tightening of the bowels, a quickening, a mounting of pressure, a gravitational pull. Her innards were dropping; she was turning inside out.

'It's coming,' her mother said.

Hands on her wrists, squeezing as she pushed, leading her back to the table. Else gripped the wood with fingers set on shredding it to splinters. Her head sagged and roared with blood as she howled.

'Again,' said her mother. 'You're almost there.'

She clamped her teeth and pushed.

'I can see it. I can see the head.'

She pushed again and felt a cleaving and a spilling down her legs. She pushed until her body quaked with an animal sound.

'It's a girl,' said her mother. 'Else, it's a girl.'

A mewl pierced the clamour between her ears and Else looked at her daughter. Her mother hugged the baby close. Tears dripped from her nose onto the purple gooseflesh of a scrawny body. She was oily with blood. Her head was smeared white, her eyes wrinkles of skin tipped by gossamer lashes. With every scream, her lips quivered and her hands searched the air. Her mother placed the child on Else's chest, then wrapped a sheet around them both.

'Come and rest,' she said.

But Else could not move. She stared at her daughter. The baby's fingers stretched and flexed, seeking blindly before closing around Else's thumb. A firm, desperate hold. Else's breasts ached. Her womb convulsed with the afterbirth. She rocked her child and said a prayer.

They were lying on the floor on a pile of blankets arranged by the oven when the hospital car arrived. Dagny opened the front door and led the midwife into the dining room. She knelt beside Else, who held her baby in her arms.

Now

2009

FOR THE FIRST few minutes, Else is alone in the barn. An arc of sunlight falls past her through the doorway, smearing her shadow over the floor in an uncanny distortion that stretches to the far wall. The air glitters with dust particles that make her sneeze when she steps inside. Her clogs clack on the concrete.

She wonders when she was last in here. Even before her mother died, they had not used the barn for some time. There was no need to once Tenvik bought the cow which, by then, had stopped producing milk. Another kindness – one of many more to come. Else remembers the sun sweltering in a summer sky during the week when she cleared the space of sawdust and manure. While Marianne galloped make-believe horses in rings around her, she shovelled it into a wheelbarrow for disposal at the edge of the property.

The recollection of her daughter as a child bolsters her now and she moves further inside. It smells of the damp that coaxes mould from the corners like fur. The stockades of the two stalls were torn down long ago and removed, along with most of the features that would remind her of her childhood. Even so, as she looks around at the gutted space, she sees her father on a ladder hammering nails into the roof. She sees a giant of a man hoisting a log towards the ceiling with his bare hands.

The girls' voices interrupt her thoughts and she backs again into the doorway.

'I'm in here,' she calls, glancing up the hill.

Marianne and Liv escort an estate agent. His gait is eager, his expression impatient.

'Oh,' he says, 'this is nice. A pearl. The location really is something.'

'Well,' says Else. 'Here's the barn. It isn't much.'

She sweeps a hand to invite him in. The estate agent – Morten, he called himself – obliges. He stops in the centre of the room and turns in a circle, screwing up eyes that dart in his head.

'You'd be surprised,' he says. 'Barn conversions are very popular these days. If summer residents can get permission for them, that is.'

Else nods. She is glad the girls are here. She would not have liked to be doing this on her own. She joins them outside to wait for Morten.

'It's strange being back here,' Marianne says.

When Morten emerges they make their way across the yard, their shoes trampling the grass where the onions used to grow. They continue to the front door, where Else hesitates, though her keys are ready in hand.

'Aren't we going in?' Liv asks.

Else fits the key in the lock. The hallway is dark when she pushes the door wide. She fumbles for the switch and a bulb illuminates the farmhouse entrance. Tenvik's man has done a good job. Only a sprinkling of dust dirties the floor and he cannot be blamed for that, given that a month has passed since he last came to clean. Else has already decided to hire him again to mow the lawn and vacuum before the viewings begin. Stay focused on the practical, she tells herself. Meanwhile, Morten slips past her and starts to calculate potential.

'May I?' he asks and points towards the dining room.

'Help yourself,' Else says, and he does.

Liv and Marianne accompany him. Else stays where she is on the threshold. Gazing at the ceiling beams above the staircase, she is surprised to find that the farmhouse is still intact. Somehow, she had imagined her neglect would have set its foundations to crumbling. A phantom house: that is what she expected. And yet, here it is, no different from how it was. Tenvik is right, of course. She should have sold it right away, but it has been easier to leave it alone.

Else follows the others into the dining room and finds Marianne and Liv kneeling next to the sideboard. They are examining the bowls that are stacked inside.

'They're filthy,' Marianne says. 'Do you want to keep any?'

'I don't think so,' Else says.

Morten calls to them from the kitchen enclave. 'It should get a good price,' he says. 'Since the council agreed to let properties be sold as holiday homes on this part of the coast, the market has opened up considerably. Of course it needs work, but we can emphasise its possibilities to prospective buyers. Knocking down the walls right here would make this space an open kitchen. A lick of white paint would make it nice and bright.'

Else lets her eyes wander over the room as if allowing herself to be taken in by his vision. What she sees are walls the grey of seagulls' wings. The door to the cast-iron oven hangs open on its hinges, exposing its empty belly, scraped clean and left cold for the longest time. In the corner above the table and chairs, which stand as if glued to their places, the windows show the barn at the end of a yard streaked with sun.

'It's different to how I remember it,' says Liv. 'Why haven't we been back here since oldemor died? It's still yours.'

'It's ours,' says Else.

'Nobody lives here,' says Marianne. 'It's just a house.'

Her tone is flat when she speaks and Else ventures a sad smile. She prefers not to think about what it must have been like for her growing up here, in this town, in this house. The strong man's daughter.

'You know your mother was born here?' she says to Liv. 'Right in this room. The hospital car was late.'

'I know,' says Liv. 'You've told me before.'

'What's next?' asks Morten.

Else leads the way through the hallway to the Best Room. The doorknob is cold in her palm when she twists it, releasing a musty smell from within. The crocheted curtains are brittle and yellow, as are the sheets that have been draped over the straight-backed chairs.

'We should probably clear out the furniture before viewings start,' says Morten. He strides inside and nods meaningfully as he approaches the window. 'Great view to the water. That could really be enhanced. If the new owners were to cut down the cherry tree and put some windows in here' – his arm sweeps the length of the wall – 'the view would be beautiful.'

Else smiles, but her thoughts have drifted. She is on her hands and knees beside her mother, scrubbing the floor with soft soap, scouring her father from the cracks. She is six months pregnant and hooking the window on its latch to air him from the four walls. Still the space smells of him.

'Marianne,' Else says, 'would you show Morten upstairs? I think I'll wait here, if that's all right.'

Morten follows Marianne and Liv into the hallway, leaving Else to herself. She pulls a sheet from one of the chairs and sits on its inadequate cushion. It is as hard as she remembers it being. While she waits, she crumples the sheet in her lap and listens to the sound of footsteps overhead.

A new door opens in her memory, propelling her back onto her feet and across the room. In the corner cupboard, a skin of cobwebs hides onkel Olav's coffee set. She punctures it with her finger and strands of silk fall away. Else reaches for a cup, lifting it and turning it under her nose. A dark residue tarnishes the white enamel of the bowl, but the exterior looks unsoiled by time. Gold leaves float on the surface of a black sea. She strokes the filigree with her thumb and recognises in the pattern a wish from her childhood.

She decides to keep these. She does not want anything else.

Else recovers the rest of the coffee set from its shelf, picking up the cups one by one and placing them on the table. As she does, the girls' voices carry down in a chatter interrupted here and there by Morten's deeper timbre. The creak of the staircase announces their return. Else retrieves the coffee pot last of all.

'What's that?' asks Liv when she arrives in the doorway.

'A gift from my uncle to Oldemor. I'm bringing it home,' Else says.

'Maybe we could take a look at the boathouse,' says Morten. 'I'm sure it will be a point of interest. It isn't easy to get permission to build them from scratch these days.'

'Could you finish showing Morten around?' Else asks Marianne. 'I want to get these packed before we go.'

'This way,' says Marianne and shows the estate agent outside.

Liv stays behind with Else. She shuffles into the Best Room and stops by the table, where she touches a fingertip to a cup. Slowly, she traces the outline of a leaf, then another, following the trail from the base in a spiral to the lip. Else takes the sheet that she removed from the chair and lays it out on the floor. She begins to wrap the first cup, stuffing its bowl and swaddling its handle with the material. Liv watches her work before rescuing a new sheet from the bench under the window and mimicking the process.

'Three cups per sheet,' Else says.

When they have packed seven cups, eight saucers, a sugar bowl, a cream jug and the coffee pot into bundles, Else fetches a plastic bag from a drawer in the kitchen. She shakes it open and crams it full with the porcelain.

'Let's go and find Mamma,' she says.

In the hallway outside the Best Room, she peers up the stairs. The corridor is dark outside her old bedroom. Its door is open.

'What is it, Mormor?' Liv asks. 'Do you want to go up?'

'No,' Else says. 'I'm ready to go.'

She and her granddaughter step out into the sun. Down by the water, Marianne is on her mobile phone. She throws back her head and laughs, and Morten jumps where he stands on the pier looking across to the Reiersen shipyard. Moored at the dock, a heavy-lift vessel sprouts four pylons from its well deck, shooting a hundred metres into the sky. Else has read about its arrival in the local paper. The accommodation unit it carries is bound for Ekofisk.

The fjord is busy with boat traffic: speedboats, sailing boats, kayakers. A waterskier hangs on for dear life. The boathouse casts a shadow, long and lean, over the lawn. It seems to sag on its stilts. It looks used up, decrepit.

Else locks the front door and climbs down to the yard. Together, she and Liv make their way to Marianne.

PETTER IS WAITING for her at the Longpier. She sees his sailing boat docked in front of Peppe's Pizza as she ambles down Torggata, the wind buffing her cheeks and washing the street with its salty, clean smell. Else pulls the elastic band from her ponytail and lets her hair fall down her back. She glances into the window of the Hong Kong Palace and carries on by.

It is a good day for sailing. Petter predicted that it would be when they spoke.

'We'll set off early,' he said. 'Get a head start on everyone else so we can choose a good spot to drop anchor for lunch. Don't forget a warm jacket.'

Else's windbreaker is tucked under her arm. A food basket is hooked over the other at the elbow. She has brought a round-baked loaf, a bag of shrimps and a tube of mayonnaise, fresh-picked blueberries and a box of chilled white wine. The shop assistant at the Wine Monopoly suggested a Grüner Veltliner. Else is in the mood for trying something new. She is wearing jeans and a smock top that she borrowed from Marianne, white linen with a pretty trim at the collar.

The migrant workers have already set up their stalls in the square. The weekend market hums with Slavic intonations. Else cuts through its centre on her way to the harbour, where the trawler is docked in its usual place. She nods her 'good morning' to the fisherman when she passes and continues up the Longpier towards the *Selene*. Petter stands on deck removing the covers from his sails. She is almost beside him before he sees her.

'Else,' he says. He finishes the job at hand and extends an arm over the rail. 'Let me take that from you.'

Else relinquishes the basket.

'What have you brought?' he asks.

'I found shrimp,' she says. 'Ninety-nine kroner a kilo.'

Petter sets down the basket at his feet. 'Welcome aboard,' he says and she steps onto the gunwale. She lifts her leg over the rail as Petter reaches for her and guides her onto the deck. While he busies himself with unknotting the mooring lines, she unpacks the food into an ice chest and settles onto a cushion in the cockpit. The fjord is snagged with short waves that race ahead of the wind. Else finds a jumper at the bottom of her basket. She shakes it out and pulls it over her head. Above her, a long stretch of cloud clots and thins like tilled soil.

The stern of the boat is already drifting before Petter leaps from the Longpier onto the prow. He steals barefoot down the length of the hull, checking his balance with a palm on the masthead and crabbing over the cabin to the helm. Else sits still while he steers them into the fjord. She closes her eyes to better feel the water.

'Beautiful sailing weather,' says Petter.

The bow dips and rises in a lulling rhythm. They have barely left shore when he switches off the motor.

'Are you ready?' he asks.

'Yes,' she says.

He begins by pulling the halyard. The head of the mainsail creeps up the mast and catches the wind. The boat pitches, sending a shiver of excitement over Else's skin. The boom swings over the deck before Petter secures his line and moves on to the jib. Now the mainsail is taut. Their speed picks up until they are winging over the waves.

When both sails have been raised, Petter rests beside Else.

'I'm glad you called,' he says.

'Shall I make some coffee?'

'I'll get it. Just relax.'

Petter ducks into the cabin and returns with a thermos, two plastic mugs and a bag of raisin buns. He rips a hole in the bag and offers it to Else, who bites into a bun as he pours the coffee.

'How do you like it so far?' he asks.

'It's wonderful.'

He hands her a mug and stands at the wheel. Else watches the water. They pass the island group and cast out into the Skagerrak.

'Have you been to Denmark yet this summer?' she asks.

'Not yet,' Petter says. 'I'll go before long. I thought I might take a trip to Skagen this year. Have you ever been?'

'Never,' says Else.

'It's beautiful,' he says.

'I'd like to see it,' she says.

Petter studies her face. 'Here. You should try to steer her.'

'No, that's all right.'

'Captain's orders,' he says and moves aside. He waves Else out of her seat and she plants her feet where he shows her. She places her palms on the wheel. Her knees are soft to the throb of the current. Else looks back at the town that is shrinking over her shoulder and holds tight as the hull tilts with the wind.

Acknowledgements

I am grateful to the taxi driver in Vienna who once told me an anecdote from the days when he travelled around Norway in a circus, so sparking an idea for a novel that later turned into *The Last Boat Home*.

The Brothers Bezrukov's circus act on p. 53 was inspired by Duo Dennys' performance on 23 July 2009 at Cirkus Merano in Arendal, Norway.

I am indebted to Roald Lund for bringing me along on his shrimp trawler, the Luro, for six nausea-inducing yet highly educational hours in the summer of 2009. Also to Gerd Mosvold for sharing her knowledge of the *bedehus* on the Norwegian southern coast and giving me an invaluable insight into that milieu.

It was on the Creative Writing MA at the University of East Anglia that I began writing this novel, so I would like to thank my tutors and fellow workshoppers, in particular Sue Healy for her words of support and careful reading in subsequent years. Other early readers include Meg Myers and Susan Aagenaes: thank you both for your encouragement, which has always meant so much.

Thank you to Åse and Jan Ødegaard, whose accounts of growing up in Norway have provided several points of inspiration, and whose mornings spent childminding during the summer months have contributed many precious hours to my writing.

An immeasurable thank you to my family: Erik and Kristina, my own personal cheerleading squad; Mom, my most devoted reader and a sounding board through every stage of writing this book; and Pappa, an endless source of encouragement and information regarding all aspects of life on the Norwegian southern coast and a great deal besides, your stories and feedback have been indispensible.

Thank you to everyone at Hutchinson for giving my novel a loving home, in particular my editor, Sarah Rigby, for her keen eye and wise counsel. To James Pusey, Sophie Hignett, Kevin Conroy Scott, Jake Smith-Bosanquet, Alexandra McNicoll and Henna Silvennoinen. And to my agent, Sophie Lambert, for her tireless efforts and discernment: I wish for all budding writers a champion like you.

Most of all, thank you to Jan André for putting up with the hard slog and having faith enough for both of us. Without your patience and support, ideas and enthusiasm, writing this novel would still be a longed for, someday-soon dream.

About the Author

Dea Brøvig moved to the UK from Norway at the age of seventeen. After graduating from Leeds University, she worked in publishing in London for eight years. She graduated from UEA's Creative Writing MA in 2009. *The Last Boat Home* is her first novel.